THE KIM'S GAME

GW00382587

STEPHANIE PERCIVAL

INDEPENDENT INNOVATIVE INTERNATIONAL

Published by Cinnamon Press
Meirion House,
Tanygrisiau,
Blaenau Ffestiniog
Gwynedd LL41 3SU
www.cinnamonpress.com

The right of Stephanie Percival to be identified as author of this work has been asserted by her in accordance with the Copyright, Designs and Patent Act, 1988. © 2017 Stephanie Percival. ISBN 978-1-910836-75-0
British Library Cataloguing in Publication Data. A CIP record for this book can be obtained from the British Library.

Designed and typeset in Garamond by Cinnamon Press. Cover design by Adam Craig © Adam Craig.
Cinnamon Press is represented by Inpress and by the Welsh Books Council in Wales. Printed in Poland.
The publisher gratefully acknowledges the support of the Welsh Books Council.

A note on 'The Kim's Game'

The Kim's Game is a game or exercise where items are placed on a tray, memorised, then they are covered up and one is removed, and the players have to identify the missing object. The name is derived from Rudyard Kipling's 1901 novel *Kim*, in which the hero, Kim, plays the game during his training as a spy.

THE KIM'S GAME

What Remains 1

Serendipity is a lovely word—being in the right place at the right time. That's how it felt then. But with my history I should have known better than to associate the word with me.

I was lolling in a deckchair, appreciating the gardening skills of my old friend. He had succeeded in making a haven of loveliness on the handkerchief plot of ground. There was something liberating about sitting in someone else's garden enjoying the noises of the adjoining countryside. I had only been here a couple of days but already the rash on the back of my hands was clearing up.

I had even removed my prosthetic foot and was allowing the stump to bathe in the warm summer light. It was a strange sensation as if my missing foot was being stroked and so much more pleasant than the phantom pain I sometimes experienced. The space where my foot should be was a reminder of what I was missing. The single cloud in the expanse of blue above covered the sun and in the brief interlude of shadow I felt worn. I had turned thirty last month. Maybe it was being back here or perhaps just the unusual sensation triggered by my missing limb. Sometimes in my dreams I was complete again. It was the same with the list of other lost things in my life; phantoms which hovered about me. I fought against the thoughts which I knew would lead me down a familiar path to despair. However, the sun chose that moment to reappear and taking a deep breath like a sigh, I became absorbed again in the soothing sounds of the garden.

In the newspaper headlines the only blight on the perfect summer horizon seemed to be the hosepipe ban and warnings about drought conditions, but that wasn't of concern to me. I'd leave Tom to worry about that when he returned from his holiday. Now that was another fortuitous happening. It was only a couple of weeks ago, as I had been listening to the radio in my bedsit, when the phone had sounded. It took me a moment to understand the signal, so rarely did the land-line ring. I prepared to pick it up and say a polite but firm 'No,' to whichever telesales person had found my number, but instead was confronted with 'Hi, Hal!'

Telesales people invariably asked, 'Can I speak to Mr Henry Bennett?' My clients also used Henry and generally contacted me via e-mail.

'It's Tom,' came the excited voice. 'You remember?'

Of course I did. Though I hadn't spoken to Tom in several months, probably more than a year, he would be considered my best friend. In fact, he had been Best Man at my wedding that never was. It took some persuasion for me to accept his invitation to house and dog sit whilst he took the family on holiday. He apologised for it being short notice but Tom had won the holiday and couldn't change the dates. 'How would I ever be able to take the family to Florida otherwise?' So it appeared good fortune had shone on us both. I had nothing better to do, could keep in contact with my few clients electronically. And so here I was, back to my childhood village, a place I had tried to forget during the past ten years.

Closing my eyes against the innocence of blue sky I felt the warmth and brightness on my eye lids. Serendipity, there it was again, not far from my thoughts.

This time the sense of comfort was short lived as a sudden sharp gust of wind eddied around me, causing the hedgerow to rattle and set off a blackbird to pipe a warning. I shivered and opening my eyes pulled a fleece around my shoulders.

The breeze continued to blow. It came in little gusts as if trying to build up to something more. After several moments of movement which riffled the edges of the newspaper on the table, it finally blew hard enough to turn the last page over.

I reached forward to replace and fold the paper up, but as I did so, a name caught my eye.

Charles Maurice Manning. It was under the obituary heading.

I shuddered. So he was dead. And some tiny part of me was thankful. The trouble was the name also caused a disturbing ripple in my thoughts, because it led straight from him to his grand-daughter, Lizzie.

The mere thought of Lizzie created a current of tension in me, one of those energies which breached both pain and pleasure and was so discomfiting I tried, without much success, never to think of her.

Picking the paper up, I read the funeral was to be held in two days time at the village church. The paper trembled in my grip.

I told myself not to go, but knew it was another step I could not avoid and on Tuesday 20th June I'd be at the church at midday. I would have a little time to build up to it, to face my past and the place of my most desperate humiliation. But somewhere I felt a spark of joy at the possibility I might see Lizzie again.

Thankfully at that moment Barklay, the collie, came snuffling around the table. I was glad of the distraction and stopped scratching the back of my hand, patting the dog instead.

'Let's go for a walk then, boy,' I said, and having replaced my foot, went to get the lead.

We took the top path which circled the village through a woody copse. The breeze didn't penetrate here and instead of the tree shade giving some relief from the heat it appeared to intensify it, so the air was sticky and cloyed with pollen. At one point the trees grew thin and led to a short grassy prominence, with a bench which overlooked the valley below. I sat down grateful for the opportunity to rest, and Barklay flopped down under the seat in the longer shady grass, panting.

There was a wonderful view down to the bowl shaped parkland below. In the distance the dark hills curved a protective arm round the Manning estate. Instead of the lushness I associated with it, the palette was more yellowed and parched, except for a halo of green circling the house itself demonstrating, in the well-tended lawns, the workmanship of Tom. The white buildings of Leverbridge Manor stretched out across the centre of the parkland like a smudge of melted snow. Heat haze rippled the atmosphere above it giving a strange appearance as if nature was trying to evaporate the building itself and leave nothing behind.

On Tuesday, with the heat and humidity increasing, I made my way up the steep incline to the church at the top. The area around the church was cobbled and as I walked I became aware of my footsteps. The cadence I had become used to was now uneven and the limping rhythm echoed under clouds becoming dense with the threat of a storm.

The toll of the bell pulsed into the sky but was reflected back by the greyness so it sounded louder and more mournful. And then there was a distant roll of thunder.

I sneaked in at the back of the church. It was a large church for what had once been a small village, but was full. I'd dressed in dark jeans, black T-shirt and leather jacket, which was my standard attire; I blended in well with the mourner's in front of me. As I entered the air became thicker than the humidity outside, the scent of lilies was overpowering and even the candles in their sconces appeared to burn low as if they had limited oxygen.

There had been a smaller crowd here for my last visit, supposedly for a happier occasion. It was impossible for me not to compare the two. A summer day, when the jewel bright colours of the stained glass had shone with an intensity I had never observed before. I remembered thinking, as I dressed in my morning suit, I would absorb every moment of that day.

I had stood, on two good legs, at the front of the church and waited like a fool for what seemed like hours before Tom led me away and told me we'd stayed long enough. Lizzie's grandmother, Grace Elizabeth, had a tear in her eye as the congregation were sent home. I had never been sure whether it was because the marriage hadn't gone ahead or because of the humiliation. Until that day I had never seen Grace Elizabeth express emotion publicly. She would consider it weakness and I wondered whether she would shed a tear for her dead husband today. One of the last times I'd seen her had been across a court room when she had given a witness statement. She was a woman able to command respect. Though I didn't like her, I had to admire her; after all she had acted as mother when Lizzie's parents had died. I tried to peer around the pillar in front of me to catch a glimpse of her - Lizzie, the woman who had jilted me at the altar all those years ago, but never left my thoughts without leaving a trace of unqualified love.

From outside the noise of thunder again sounded, an ominous accompaniment to the organ music. A draught of warm air made the door creak beside me and I suddenly felt desolate. I had never discovered why she had not arrived at the church. The police had checked her plane ticket, the one to our honeymoon destination in Bali, and found she had used it. My nails caught the back of my hand. There was a drop of blood. But somehow the physical pain eased my emotions and stopped me from crying.

I could see an edge of the coffin and wondered what outfit Maurice Manning had been buried in. Perhaps his hunting dress. In the Manor there had been a portrait of him in his scarlet coat. When I had first seen it at the age of six, it terrified me. The figure was so vivid he looked as if at any moment he might jump from the frame and beat me with the whip he clutched in his right hand. On the fist and on his face was a trace of red, revealing what I thought of at the time as anger but later, when I knew him better, thought was intended to portray passion. I suspected the flush on his cheeks had now been erased by death, and I had difficulty imagining his face without it.

The service wasn't lengthy, a couple of well-known hymns, to which I made no effort to contribute and some short prayers. The tribute was given by Nigel Phelps. I could not see him well, but from what I could tell he had filled into the middle aged man I had suspected he would. A little older than me, we had played together as children, but now his hair was thinning and he looked stout. He spoke well enough about Maurice Manning's achievements as local landowner and business man, his work for the village and community and his role as master of the hunt. I watched the bowed heads on the front row desperately trying to work out which was Lizzie, but from my position I could not.

Organ music started to fill the church, and was accompanied by the movement of people as they stood in the pews waiting for the family to proceed to the church doors. I was aware of my heart thumping as I rose to join the end of the procession. I was trying to work out what I would say to her but although phrases whirled round my head they all seemed trite against the landscape of time. I flinched as I dug my fingernails into my wrist.

I was in front of the family, trembling as I shook the hand of Grace Elizabeth. Though the fingers were slender and pale, there was nothing fragile about the strength of the movement. If she recognised me she did not show it; not even a glimmer from the marble façade, a look she had perfected. Perhaps the stone like quality was even more noticeable framed by the black drapery of mourning. She was not a tall woman, but under her perfect make-up she achieved the appearance of unmoveable dominance.

Approaching the next veiled woman in line I didn't dare lift my bowed head. But as I grasped her hand I realised something was wrong, and I looked to see the familiar features of Gracie, Lizzie's identical twin sister. Nigel Phelps was the next person in the line-up and I felt my knees give slightly with the horrible sensation of disappointment. Lizzie was not here.

'Where's Lizzie?' I asked.

'I'm sorry?' questioned Gracie. She regarded me for a moment, 'Hal?' I thought she was about to say something more, but I interrupted.

'Where's Lizzie?' I demanded in a voice that was too loud for the occasion. An echo of my disruption remained, pulsing outwards, saturating the atmosphere with a single thought...*Lizzie...Lizzie...Lizzie.*

Gracie looked uncomfortable.

'I'm sorry but didn't you know?' She hesitated. 'Lizzie's dead.'

I was on my knees and weeping, without noticing the boundary between standing and falling. Great shudders of grief shook my body and I gulped the air which gave no oxygen. I was aware of foot fall around me, and a cough of embarrassment. I had occasionally had panic attacks before, and the plunge into darkness was like being pushed into a pool of cold, stagnant water. I was drowning. Then an arm linked in mine and pulled me gently but firmly upwards and towards a pew. The woman who'd pulled me aside pushed a tissue into my hand and said, 'There, There,' as though I were a child. Gradually my breathing steadied.

She said, 'It's little Hal, isn't it?'

I nodded; glad I didn't have to articulate my name.

'I knew I recognised you.' She smiled. 'Little Hal. I used to work at the Manor.'

She must have been around sixty. Her hair was silver-grey and scraped back into a bun. A small black beret was stretched on top. The face was familiar, but with the weight of despair clouding my thoughts, I could not think of her name.

'Annie Taylor,' she said, at my perplexed look. 'Come on; let's get you to the Big House for a cup of tea to settle your nerves.'

Annie, of course it was Annie.

Though I had mastered walking with my artificial foot some time ago, my legs felt unsteady as I walked into daylight. Outside was even warmer, as if the village had been draped with a canopy enclosing heat and muting sound. Annie was saying something to me but her words seemed to come from a great distance.

I was aware that again I had left the church feeling hollow, as if I was forced to grieve my fiancée and the future life I had been expecting for a second time. Obediently I accompanied Annie along the path to her car. She had still used the words 'The Big House' for the Manning estate.

It was a short drive to the outskirts of the village to access the main entrance. The metal gates were still in place, but open today. They had been modernised but still bore the Manning crest interlinked between the bars. I remembered tracing the letters with my fingers whilst kissing Lizzie goodnight. I would watch as she tripped down the drive until she was swallowed up by darkness, disappearing behind the copse of trees in the dip of the driveway. If I waited long enough, which I always did, I would be rewarded with a final sight of her shimmering under light spilling from the lamp in front of the main house. I always hoped she'd turn, notice me, and wave. But she never did.

Annie drove slowly through the gates giving me enough time to absorb the dilapidated state of the Gate House which had once been my home. It squatted in the wooded area behind the gates. The high wall bordering the gates and the canopy of trees kept it in constant shade. But when the sun shone, stray sunbeams managed to penetrate through, giving a fairy tale atmosphere. Ivy, undeterred by the drought was endeavouring to hide the building. The little I could see of the leaded windows showed an age of grime and there were old autumn leaves still in a pile by the front door, as if nobody cared for my former home. I must have physically shivered as Annie asked, 'Somebody walking over your grave?' I don't think she realised the truth or the tactlessness of her words, but she patted my knee and said, 'There, there.'

We continued our way down the drive, Annie driving at a stately pace. I was aware of her speaking to me, but ignored her chatter. Her voice seemed to emanate from a different world as if on this strange day I had been caught in a trick of time where my present existence and memories had become confused.

The copse of trees in the dip in the drive had aged. They too were draped with dark green ivy, giving a strangled effect, but below, summer undergrowth softened the ground. I had a sudden desire to stop and climb out of the car. I would wander the pathways of my youth. The tracks through the woods, the secret passageways in the garden, the walkways and follies and finally down to the lake. But I remained still as Annie took the driveway round to the less picturesque side of the house and parked there. I noticed the sign directing visitors to 'The Stable Cottages,' and guessed they had put the plan to turn the stables into holiday lets into action.

We went in the back door. Annie put her head in through a doorway where cookware clattered and voices could be heard, and asked, 'Everything under control?' I waited and when voices had assured her all was well, I

13

followed her up a short flight of stairs into the rear of the grand hallway.

A knot of people was dispersing into the wider reception area, being served cups of tea from uniformed staff behind a long table. I joined the queue and was pleased to quench my thirst with the lukewarm beverage from fine china. But after the news of Lizzie, I craved alcohol to settle the uncomfortable sensation in my head; an old addiction entering my thoughts. I returned for another cup of tea and added three teaspoons of sugar. It would have to substitute.

Moving through the reception area to a smaller lounge I nearly dropped my cup. In front of me was the familiar face of Maurice Manning. The portrait had been given centre position on an easel at eye-level, as if he was in the room. The manner in which he carried himself and features which the portrait captured could not be ignored whether living or dead. He could have been summoning the hunt.

It was impossible to believe he was dead. Just as I could not believe his grand-daughter was dead. She had a similar charisma and colouring. I suppose they would be nick-named 'ginger' but their hair was more like gold. Feeling unsteady, I made my way to a window seat and placed my cup on a small table. I looked out of the window at the striped green lawn leading down towards the lake. It was only when somebody sat next to me that I became conscious of scratching the back of my hand again.

'I'm so sorry you had to find out like this,' said Gracie.

I looked at her and in the identical features could only see a ghost of Lizzie. Her hair was the same colour but lank. Gracie was too thin so her cheek bones jutted out in sharp ridges and her eyes were prominent without flesh to soften them. She was pale, as if she never went outside, whereas Lizzie's skin always had a golden glow.

'What happened?' I asked, not sure I was ready for the answer.

'We really don't know. She went away after the wedding and never returned. Grandmama hired a private detective but there was never any news. She became another missing person statistic.'

I didn't correct her about the wedding that never was but asked, 'But did you have a funeral?'

'No, I don't think Grandmama could face it. But Lizzie was declared officially dead three years ago.'

Remembering Lizzie running down that green lawn towards the lake, so full of life I suddenly had the mad idea, maybe they had it wrong. 'And you think she's really dead?'

'There's no reason to think otherwise.'

'But she's your twin. Don't you have a sixth sense about her?'

Gracie shrugged. 'When we were small I always thought we did but not later. I only know if she was alive she'd have let me know, to stop this pain.' As she spoke she pressed her hand across her heart and her skin looked even paler, taking on a green tinge, as if reflecting the view outside. I noticed a wedding band on her ring finger.

'You married then?'

'Yes, I married Nigel in 2004.' So that explained his role as spokesman at Maurice's funeral. But Gracie was saying more, 'and we have a daughter, Eliza; she's nearly six.'

I looked back at the garden. I'd been about six when I'd first been invited to play at The Big House. I had memories of those early days but though I had contemplated it often I could not remember my first meeting with Lizzie. Now I would never see her again, I wished I could.

Gracie moved away but I stayed by the window. The room had become more crowded with people standing around the portrait admiring it and speaking about Maurice in respectful voices. One or two people looked familiar. My childhood companions becoming middle aged. Although older, the Manning cousins were still conspicuous. Their aristocracy radiated from them, making everybody else look plain. Especially eye-catching was a tall blonde, Tara. She was beautiful, her hair tousled in a stylish crop. She was laughing too loudly, throwing her head back with her mouth open wide as if she were some actress who had stumbled into the room mistaking it for a theatre stage. A spiral of smoke drifted upwards from her cigarette. I would not have dared smoke in here; any moment I expected Grace Elizabeth to bustle through and extinguish the cigarette.

Being back prompted a stream of memories. We had spent time in this room as children. In heavy summer rain, water cascaded in ripples down the large window-panes. We'd played pirates and when we were exhausted with piracy had been forced to sit and play Kim's game. Grace Elizabeth had insisted we play quietly and would bring random items in on a covered tray. We would try to memorise them and one by one they were removed. It was important to remember the object that had been taken but you could only do that if you recalled what remained. I was the poorest player, becoming easily distracted either watching the rain on the windows or stroking Maudie the black Labrador as she chased sheep in her dreams.

On the tray one day was a lovely snow globe; I could not resist picking it up and playing with it, dropping its weight from hand to hand. The miniature cottage within swirled in a snow-storm. I watched and let the flakes fall. The globe fitted perfectly in my hand, a cool orb on my sweaty palm. When the flakes were still again I continued to juggle it between my hands, more careless with each toss. I think it might have been Lizzie who warned me, 'Stop that Hal, it's very precious.' I ignored her, caught up with the cottage and snow and the way the light made it glitter, as if I were a magician casting a spell in a story book. And then, just as Grace Elizabeth entered the room, I dropped it. It rotated in slow motion, a glassy eye blinking at me as it fell, its snowy precipitation whiteout. I heard the globe screech across the floor, it winked in the light before cracking like ice. Fragments of the cottage lay at my feet, like tiny bones amidst a slush of water. I thought Grace Elizabeth was going to slap me. She walked towards me with such purpose. Her words cut the air, straight to my heart, like a curse. 'Henry Bennett! Look what you've done. It's gone forever.' For a moment everything was quiet whilst we all looked at the destruction I had caused. Then Grace Elizabeth continued, 'Something precious has been lost because of your clumsiness. You must concentrate. If you are so easily distracted you will miss so many opportunities in life.' She looked at me unblinking and I was aware of my eyes widening, as if my eyeballs might explode like the snow globe. I looked away and when I turned back she was already asking the others, 'Are you ready for the next one?'

Suddenly, the atmosphere changed as a young girl ran into the room calling, 'Mummy, Mummy.' She had been dressed in a black frock but it only served in making her red hair more vivid and her freckled complexion more alive. She looked confused, staring up at tall adults trying to find her mother. Then she found Gracie and tried to get her attention.

She tugged at Gracie's hand. Finally Gracie turned and said, 'What is it? You know not to interrupt me when I'm talking.'

Gracie tried to continue her conversation with the woman beside her.

But Eliza would not be ignored. 'Mummy, Mummy,' she hissed in what she considered to be a whisper. Gracie turned and looked down at Eliza her forehead furrowed.

'I will not tell you again Elizabeth!' She again tried to turn back but the audience was fully entranced by the floor show.

Eliza had begun to sob. Still looking up at her mother she sniffed and taking a deep breath managed to choke out the words, 'But Mummy, we found something in the garden.' She had large eyes like her mother's and these stretched even wider as she said, 'It's a body.'

If the room had been quiet before it was now completely silent. Even Maurice Manning in portrait appeared more attentive. It was so still we could have been playing a game of musical statues. Thunder rumbled again, prowling the ridge of the estate, getting ever closer.

Grace Elizabeth arrived in the doorway asking, 'What's going on?'

People moved back, allowing her passage through to Gracie and the child, her stick tapping on the parquet flooring.

'Where did you find this body?' she asked, and looking around at the staring faces of her guests she said, 'It's probably the pets' grave yard; the ground has become so dry. Come on Eliza, you show me,' she said firmly, taking the young girl's hand.

We made a curious procession as we trooped outside. The little girl with the red hair holding the hand of the old woman in black, a couple of children, then the rest of us in our dark clothes moving forward under an ever darkening and restless sky.

We passed through a formal garden and a walled area behind the house, then took a pathway to the edge of the wood. Grace Elizabeth kept a good pace even with her stick and young Eliza dutifully walked beside her, still holding her hand.

As we walked down the slope the humidity increased so I found it was difficult to breathe, as if we had been walking at high altitude. In the glade, muted shadows rippled across the space known as Pet's corner. There were stones marking various graves. I recognised Maudie's name and also Box, the Jack Russell who had been part of the family in the days I had spent here. There were several other graves and the pathways through the plot had become ridged and furrowed due to the heat. I could sense the disappointment of the crowd as we realised what Grace Elizabeth said was probably true, the bones found were a family pet. However, Eliza led us deeper into the wood. She stopped under a beech tree, its full canopy of green barely moving but allowing the light to ripple over its contorted roots revealing a deep crevasse. Again I thought it was likely an animal burrow and there would be nothing to see. But then Eliza pulled something from the ground. Even to my untrained eye the long bone she held in her hand looked surprisingly human. Grace Elizabeth looked round, the stroboscopic light giving her skin an ancient mottling, for the first time I sensed she was anxious.

'Oliver, are you there?' she asked, requesting assistance from the family doctor. He stepped forward in his sombre suit. His hair a dense grey, his figure more stooped than when I saw him last. He nodded as he took the bone from Grace Elizabeth and murmured something to her, probably confirming what we all knew, that the bone was a human femur.

Grace Elizabeth clapped her hands; a startled pigeon took flight from the tree. I felt sick. Everybody listened.

'It does look as if we have a human bone here. I'm going to contact the police. I ask you all to go back into the house now.'

There was no hope of a mobile phone signal there so the call would have to be made from the house. It was a measure of Grace Manning's position in the village that there was not one dissenting voice. Everybody turned to leave, but I could not move.

I was unaware of time but was eventually conscious of large raindrops striking my face. The movement of rain and breeze rustled through the trees as if the elements were trying to close the wound below the tree roots and hide what should not have been disturbed. Somebody moved beside me. I knew it was Gracie. I could sense her freezing fingers through my leather jacket as she put her hand on my arm.

'We'd better get back to the house,' was all she said.

The rain was falling more heavily and my hair was plastered against my forehead. By the time we returned to the house I was shivering. Annie was waiting at the door shaking her head.

'You're going to make yourself ill,' she stated, and it could have been a premonition because I already felt feverish. All I wanted to do was curl my body into warm bedding and inject myself with pain-killers.

What Was Taken 1

It is one of the unwritten rules of childhood that you will create the most terrifying games that test your strength and resolve to the limits and scare you witless.

As we prepared for the annual summer camp in the grounds of Leverbridge Manor little did we know we would excel this year. Nor could we know it would be the final camp. Much later Gracie said she'd had a really bad feeling about that night, but I think we all sensed it; everything was different.

Tradition held firm on the date being the third Saturday of July, but due to some flooding we couldn't pitch the tent in the usual area of rough grass at the back of Leverbridge Manor lawn but had to go further up the ridge towards the edge of woodland. There had always been six of us. That year, not only was there a different official six who set out, but a seventh person joined us later. Those alterations skewed everything.

Lizzie and Gracie's cousins were present, but Tara, at fourteen, had decided such games were beneath her; she was going to be self-sufficient in the groom's digs above the stables working as stable hand, the job my mother had once done. Tara's brother Leo was at the camp. At thirteen he was the same age as Nigel, the family friend who was always invited. Those two boys had spent several terms at boarding school and were in a particularly competitive mode; vying for the attention of the girls, and at the age of ten I didn't understand that I was part of that rivalry too.

The final legitimate member was little Alicia, the twins' youngest cousin. She'd been promised that when she was six she could join the 'big' children camping. When Tara decided not to accompany us there had been some talk of reneging on this arrangement, but Alicia was having none of it. 'I'm going and you can't stop me!' she decreed, stomping off in her wellies before the parental argument could be finished.

'We'll take care of her,' Lizzie and Gracie said in unison. So Alicia got her way.

Despite her age, Alicia was helpful when we put the tent up. It was a huge old scout tent big enough to hold twenty children. Alicia sorted the colour coded poles; she collected guy ropes and held tent pegs, not flinching when the mallet struck the top.

We were given the usual lecture by Grace Elizabeth, on being careful. No lighting fires, no going near the lake or walking in the woods. We half listened, knowing the rules had to be spoken before we could start the camp.

It was particularly windy that night and the tent rattled around us. The canvas made a booming sound like a slap of a giant's footsteps. Inside, our shadows were enlarged by the torchlight so a circle of huge shapes mimicked us. As the canvas moved the shadows contorted, like grotesque caricatures.

I wasn't surprised when Nigel and Leo started picking on me. Though I had lived on the estate all my life they saw me as little more than a servant. For the previous years we'd had Tara bossing us about curbing our boisterousness, but without her there might be no limit to the teasing.

'So skivvy boy, why are you here?' demanded Nigel, standing up and swaggering around the tent so his shadow captured me in its umbra.

Before I could reply Leo joined in, 'If you were at school with us you could fag for us, Skivvy.' They both laughed but only Nigel's had an edge of venom to it.

'What's a fag?' asked Alicia.

There was more laughter and Leo said, 'Well, at school the older boys have a fag to do chores and run errands for them.'

'Like a slave,' added Nigel. 'My own personal servant, eh Skivvy?'

He was not tall, but his stocky figure meant I could not escape the darkness of his shadow.

'Are you really a servant, Hal?' asked Alicia, innocently.

I still couldn't speak.

'No, of course he's not,' Lizzie said with some force. 'Hal's a friend.'

'But his mother's a servant,' continued Nigel.

'No, she isn't, Nigel,' said Lizzie, 'She's an employee. There is a difference you know.'

How long the bickering would have continued I don't know but a moment later there was the hoot of an owl and the tent flap was flung open to reveal a laughing figure. The screams of the girls were very satisfying as Tom came into the tent and threw down his sleeping bag and pack.

'Tom you scared us!' said Lizzie.

'I wasn't scared,' said Alicia.

Tom was my friend and I was pleased to see him, even more so because now I had risen a place in the pecking order. As the lowly gardener's son, Tom did not belong in our group and was not invited. But I'd asked him this year. Had Tara been here I would not have dared.

'You weren't invited, Tom,' Nigel said.

'I invited him,' I replied stubbornly.

'We should vote on it,' continued Nigel walking towards Tom.

'No, wait,' called Leo, 'How about Tom tells us a story, a really scary one. If he scares us enough he can stay.'

Nigel shrugged, reluctant to give up the opportunity of a confrontation but intrigued by the idea. 'Okay, but it better be good,' he said as he sat back down.

Suddenly I was nervous for Tom; he wasn't the story telling type. But I needn't have worried. I was riveted by the awful tale he told of flesh eating plants taking over the world. As the wind continued to blow and the shadows of the trees moved over the canvas we were terrified, though none of us was prepared to show it. I could see Nigel's usually healthy skin tone become pale in the lamplight. Only Alicia appeared more interested than afraid, and when Tom finished she asked him various questions about whether plants really could eat flesh. Tom answered her in detail about the mechanics of the Venus Fly-trap. I was impressed and the others must have been too because there was no further mention of votes or Tom leaving. However, the story telling had begun and we each told tales in turn, digging deep into our limited knowledge for the things which would scare us the most.

After that the dares began. It was tradition that the first two names drawn would go and get a midnight feast from the house. This had to be done secretly without disturbing any of the adults. Nigel and I were chosen. I followed him to the kitchen. We did not turn on the lights but the interior of the fridge gave illumination as I started filling my back-pack with cheese and ham, sausage rolls and tomatoes. When I turned, expecting to see Nigel packing his bag with bread rolls and cakes, I was surprised to see his torch spotlighting the key rack. He removed one and tiptoed towards the cellar door.

'What are you doing?' I hissed, closing the fridge.

'Thought we'd have a real feast tonight.' He unlocked the door and disappeared, taking the glow of torchlight with him.

I waited in the dark kitchen, more fearful as each moment passed. Every few seconds a new noise would make me jump. I told myself it was the wind catching window frames and doors. But I was certain I heard footsteps. It would be a real failure to be caught. I willed Nigel to hurry. Then I heard him and realised he was locking the cellar door. We ran outside and hid below the window as the overhead lights went on in the kitchen.

'I think we've had mice,' a loud voice said in the exaggerated tone of a fairy tale ogre. But though it had been close we had not been seen.

We hurried back to the tent feeling exhilarated.

'Look what I've got!' said Nigel swinging two wine bottles in the air like a band leader.

We had never had wine at the feast before. Had Tara been there she would have made us put them back. It was difficult to remove the cork but once that obstacle was overcome we all took a swig. It was Lizzie who stopped the bottle being passed to Alicia. 'Not for Alicia,' she said. Nobody argued, not even Alicia.

'Good vintage,' Nigel said as the bottle was passed round, trying to sound like an adult. The liquid was foul. It tasted sour and dry with bits of cork in it, leaving the tongue feeling rough. The bottles were covered in dust and felt horrible against the fingers. But nobody complained and everything started to seem funny.

Tom and Leo were picked for the next dare. Ignoring the rules, it was decided they had to swim in the lake. We followed them across the expanse of grass down to the water. Trying to be quiet, we made our way through a gap in the surrounding bushes to a small shore.

'I want to swim too,' Alicia said, but she was told it was against the rules to do somebody else's dare. She appeared to accept this.

Clouds scudded across the sky occasionally allowing a glimpse of moon to break through. The wind made wavelets on the usually placid water and the moonlight illuminated them into jagged teeth. But Leo and Tom did not hesitate; they stripped and stepped into the dark water, splashing about for a couple of minutes, trying to keep quiet so as not to disturb the inhabitants of the house. Then we all ran back to the tent trying to stop shouting and whooping at our bravado. When we returned the rest of the wine tasted better.

Lizzie and Gracie were picked next. They had to go to the Gate House and spy on my mother. It was not my suggestion and I felt uncomfortable with the idea. A slight nausea filled my head which I put down to the wine. Considering the Gate House was at the other end of the park, they came back quite quickly. Later I wondered if they'd really gone there at all. I had hoped they would return with bored expressions saying the lights were out or Mother had been sitting watching the television. But as soon as I saw the excited identical glow on their faces I realised they had seen something.

'Hal's mother's with a man,' chanted Gracie, she repeated the dreadful lie and began dancing round the tent. 'We saw them snogging.' She giggled and then, hugging her arms over her shoulders, she wiggled her back to us suggestively making horrible sucking noises, pretending she was kissing somebody. Even in the low lamplight my face must have taken on a stricken expression.

Lizzie was kinder though. 'It's true, Hal, somebody was there,' she said. But she didn't elaborate on the kissing.

I had to get out of the tent and lunged into the dark night. I was going to run away but I only got a short distance before I was sick. I went back into the tent wiping the bitter spit on my sleeve. Nobody said anything but Nigel looked at me with a smirk across his face. If my head hadn't been spinning I might have punched him.

We had made the unspoken decision that we'd had enough and I was making myself comfortable in my sleeping bag, when a voice said, 'It's my turn.'

We had forgotten Alicia. All of us were tired with heavy heads, unused to the consumption of wine.

'It's my turn,' she said a little more firmly.

'You're too young,' somebody replied.

'That's not fair. I couldn't have the wine, and now I want to do a dare.'

Alicia was standing up. She had her wellies on and was waiting by the tent flap ready to go, with her arms crossed tightly in front of her. In my fugged brain I thought she had suddenly grown tall and was towering over us like some powerful queen. Leo must have had a similar vision because he said, 'Alright, go on then. What do we want her to do?'

It was some moments before the dare was given.

'I know,' slurred Nigel, giggling to himself, 'Seeing as Tara has decided she likes horses better than us, this is what you've got to do. Go to the stables and get some horse dung, then get into Tara's rooms and try to put it as near to her bedroom as you can.' He finished with a strange gurgle which I presumed was laughter at the thought of Tara waking to a pile of horse shit outside her door.

It seemed funny at the time, several of us joined in with his merriment. It was only Lizzie who suggested, 'Shouldn't one of us go with her?'

'We've all done our dares,' came the reply, 'She'll be fine.'

We were numbed with alcohol, my eyelids were heavy and I could already hear the faint snoring from Tom's sleeping bag.

We let Alicia go.

The track of time slipped as we waited. I dozed until Lizzie said, 'Where's Alicia? She should be back by now?'

Leo said, 'I expect she's gone back to the house.' His voice sounded reasonable.

Then Nigel added, 'Yeh, she'll have got spooked. She's only little.'

We were too stupefied with wine to recognise that Alicia would never have given up. Had I been sober I would have done something. As it was, I drifted back to sleep.

I woke early, the sound of rainfall pattering the canvas like agitated finger drumming. My head ached, my mouth was sour. My first thought was to get Tom away before he was noticed. I shoved him and after some grumpy words he appeared to be awake.

'You'd better clear off,' I told him. He didn't argue, just packed up his belongings.

As he was heading out Nigel spoke, 'Here take the wine bottles; we don't want them to know.' He moved his head in direction of the house and I was impressed he'd been able to think of such a thing. Dutifully Tom pushed them into his pack and quietly left.

It was tradition to have a huge fry up the following morning of the camp and the smell of bacon greeted us as we returned to the house. After tidying ourselves, we made our way into the dining room and tucked into the food waiting for us on the hotplates at the side of the room. This was a breakfast like no other. It was the one time a year I was allowed to eat in the Manning dining room and it seemed like a banquet for a king.

I loaded sausages, bacon, fried and scrambled eggs onto my plate, finishing with a garnish of mushrooms, tomatoes and kedgeree. The food looked even better today. There was no talking just the scrape of cutlery against china and sipping and supping noises.

Annie Taylor was serving that day and she came in to replenish the dishes. She beamed at us and said, 'Well, somebody had a good feast last night, the fridge is almost bare!'

We didn't answer her but exchanged a secret look of knowing between us. The addition of wine to the feast had been a total success. Nigel winked at us. Gracie giggled. He had succeeded in impressing the girls and I felt disappointed it hadn't been my idea to steal the wine.

The adults gradually joined us. Leo's parents, Eleanor and James, and then Alicia's father, Charles. Clarissa, her mother, 'was having a lie in.' Victor, the twins Great Uncle, was also there, his plate piled higher than everybody else. As he put yet another spoonful of tomatoes or eggs or slice of toast on his plate he would wink at me. In fact, I don't think Victor ever said a word or made an action without a wink. Of all the Manning adults, he was the friendliest. His brother Maurice always looked cross and

Grace Elizabeth expected perfect behaviour, so I became nervous when she looked at me and would always make a mistake.

We were told Maurice wouldn't show until later but Grace Elizabeth made her entrance shortly after we arrived. She was full of questions as to how the camping was. Sometimes I thought she wished she joined us. Today though, instead of questions about the weather and the temperature overnight she asked, 'Where's Alicia?'

I don't think any of us had thought about Alicia for some time.

'She came back to the house,' Leo said.

'No, she's with you,' Charles said, a forkful of kedgeree half way to his mouth.

Whilst a doubt wriggled into my mind, Nigel continued in a sure voice, 'No, she came back to the house early.'

'Well, I'm certain she's not here,' said Charles. He put his fork down, a little rice scattering onto the table beside his plate. 'I'll go and check,' he said, obviously disgruntled at having his breakfast disturbed. He crumpled his napkin and threw it onto his vacated chair and strode from the room.

It was some time before he returned. 'She's not in the house. Now is this some sort of joke?'

We all shook our heads.

Lizzie suddenly said, 'She could be with Tara.'

The adults agreed this was possible and Lizzie was instructed to go to the stable block. Gracie followed her.

They returned shortly afterwards, a sleepy-eyed Tara with them. Tara was a tall figure behind the twins; a beautiful, slender girl with a delicate bone structure. To call her a girl was inaccurate; though not one of the adults she had definitely outgrown our childish group. She had a satisfied smile on her face as if she was still on the verge of some lovely dream and not quite awake. Her blonde hair was tousled and she reminded me of a cat, the way she rubbed her eyes with the heels of her hands and gave a delicate yawn. I thought instead of talking she might just purr.

'Tara,' said Charles, making her jump slightly, 'Did Alicia come to you last night?'

'No,' replied Tara, her voice husky and low. Her lovely forehead frowned. 'The twins found some horse dung outside my room.'

The children exchanged knowing glances. Had Alicia not been missing, we would have smirked and later laughed, but now the dare seemed ridiculous rather than amusing. The adults had no way of knowing how pertinent this information was.

'Never mind that,' said Charles. 'Where's my daughter?'

We were quiet then. Eating had stopped and half full plates were congealing in front of us.

'Did you make her do something stupid?'

We all shook our heads.

If the silence had lasted I would have had to say something, to fill the heavy atmosphere that was building with blame. I would have told them about the dare, maybe even about the wine but it did not last and I'll never know whether it would have made a difference for the police to know Alicia's last known position. I'm certain nobody ever told them about the dare, but they did discover the missing wine and Tom was blamed for that.

Grace Elizabeth clapped her hands and stood up at the head of the table and spoke. Her claps worked like the commands of a sergeant major and everybody in the room was immediately attentive. We listened, grateful that somebody had taken charge.

'Now, here's what we're going to do,' she commanded. 'We search the house and then the grounds.'

The adults were commissioned to do the indoor search in the dry and the children were sent out.

It was still raining, so it took a while for us to get ready with boots and anoraks and then Grace Elizabeth gave us our instructions. Lizzie and Gracie were to go down to the lake accompanied by Maudie; Tara was to search the stable blocks and outhouses. Leo, Nigel and I were to go to the woods behind the tent.

Whilst Leo and Nigel headed off as instructed towards the woods, I took a detour, making some excuse. At that point, I wasn't worried about Alicia; she was feisty and had probably gone off on her own or was hiding somewhere in the house. Perhaps playing a trick on her older companions. More pressing in my mind was the information I'd had about my mother kissing a man.

I suppose I was rather possessive of my mother. I'd never had a father about and considered myself the man of the house, and Mother encouraged this. So I marched up to the Gate House and stamped into the small kitchen, my boots muddy enough to make footprints on the worn tiled floor.

Mother was making tea. She turned from filling the kettle and smiled at me. My mother had the most beautiful face; perfectly proportioned with a creamy complexion and unusually green eyes. Her nose was small and her lips slightly bowed, so she always appeared to be smiling. Her hair was long and dark blonde with silvery strands which caught the light when she moved.

As I looked at her for evidence of her deceit she smiled at me as if I was the only important thing in her life. I was sure that Gracie and Lizzie had lied. I ran to Mother and hugged her.

She laughed and said, 'You missed me then? Didn't you have a good time?'

'Yes, it was great,' I answered though without much conviction. 'Alicia's gone missing though.'

'Well, she can't have gone far,' Mother said whilst stroking my hair.

'I've got to help look for her,' I said with the important tone expected from the man of the house.

'Alright,' Mother said without any fuss, and then added the usual refrain. 'Do as you're asked and remember to say 'Thank you' to the Mannings for letting you stay.' It was Mother's constant mantra that I do what the Mannings asked, and I was reminded of Nigel's jibes from the previous night about us being servants.

She bent and kissed my cheek and, reassured that nobody had been with my mother, I raced to catch up with Leo and Nigel.

Under the canopy of leaves above us the ground was reasonably dry, though the air surrounding us was suffused with the odour of damp vegetation. We split up and each took a separate path, calling Alicia's name as we went. All of us knew the woods well and had no difficulty in searching the pathways and then winding through less well known passages choked with thicker undergrowth.

Finally we met together in a glade by a stone folly. It was a square building, with two pillars carved either side of a glass-paned entrance. The doors were unlocked and we opened them and peered inside. Nothing was there except dried leaves and the smell of disuse. I didn't go in. It was exactly the sort of cupboard-like trap that Nigel would have delighted in locking me into as a joke. A path led from it to a central pavement where a statue greeted us, her bare arms outstretched. The space was open and the rain had stopped. We stood by the statue and moved round it as we talked.

'Where do you think she is?' asked Leo, 'I thought we'd have found her by now.'

The statue regarded me with a blind stare, as if demanding an answer.

'Yeh, but she's probably in the house, nice and warm and dry,' said Nigel, stamping his feet with impatience.

I had no idea what could have happened to her, so said nothing.

'Let's go up to the top ridge, see if we can see anything from there,' suggested Leo.

Nigel huffed a bit and I thought he might decline but he followed Leo as we climbed a muddy trail to the line of trees bordering the estate. At the view point we looked out, the house and hills misted with the damp air. We saw no one, not even the girls down by the lake. The dark surface reflected the sky in a mosaic of grey giving no clues.

We ambled back to the house, occasionally calling for Alicia but not expecting any response. By the time we reached the edge of the lawn we had given up calling her name.

Everybody had gathered in the dining room again with the addition of Clarissa and Maurice. Maurice now replaced Grace Elizabeth at the head of the table. His cheeks had their usual red glow as if he had been searching high and low, but it was obvious he had not been involved in the search when he said, 'Now what's all this fuss about?'

Grace Elizabeth spoke in a quieter voice, 'We've searched everywhere and can't find Alicia. I'm going to call the police.' She started to walk to the door but was halted by Maurice.

'Now we don't want to do anything hasty, surely she's going to turn up. She can't have gone far.'

'With respect, Uncle,' came Charles's voice, 'She's my daughter, and she's disappeared. She's been missing since last night. What if she had an accident coming back to the house in the dark?' His pitch was increasing a little; beside him Clarissa was twisting a serviette in her fingers. I thought of the dark lake, its phantom haunted the room. From the window a tiny speck of it was visible through the thick trees and vegetation that surrounded its banks, and for a second I thought I could smell it, as if it had become stagnant.

Maurice shook his head. 'She'll turn up any minute. But if you must, we'll phone the police.'

'I think that would be best,' said Charles.

'I'll take care of it,' said Maurice, 'I know the Inspector.'

I was surprised at how long the police took to arrive considering it was a directive from the Big House. It wasn't until the middle of the afternoon that they appeared. The rainy skies lingered and though still day time there was a sensation of dusk falling. There were several policemen and also a police dog handler with an Alsatian. Though we wanted to be involved in the search, we were told to stay inside.

One of the benefits of the Manor was windows facing in every direction. From Lizzie and Gracie's bedroom and the playroom on the upper floor we had a good view of the figures moving round in the hazy light.

They seemed to spend a long time by the lake and I wondered whether they were looking at the foot prints we had made last night and were thinking Alicia might have drowned. I recalled her saying she wanted to swim and I shuddered. Perhaps she had returned there on her own.

As true dusk fell the policeman in charge came to talk to Maurice and Grace Elizabeth. Charles and Clarissa were not present in the hall as the chief spoke. We children were huddled on the landing above, trying to catch any words drifting upwards. We couldn't hear much, only that Alicia had not been found and they would bring divers to search the lake tomorrow, when it was daylight.

I returned to my home with a new feeling; one of anxiety at Alicia's disappearance, mixed with excitement at the idea of police searching the lake. This sensation kept me from sleeping and I spent the dark hours listening to the wind moving in the trees surrounding the cottage. At some point I thought I heard Mother talking quietly in the hallway. It sounded as if she was reciting prayers. In the morning I wondered whether it had been part of a dream.

I got up early and took Mother a cup of tea. I told her I was going down to the lake and she said she might join me later. Instead of going straight down there though, I walked into the village and knocked for Tom.

Though still early, as we approached the lake we could already see vans and uniformed figures moving about at the misty edges of the lake. A senior officer gave us a brusque 'good morning,' and told us we could stay only if we didn't interfere with the search. We made our way to the lakeside and sat down on a damp patch of grass where we sometimes fished. And then we watched.

As the veil of morning mist lifted from the lake's surface, the colour changed from uniform grey to a mosaic of greens like a photograph being developed. We said little as we watched the divers make their preparations, wade into the water and then disappear under the surface.

Every so often they would re-appear and signal to the officer on the bank. Nothing.

Some of the others wandered down from the house at intervals, Charles appeared once and stood so still he might have been transformed to stone. He did not stay long and said nothing.

Then the vans and police were gone, leaving ruts and footprints on the muddy grass. They had not found Alicia or any trace of her.

After that the focus of the search moved. In the village the police made enquiries and there were some bulletins on the television and radio. Alicia was not found.

As summer ended the atmosphere at Leverbridge was strange. The Manning house and household appeared to be holding their breath as if expecting Alicia to suddenly return. She did not.

The natural cycle of the year turned and as the vibrancy of autumn passed into winter I thought Leverbridge Manor had lost something of importance, a colour which would never be replaced. For a long time afterwards I always thought of Leverbridge Manor as a black and white postcard, caught in a perpetual winter.

What Remains 2

I had no memory of falling. I came round to a murmur of voices and for a moment I could have fallen asleep at home leaving the TV on. But my body felt bruised, my emotions too. Slowly I opened my eyes. The room was dim. I was lying on a couch, a rug draped over my legs. I had to check my memory because Lizzie was leaning over me, a concerned look on her face. She held my hand between her cold fingers; they were so icy and her face so pale I thought perhaps she was a ghost.

'Hal, you gave us such a fright,' she whispered. I noticed the colour of her dress, the wedding band on her finger, and as I opened my eyes fully I realised it was not Lizzie at all, just Gracie.

Looking up I could see an expanse of sky at the window, shadows of variegated grey swept past and there was the noise of rain against the glass. The world appeared skewed as if I was looking at it through a water droplet. A wave of pain pulsed through me, from my missing toes up into my body. For an instant I relived the sensation of being thrown from my motorbike, sliding across tarmac, feeling my foot being torn from me.

'What happened?' I managed to stutter.

'I think you must have fainted,' Gracie told me, only partially answering my question. I had a vague memory of feeling giddy as I returned to the main house but I was unsure of what had occurred before. Did we walk across the grounds and find a human femur?

Gracie continued to focus on the most recent event. 'We moved you in here, but it was difficult. What happened to your foot?'

I wasn't a particularly big man, but in a state of semi-consciousness my foot would have dragged and, as they put my feet up on this chaise longue, they would have noticed my disability. It was a topic I had no intention of discussing.

'It's a long story. Maybe I'll tell you some time.'

Thankfully, Gracie seemed to take the hint, and simply patted my hand. 'Annie's gone to fetch you a cup of tea,' she said.

My body felt drained of energy. The phantom pain throbbing from my foot continued but it was the ghosts wrested from my brain which caused me most distress. I closed my eyes and shuddered.

What Was Taken 2

After the debacle I refer to as 'the wedding that never was', I left Leverbridge. I waited a few weeks, long enough to know Lizzie had deserted me. With her absence I whirled unbound like a particle of sand eroded from a rocky place.

I hitched rides northwards, but my lifts petered out around Milton Keynes. So that's where I stopped. It was north of the Watford Gap and the landscape had changed from the narrow lanes, hedges and hollows of Leverbridge to rolling arable land. The town with its grid pattern and roundabouts was strangely appealing in its regularity.

I rented a basic flat and found a job at a high street bank. I had been there about two years and on the outside was making progress. The job was alright and I was doing an evening course in accounting. I spoke to the people at work and to customers with a fixed smile on my face. It offered a little protection.

Yet I ached. Sometimes I would catch a glimpse of golden hair or a movement in the crowd which reminded me of Lizzie and my stomach would flutter with the hope of seeing her, then it would drop when I realised it was not her and I felt sick. It was like living on a rollercoaster.

Eventually my colleagues at work and college stopped inviting me out. They knew the answer would be no. I guess they thought I had a family or friends at home who I socialised with. In fact it was just a bottle, my motorbike and me. A trinity of sorts. If I was feeling low I'd take the bike out and we'd speed through the surrounding countryside. Moulded to its frame by speed I could distance myself from life. I drove as if I were a stone flung from a careless hand without direction.

It was only a matter of time before the equilibrium was disturbed. Her name was Lauren.

On my evenings at college I usually managed minimal contact with my fellow students. The wall I had built around myself deterred most people. But not Lauren. I should have been forewarned when during our coffee break she would produce a magazine from her bag and proceed to tell anybody who would listen their horoscope for the week. I guess there were also pseudo-psychology tests in those journals because that was her approach to me.

'I'm very good at working people out,' she announced most weeks. She was pretty, but would have been more attractive if she used less make-up. She wore tight clothing, which emphasised her figure in a pleasing way. Generally I sat as far from her as I could, but I couldn't help listening as she annoyed others with the insights gleaned from her glossy magazines. Inevitably my turn came. Her lesson in the coffee room that week was 'attention seeking'.

'Take Henry for instance,' she said. 'Look at him, sitting over there trying to keep his distance. He's so desperate not to be noticed he makes himself stand out. It's the same as attention seeking by being noisy.'

I wanted to tell her I had no desire for attention.

'I think he's been used to getting attention in the past because of his good looks,' she talked as if I were a rat in an experiment with no feelings.'But now he's finding the strategy doesn't work so well anymore.'

Some of the heads had turned to look at me, their eyes appraising me and my fading looks. There were nods of agreement. I drained the last of my coffee, crushed the polystyrene with my fist and walked out. Once back in the lecture room everybody ignored me as they took their places. We continued to discuss 'loss contingency' but I couldn't take it in. Beneath my protective wall, I burned. I kept looking at the back of Lauren's head, hoping the heat I generated would scald her. But the shiny brown hair simply swung from side to side. A silly movement, and I imagined her face working in little pouts, sucking her pen as she thought deeply about the subject of spreadsheets. That I recognised this mannerism later made me wonder how long I had been watching her from my voyeuristic position at the back of the room.

On the way out Lauren caught up with me. She was a little out of breath because I had left as quickly as I could.

'Hang on a minute, Henry,' she said her hand across her chest. She was shorter than me and I was aware of the heave of her breasts. Although summer, it was a cool evening and I could see her nipples pushing the stretched cloth of her shirt. I had not meant to slow down but I realised we had stopped. The breeze lifted her hair; she brushed it from her face.

'Now Henry, I don't want you to be upset by what I said earlier. I like helping people.'

'It doesn't matter,' I mumbled and turned to walk on. She grabbed my elbow.

'Look, I can tell you're lonely. Please just wait a moment.'

I walked on but more slowly so her shorter stride could keep up with mine.

'Let's go for a drink,' she said, 'The Crown's just along the road. Come on.' Again I felt her grip on my arm. I could have pushed her away but didn't. Alcohol appealed. I could already sense the taste of it.

The Crown was a basic public house on a busy corner. Though close to the college, its clientele weren't students. We went into the bar. The upholstery and decor was shabby and it had a yellowish ceiling ingrained with smoke. I bought myself a beer and a pint of cider for Lauren. I took out a cigarette and offered her one.

'No, that's a terrible habit,' she chided. 'You know they're going to ban smoking in public places soon?'

I shook my head. 'Can't see that ever happening,' I said, 'This lot would have a fit.' I used my cigarette to point at

41

the huddle of smokers at the far end of the room. The coil of smoke remained for a moment like a line in the process of being erased.

I can't remember the conversation we had. I recall it like the buzzing of insects, but during our drinks Lauren moved closer to me and started insinuating herself into my body as if she were trying to solve some mathematical puzzle; to see if her curves would blend with the angularity of my limbs. The necessary function must have been proved because the next thing I was aware of was Lauren moulded to me on the back of my bike. Her hands gripped my thighs, her breasts pushed firmly into my back; even with my helmet on, I heard the sound of her laugh in my ear.

The bike had barely come to rest before she was tearing at my clothes. I slowed her down enough to remove our helmets, but then her mouth was on my lips. Her lipstick, which she must have reapplied before we left the pub, was sticky on my skin. Her mouth wet and open, pushing her tongue with little jabs to part my lips and writhe into the space.

Her hands were on my fly and belt as I fumbled with the keys in the lock. She hesitated only a moment before pushing me inside; we didn't reach the bed. She had exposed me in the hall and was tugging me towards her, pressing my hands against her parted thighs. I don't remember removing her underwear but there was no barrier as I pushed inside her and was taken over by the bliss of heat and pressure and release.

We were lying on the floor. I was becoming aware of the cold linoleum pressing my buttocks but also the warmth of Lauren beside me. I wondered if she had been right, that my removal from the group had been attention seeking after all. That I had wanted her all along. Even in this uncomfortable position it was pleasant listening to her breathing. I leant over and smiled at her.

She didn't reciprocate but glared at me with narrowed eyes. I looked at her again; lipstick was smudged around her mouth, a dark whip of hair stuck against the sweat on her cheek, the pushed aside shirt and bra. Her mouth opened to speak. It was grotesque with its distorted paint. I thought she might be about to shout 'Rape'.

The words she did speak had a similar weight of terrible accusation.

'Who's Lizzie?'

I jumped back. How did she know about Lizzie?

'You said her name.'

I was bewildered. I was sure I hadn't said anything.

'Are you sure I said that?' I asked. I still had the feeling I couldn't vocalise the word 'Lizzie', let alone do it without knowing. Lauren's eyes looked darker and smaller, her mouth puckered and I thought she might spit at me. If I had called Lizzie's name what else had I done or said without being conscious of it? Had she told me to stop and had I ignored her? I took in her rumpled clothing. Was her shirt ripped? Was there a scratch on her neck or just a smear of lipstick? Looking at her lying dishevelled in front of me, I wondered how rough I had been. Was she about to scream?

'Who's Lizzie?' Then again, 'Who's Lizzie? You told me you didn't have a girlfriend.'

'I don't.'

Sulky huffs were the only response.

'Tell me,' she ordered. I thought it best to comply.

'She was my fiancée. She broke my heart.'

Whilst I contemplated the notion that I had simplified my relationship with Lizzie to eight words Lauren put her face near to mine and said, 'You're sick.'

Her sticky, sweaty face was too close to me. I could smell her perfume, a sugary scent overlaid with the sourness of sex. I wanted to shove her away but managed to hold back. She left me sitting in the hall whilst she went to the bathroom. It was dark now and I could only just make out the shape of my coat hanging from its hook, it looked lonely and empty. Though the air was still, everything seemed unsettled. Vocalising her name had caused a ripple in time.

Of course, I had shouted 'Lizzie' at the moment of climax. She still lived with me. Every time I spoke, her name underpinned whatever I said; every thought involved her. Without Lizzie I was dead.

Lauren's voice came from a long way off. She was standing at the end of the passage way.

'I'll call a taxi,' she said.

After Lauren had gone I could only think of Lizzie. I had called her name. Lizzie, Lizzie, Lizzie. It was a mean trick. She had deserted me but somehow remained with me. Her name repeated in my head as I washed in the dark bathroom, watching my reflection moving around like a ghost. And with each repetition the name brought her memory closer to me. I hadn't had much to drink but felt inebriated. In an effort to clear my head of Lizzie, I started smashing things. My toiletries from the bathroom shelf were swept aside, the bin kicked over, laundry thrown and then I heard the front door slam, my keys rattle in my hand, and my helmet was shoved onto my head.

I threw myself onto the bike. With the noise and vibration of its engine and the muting by my helmet, for a moment I was relieved of Lizzie's whispered name in my mind. But then we were cruising and I began to hear it again, Lizzie, Lizzie, Lizzie. I opened up the throttle and accelerated.

It had begun to rain. I was glad of the sound which pattered against the visor. As it blurred my vision the jumble of my thoughts was dampened. The rainfall increased until I could hardly see, lights slashed into stars through my visor and the surface of the road gleamed like glass. The wind rose trying to blow me off course and rain wraiths twisted around me whispering Lizzie's name. The faster I went the heavier the rain became, the beam of my headlamp creating a grey wall. I kept driving at the wall; I knew I would eventually reach oblivion. Still the crash took me by surprise. Not the impact, but the pain; it felt as if my body was being ripped. The bike beneath me screamed as we slid across tarmac and bumped over softer ground, and then was still. I was embraced by darkness out of which a small word whispered. Lizzie. Then sirens sounded, they shrieked, Lizzie, Lizzie. And finally footsteps and voices around me, speaking in tongues, a language comprising just one word. Lizzie.

I was in hospital for several weeks, by which time the group I was attending college with had completed their year. Nobody came to see me from work or my study group. I wondered whether Lauren might visit, but she did not.

When I was released from hospital my rehabilitation took time. I attended appointments for fitting my prosthetic foot and had physiotherapy to get used to moving with it. But eventually I returned to work and my studies and learnt to live with my modified body. Occasionally I would get phantom pains and during the intense twisting sensation, when it seemed as if my tissue was being wrung out like a rag, I thought of Lizzie. It was the same sensation; I had tried to rid myself of her but the pain remained worse than ever.

What Remains 3

'Are you alright?' Gracie asked with panic in her voice, 'Hal, Hal,' she said, slapping my hand, which stimulated the anxiety rash to a prickling heat.

I heard Annie come in, 'What's happened?'

'I think he's fainted again,' Gracie replied.

Forcing my eyes open I managed to say, through gritted teeth, 'It's alright, I'm alright.'

I tried to breathe deeply and relax my shoulders in the way I'd been advised by the pain clinic. It eased the agony in my missing limb slightly. They were both staring at me. After a moment Annie knelt beside me and proffered me the tea cup. 'Try to sip this,' she said.

They helped me sit up and pushed cushions behind my back. The fine china rattled against my teeth as I took small sips. Annie had made it so sweet it was like linctus. But it was soothing and, as the pain subsided, I felt a little better.

'What about the bones?'

The women exchanged a look between them as if deciding whether to tell me anything, as adults might before speaking to a child. It appeared Annie had deferred to Gracie and left the room.

Gracie said, 'We don't know much. The police are here now.'

'What about the wake?'

'Everybody's gone.'

I made to get up, realising I had managed to outstay any welcome I may have had, but Gracie pushed my shoulder gently. 'You don't have to go anywhere. You must stay until you're feeling better. Where are you staying?'

'At Field Lane. Tom Sheldon invited me down to house sit whilst he's away.' Gracie didn't react to the information but merely nodded. I wondered if she remembered Tom joining in our childhood adventures, or whether she dismissed him as merely 'the gardener'.

'I need to check on the dog,' I said, trying to move again. It was not my normal state to show concern for others but suddenly I felt agitated that Barklay hadn't been walked or fed.

'Barklay isn't it?' Gracie said.

'Yes. I'm meant to be looking after him.'

'I can run you home if you like,' Gracie volunteered, and I nodded acceptance.

I stumbled out of the house, it was still raining. However, the cloudy sky appeared to hang above the bowl of the Manning estate with light radiating over the horizon beyond. I wondered if it was me or the Manor which was the focus of the gloom.

After the crowd from earlier, the hall was echoing silence. I did not see Grace Elizabeth or Annie to say goodbye to. Walking beside Gracie, I leant on her arm like an old man. I was not sure if I could balance on my own.

There were various cars on the gravelled area in front of the house, probably police, and I couldn't help but remember the previous vehicles and dogs, which had arrived when Alicia had gone missing. I gripped Gracie's arm more tightly but if she noticed she said nothing.

We travelled in silence in the Range Rover and I watched the wipers swish their steady rhythm across the windscreen. Gracie had once told me she would never drive. She had obviously overcome her anxiety because she manoeuvred the vehicle easily through the village roads and across the narrow bridge.

As Gracie dropped me at Tom's front door she asked if I'd be alright. 'Yes, I'll be fine.'

'Come and see me again,' she said. And it was not until I'd heard the engine noise fade and was unlocking the front door that I realised she'd used 'me' rather than 'us'; not a

47

general family invite through politeness but a personal request.

Barklay did not live up to his name but came to greet me with happy wagging of his tail, jumping and snorting. He found a cushion, which he presented to me, and I wondered why I had never thought of having a dog, when it appeared they were so easily pleased. I could not think of any other occasion when I had been greeted with such open and unquestioning affection.

Though the afternoon light was fading and the rain continued, I decided to take Barklay for a walk to reward him for his loyalty. We took the path into the village and I reminisced about the buildings and tried to remember places I had known as a child.

The layout was recognisable but with new houses and buildings nestled in spaces I did not remember as spaces. I thought there had been a garage once and perhaps a warehouse. The new constructions in the main had been sympathetically designed. The only thing that grated was the prominent signage of the corner shop, which was now an express supermarket. Otherwise the post-office was still there and the bakery nestling at the bottom of the hill where the church dominated above. On the hill, one of the village pubs didn't look much altered except it had been repainted and the sign changed. It was called 'The Huntsman'. The picture showed horse and hounds and a ruddy faced rider who resembled the portrait of Maurice Manning in Leverbridge Manor. On the opposite side of the road was a boarded up shop with peeling paint work. You could just read the name Sheldon, Tom's family name. It had been the shop where they sold organic veg, grown in their market garden. It had never been palatial but now had a shabby neglected air. It reminded me of the Gate House and how things change without us noticing. I had a sudden impulse to see what had happened to Tom's folks place.

The walk took us a little way out of the village centre and Barklay snuffled in hedgerows but every now and then looked back towards me. As we walked the rain lifted and late afternoon sunshine lit our way. It glinted off the wet leaves at the roadside. I was expecting the same small lane and track that led to the market garden and bungalow which had once been Tom's home so was surprised by the new road lay out. A large sign indicated, 'Leverbridge Garden Centre', it had a floral border and a sponsor logo.

I put Barklay on the lead as we walked at the side of the driveway, passed by several cars. I could work out where Tom's old bungalow had once been but now it had been absorbed into a new enlarged building. Automated doors slid open and I entered a glazed atrium with displays of plants softening the edges of the white decor. Directly inside the entrance a prominent plaque told me Maurice Manning had not only opened the Garden Centre but it was through his generosity that the project had been funded. The entrance way led us to a covered area at the rear, filled with rows of demarcated spaces filled with plants aligned alphabetically. Further away I could see one of the sales assistants, in a distinctive green uniform, spraying plants. The arc of water caught the light causing a rainbow to form; it was a sight which made my heart lift. Such a simple thing that seemed so magical. Mother had always referred to it as heaven's kiss and if we had been together when rain and sunshine met we'd run outside to see if the rainbow's end had landed on our cottage, suggesting there was gold to be found. I shivered at the thought of the Gate House; once upon a time it had captured the sense of existing in a fairy story, with the potential for harbouring treasure, but now I was reminded of its emptiness and decay. Barklay and I walked the rows looking at the plants with their intriguing names. During the months when I had lived with Tom I had helped with the basic care of plants and though I didn't know much about them, it was soothing to wander in peace absorbing the fragrance of greenery.

There was a paved area which served as a cafe and I ordered a coffee and Barklay was given a bowl of water. Whilst I sat, I tried to imagine where I was in terms of the past structure I had been familiar with, but the more I thought the more disorientated I became.

After a time we made our way back to Tom's new house, Barklay close at my heel. I opened the door wondering what might be on the TV that evening and was surprised to find an envelope lying squarely on the doormat, its whiteness striking against the black of the mat. I did not recognise the handwriting, a looping elaborate script flowing over the paper with my name. Formal. Mr Henry Bennett.

Once, I would have been impatient and torn the envelope to reveal the letter inside. I had lost the ability to be excited and thought only it could not be good news. I left the letter on the side as I fixed Barklay his supper and made myself a cup of tea and a sandwich. Only then, when I had kicked off my shoe, removed my prosthetic foot and slumped on the sofa, did I pick it up again. It took a moment to open the seal and as the card was pulled from the edges of the envelope it made a sucking sound. The same black handwriting invited me to attend Leverbridge Manor, for the reading of Charles Maurice Manning's will at 10 o'clock the following morning. There were neither pleasantries nor any signature. It was an order, of that I had no doubt, and I presumed must have been written by Grace Elizabeth herself. I knew I would attend. If you were summoned by the Mannings you did not argue.

My overriding memory of Maurice Manning is of him demanding that Mother see to the horses. It didn't matter what time of day or night it was, she was always on call to him. He would come to the door stamping his feet impatiently like a truculent child. 'Is your mother in?' he would ask without saying 'hello' or 'good evening'. I don't think he ever spoke my name. I wouldn't answer but went straight to get my mother. She might come to the door drying her hands from the kitchen or from the garden, with secateurs in her hand.

'The horse is unsettled,' Maurice would say, still red and breathless as if he had run from the stables in a hurry.

Usually Mother would go straight away telling me 'I won't be long.'

Only once do I remember her saying, 'Just give me a minute, Maurice, I've just got to...'

But she didn't finish the sentence, Maurice was already saying, 'Now!'

So Mother would go with him. I would watch them walk down the drive, Mother taking two steps to each of his strides. He walked in front staring ahead and Mother followed him as if she had no choice. It made me angry he had such power. Minutes before I might have been asking for something and she would say, 'Not now, Hal, I'm busy.' Yet he would turn up and she would go. When I was older I asked her why she did it and her response would always be the same. 'The horses are my job, Hal, and most important to Maurice. He's my employer.' Once, when Mother was not strictly a groom and employee of the Mannings, I'd said, 'But you shouldn't be on call all the time. Especially now.'

She shook her head at me, 'You don't understand, Hal.' I was already annoyed by her patronising manner; usually she would talk to me as an equal. She continued, 'You don't know how much I owe them, Hal. They changed my life.' It was as much of an explanation as I ever got. I never asked again, but my hatred of Maurice Manning grew each time he appeared on the doorstep.

As I thought about Maurice Manning my body tensed. Coiled into the corner of the sofa, I tried to relax, remembering, 'One should not think ill of the dead'. But I couldn't do it. I stayed on the sofa for the rest of the evening, pondering what the will reading would bring; I could not imagine it held anything for me. The writing on the card could have been Gracie's I supposed, wanting me there for moral support, but I did not think it was her style; she would have asked me if she wanted me there. I scratched the back of my hand as I wondered; occasionally stopping to pat Barklay as he shuffled at my foot, presumably thinking it was too quiet without his family around.

The following morning, not knowing how to dress for the reading of a will, I chose the standard black jeans and T-shirt. The T-shirt was the first that came to hand from the pile in my suitcase which as yet remained unpacked. The top had the opening paragraph from Crime and Punishment. Where I had acquired it from I could not recall and it crossed my mind that it was probably inappropriate but by then I couldn't be bothered to change.

My hand was sore so I went to find some antiseptic cream. The bathroom cabinet was locked which I presumed normal for a house with young children. After a bit a searching I found the key just on top of the cabinet. At first I was shocked by what I found. It looked like syringes. However on closer inspection I realised they were cartridges of insulin, ready fitted to a needle applicator. Beside them was a tub of test strips. Somebody was diabetic. I looked at the prescription label and read 'Mr Thomas Sheldon'. So it was Tom. I wondered when that had been diagnosed, as he had never mentioned it to me. There was also a tube of antiseptic cream and as I rubbed it over my hand I told myself I needed to be more disciplined and not to scratch. This was part of the reason I decided to take Barklay with me to the will reading. I reckoned stroking him served as a distraction. It was also a lovely day so the car was unnecessary.

Looking up at the blue sky, the rain of yesterday was a distant memory, a blot on an otherwise perfect summer. As it was dry we took the back way to the Manor, using the footpath that leads along the ridge then through a wooded area which took us to a five bar gate. It had a sign on it, 'Private. Keep Out', which I ignored and I climbed with some difficulty into the Manning estate.

I liked the trees here, a mixture of various greens and different leaf shapes. There was one particular silver birch which I hesitated beside. Yes, although barely discernible, the mark was still there; a heart poorly scratched on the trunk. Just above it was the place I had peeled a silver strip of bark away. I had taken hold of Lizzie's hand and carefully tied it around her finger. Throughout this process Lizzie giggled but my face was serious. I asked her to marry me. She had continued to laugh as if it was a joke but still she wore the mock ring for the rest of the afternoon. That was a long time ago, before our official wedding plans had ever been discussed. I patted the tree as if we were old companions reminiscing.

We left the woods and started to cross the expanse of lawn. Barklay trotted at my side. Half way across somebody came out waving their arms in the air and Barklay bounded towards him thinking the man was pleased to see him. He was not. As I got closer I recognised Nigel, rather flustered and red in the face. 'What the hell are you doing? This is private property,' he shouted. Then, as our eyes met, he said in a feeble voice, 'Oh, it's you.'

'Sorry,' I shrugged, 'I didn't think. Just thought I'd take the old route.' Neither of us said anything for several moments and I wondered if he had been thinking about those days as children when we had used the estate as if it was ours, even though we were both interlopers. My hand prickled but before I scratched it I reached out for Barklay and slipped the lead round his neck.

'Nice dog,' Nigel commented.

'Yes, I'm house and dog sitting for Tom.' I followed with, 'Tom Sheldon, the gardener?' And wished I hadn't because there was another palpable shift in the atmosphere.

'What are you doing here, anyway?' Nigel finally asked.

'I've come to the will reading.'

Nigel's look became round with surprise and not without a good amount of doubt. As he looked me up and down, taking in my informal outfit, I realised what I should be wearing for a will reading. He was dressed in a pale blue shirt under a dark suit and a black tie with a crest I could not identify embroidered on it.

To help him out I said, 'I had an invitation.'

I had left the invitation; such as it was, at home, so could not prove it.

Nigel had obviously changed in the intervening years because he did not demand to see it, instead he simply turned and said, 'Come on then.'

I followed him down to the house.

I was again ushered into the house through the back door rather than the front entrance, and followed Nigel into the main lounge. The furniture had been moved and laid out in formal rows facing a table and chairs occupied by what I presumed were a legal team. There were three of them. A man younger than me sat at the far end, the junior member of the team. Next to him a striking woman with cropped red hair and beside her an older gentleman with distinguished silver hair and a benign expression which I thought he had probably perfected over many years; one that gave nothing away.

The room was already full; nobody looked round at me and Nigel abandoned me as I took the seat nearest the door, Barklay lying down by my feet. I could make out Gracie beside her grandmother on the front row. Neither acknowledged my presence but the lead solicitor took my entrance as a cue.

'If we're all present I'll begin,' he said. He introduced himself as Paul Woodhouse and then proceeded with the information that this was the last will and testament of Charles Maurice Manning.

As the details were read I scanned the outside world feeling removed from it, but not included in the present. I could view the lawns and see the path I had taken earlier; my trespassing would have been obvious to anybody looking out. Nigel must have known I had been invited; his deception when we met struck me as typical. I half listened as the list was read, each with a brusque comment I could imagine Maurice saying in his clipped tones.

Suddenly, I heard my name. Mr Henry Bennett. I did a double take wondering if I had heard correctly but did not have time because the next words were even more disorientating.

'...The building known as the Gate House and all its contents. Also, an oil painting of Chantelle Bennett.' I waited for an explanation; a sentence that would tell me why I had been left the Gate House and a painting of my mother. I'd no idea about her portrait being painted. No explanation came. I told myself I must have misheard, but it was unlikely as I became aware of a collective scrutiny as the creak of chairs signalled people turning to look at me. Barklay sat up, aware of the attention. Paul Woodhouse, the solicitor, looked at me with a steady gaze and nodded, as if to confirm the bequest.

Out of the corner of my eye I could see Maurice's brother, Victor, smiling. He winked at me and gave me a thumbs-up. I did not return his smile but continued to stare straight ahead, as if caught in some misdemeanour. Gradually the faces turned away and Mr Woodhouse continued with the reading. Even when the final legacy had been read and the proceedings had been closed I continued to sit, staring straight ahead, my only movement one hand moving across the back of the other pulling at the skin.

The solicitors packed their papers away and then Nigel led them out. Grace Elizabeth stood and addressed us. 'Refreshments will be served in the Blue Room.' That was the dining room. The company started to talk and shuffle their way to the doors. I continued to sit. For some reason I couldn't identify, I did not think the bequest had been made with generosity, but had been hurled at me like a curse. I tried to tell myself not to be so stupid. The inheritance of even a small property these days could only be a blessing. Surely? However, I knew the last time I had been there I couldn't wait to escape it.

What Was Taken 3

In fairy tales, often places or people are not what they seem. It was like that with the Gate House.

With its white-washed walls, leaded windows and its uneven red roof tiles it had a charming presence as it nestled under the canopy of trees. If you had drawn it as a child, which I had no doubt done in my school books, you would think it an enchanting cottage.

For most of my life I had viewed it that way too. Until Mother died.

Now it was stained with painful memories, which had transformed the cottage into a witch's hovel, squatting with malevolence at the end of the drive.

The years of my sixth form were not trouble free, but I had been content, returning each day to the cosy comfort of the cottage and Mother, who always welcomed me with a smile whatever time I chose to arrive, as if I was the one thing that always gave her pleasure. I did not tell her everything, but I knew she would forgive my misdemeanours such as they were, without question.

How did I manage to let her down so badly? The idea of going to university had never crossed my mind. I enjoyed school and without much effort passed the tests and exams I was set. The secondary school was in a larger town six miles away, Bainsford, and the few students from Leverbridge would catch the bus in each day. Tom and I used to enjoy the journey but by the sixth form Tom had left to work with his father. Being more isolated concentrated my school-work, my results got better with each term. At school I was not distracted, I didn't play sports or join in clubs, my focus was school-work and Lizzie. We had become closer during the last year and I was desperate for the little time we spent together. Lizzie and

Gracie went to a private school which had longer hours than my school, though the terms were shorter.

But during the autumn of my final school year, I realised I could never be with Lizzie unless I made something of myself, became a better man. It must have been towards the end of November and I was at the cottage alone. The day was not bright and the interior of the cottage dim under the clawing bare branched trees. At this time of year there was always a damp smell of decaying leaves in the air that I rather liked. Shut up in the cottage under the canopy of interlocking branches and with fallen leaves below, I felt like an animal preparing for hibernation tucked up in his hole before winter set in.

There was a knock at the door, not a polite rapping, but a *Boom, Boom, Boom* of the knocker, making the cottage shudder. As I opened the door I noticed the final falling of leaves from the surrounding trees as if they had at last been shaken free. Charles Maurice Manning was too big for the door. He looked swollen, standing there with his red cheeks and puffed out chest. His manner was different from the times he came to summon Mother. He wasn't ignoring me like an invisible bell boy but looking directly at me.

I could not find the words to greet him so meekly said, 'Yes?'

'I understand you are seeing my granddaughter?' It wasn't really a question but a statement shouted out.

I could feel his angry breath on my face and thought if he had a mind to he could probably blow me over. I managed to stutter a pathetic, 'Yes.'

Lizzie and I had been secretive about our courtship. I wondered how Maurice had found out.

He continued shouting, spittle spotting my face.

'It's got to stop. Do you understand me? You are not worthy of her company let alone courting her. I took your mother in when she was in need, let you stay here for a peppercorn rent, and I don't want repaying by her snivelling son thinking he can seduce my granddaughter. Do I make myself clear?'

I was nodding like a toy dog in the back of a car, unable to control myself and like that ornament my head was empty, as if I had lost the mechanics for speech. Mother had instilled the fact that we were little more than servants, she had been given the opportunity to work as a stable girl and live in the cottage and I was to remember that always and be grateful for it. Had this been Victorian times I would have been expected to touch my forelock and genuflect. I may have done so in the face of his glare. Maurice continued, 'You do not see her again, you hear? You don't even think of her again.'

With that, he turned and marched away. I stood at the door for a long time, waiting until my breath had returned and watched a final yellow leaf sway in the air and then settle on the ground. The walk back to the warmth of the living room seemed disproportionately long. I stumbled to my armchair repeating to myself that nothing could stop me seeing Lizzie again. Of course I agreed with Maurice, I was not good enough for her. I also comprehended my lowly position in respect of the Manning family. So, Maurice didn't have to tell me I was unworthy, I knew I was. But whilst Lizzie needed and wanted me, I was never going to give her up, not even with the bullish Maurice Manning charging in.

I watched logs creak and crack in the grate and as they did so my thoughts settled. Rather than it being a hopeless case, I took Maurice's outburst as a challenge. I would find a way to prove myself to the Manning family.

Sitting in the armchair I brooded for the entire afternoon and I worked out my plan; I would try for university. I chose Law simply because I thought it would give me credentials of worthiness. The following day I asked at school and was given nothing but support. The tutor told me what I needed to do and gave me suggestions for the best universities to study Law. She helped me with the paper work, additional forms and preparation for my interview and before I knew it I was there.

Through the process Mother had been supportive. She had never questioned the decision and I think she presumed it was what I wanted. Foolishly, I don't think I ever asked her for her true feelings. In any event by then it would probably have been too late. Even Grace Elizabeth had become involved; I presumed Lizzie had mentioned it to her. She could not have been more helpful, coming to the cottage and speaking to both Mother and me, asking if she could help with funding or anything else. I remember her standing in the living room like a Lady Bountiful trying to smooth my path. I took it as a good omen that she should take so much interest, supposing it to be confirmation that this indeed was the act of a legitimate suitor for her granddaughter.

My meeting with Maurice still makes me shudder. Perhaps that's when the cottage changed its nature; not with Mother's death but with the premonition of disaster.

So towards the end of September the following year, I was waved off from Leverbridge like royalty. Mother hugged me and said she was proud of me, I accepted her comment as an honest one. Tom was there to slap me on the back and say, 'Good on you.' Victor came and winked and shook my hand, clumsily pressing several twenty-pound notes into my palm as he did so. Even Grace Elizabeth came to say goodbye and confirm what a fine young man I was becoming.

Lizzie was going to drive me the two hour trip to Warwick. We'd packed her car, the one she'd been given for her 17th birthday a year ago, and she apologised Gracie couldn't wish me goodbye. With Gracie's health problems I didn't take it personally.

*

My transition to university student was not the disaster some might have expected. I had a pleasant room in an accommodation block, everybody was friendly and the course was interesting. I soon had a working structure arranged and time to go out and drink. I did not socialise in the true sense because I didn't really want more friends. I had those in Leverbridge. It was a time just before everybody had mobiles so I spoke to Lizzie on the communal phone each day and we wrote letters. She told me Grace Elizabeth had suggested she did not drive up and see me in the first term so I could have the best chance of settling in, and it would allow Lizzie to take her studies at a local university seriously. The way she reported it made it sound like sensible advice, given with the best of intentions.

I spoke to Mother almost every day. She told me she missed me, but from what she said I thought she was coping without me just as I was learning to live without the certainty of her companionship in the next room. It was a learning curve for both of us but one we both acknowledged had to happen at some point in our lives.

The most treacherous part of life is when everything appears to be going well. Whilst I was looking along the path of enlightenment, to a future with Lizzie, something terrible occurred.

I got the call mid-morning, just after I'd finished a lecture on European Law. We had been discussing the laws regarding direct and indirect effect and I was still contemplating the subject.

There was a sobbing voice at the end of the line, 'Hal. Hal.' Each word was punctuated with a gulp for air. 'You've got to come home, something dreadful's happened.'

Several horrible notions rushed through my brain as Lizzie choked the message out. Lizzie had hurt herself, something had happened to Maurice or Grace Elizabeth or...my god...Gracie; Gracie had finally succeeded in committing suicide. I don't know why all the terrible things which twisted in my thoughts applied to the Mannings, not to me.

Whether Lizzie was calmer when she said the words I don't know. It may simply be that the words were too horrific for anything else to be comprehended when they were spoken, but they came down the line with the power of nuclear weaponry. Three little words, which would change my life and spin me off the noble course I had recently chosen.

'Your. Mother's. Dead.'

The phone clattered from my hand and I was found in a heap on the floor. Some poor soul volunteered to drive me home. But I was still struck dumb. I didn't say a word to him as we drove to Leverbridge. Nor did I thank him or say goodbye when he dropped me at the gates of Leverbridge Manor. In fact, I don't think I ever saw him again. I did not return to Warwick. My things were packed up and returned to me, I never asked how.

The scene that faced me when I arrived at the Gate House was not as I expected. I had imagined chaos; policemen, medics, perhaps a priest. Where were the emergency services? Where were the blue flashing lights and sirens, to indicate people were trying to save Mother? There was nobody. There was not any sound. Birdsong had been muted; even the trees were noiseless as if stunned by what they had witnessed. I approached the cottage door and turned the key in the lock. Instead of the usual click as I pushed the door ajar, it was silent. I tried to step over the threshold but my leg couldn't move against the weight of stillness within.

Then from far away something stirred. A voice had called out but I could not decipher the words in the vacuum around me. It might have said my name, but I could not remember what my name was. Lizzie rushed up to me like an angelic apparition. I hugged her, reassured by her realness; the warmth of her body, her breath against my neck, a strand of her hair against my mouth. I kept hold of her as if she were the only fixed point on earth as the rest of the world swayed about us.

'Hal, come to the house. You can't do anything here.'

I let her guide me down the driveway towards the Manor. Behind me I imagined an ambulance door opening and a stretcher with a black body bag being stowed inside. I vomited. It was a thin, sour liquid as I had only had coffee for breakfast that morning. Coffee in a red mug seemed like a distant dream of normality.

Lizzie didn't comment on the splashes of sick on the path, she just handed me a tissue and we continued to move forward. We sat in the kitchen and Annie Taylor made me sandwiches and sweet tea. But the food dropped into my stomach as it might a well. That is the closest I have come to an out of body experience because it was as if my physical body had become stone and I was simply an entity floating in space.

Annie fussed around me, not knowing what to say. She spoke about the minutiae of the moment. Was the tea sweet enough, the jam had been bought at the Summer Fayre, she thought it was from the batch that had won first prize, it was a shame she hadn't baked a cake, and on and on and on, whilst she clattered clean pots and pans around as if she had an important function to arrange.

Lizzie sat beside me, completely still. I knew she was watching me and I was glad she said nothing. There was nothing that could be said. I saw her hand clutching mine but I could not even feel the sensation of her fingers.

A little later Lizzie left me and I could hear an argument in the corridor outside. Lizzie rarely raised her voice but she did so now. 'That is so unfair. You can't throw him out. I won't let you.'

The other voice was quieter, measured. I did not hear the words but could understand the response by their certain rhythm.

For a time Lizzie continued her sharp retorts but the solemn reply was unwavering.

When Lizzie returned she again sat beside me and held my hand. 'I'm sorry Hal, but you can't stay here tonight. Shall I ring Tom and see if his parents will put you up?'

So that's when I moved in with Tom and his parents. I never returned to the Gate House.

During that time I knew I was still alive because at night I could hear my heart beating inside my hollow chest, so loud it drowned out the snores from Tom's side of the room. I looked up into the darkness not wanting to go to sleep because my dreams always ended with waking and the realisation all over again that my mother was dead. Worse still, people were saying she had committed suicide. This I would never believe. If Mother had been depressed I would have known when we'd spoken on the phone; we were so close I would have sensed it. She loved me too much to leave me like this, without an explanation. If she had killed herself she would have left me a note. I lay awake in the darkness listening to the steady rhythm of my heart, wishing it would stop.

So I existed in a state of semi-coma for days, moving about without sensation. Tom's parents were welcoming and kind; I could understand why they were such good gardeners because I imagined they had the same effect on plants with their gentle nurturing. Each day they would give me a job to do in the nursery, it was usually weeding or hoeing or collecting leaves and in the beginning I did it without feeling. Then one day, I realised I was cold and getting wet. It was raining and had probably been doing so for several days without me noticing. I went indoors and asked for a cup of tea. Mary, Tom's mum replied, 'Of course,' and smiled at me. It was only then that I realised it was the first time I had asked for anything since arriving. From then my recovery quickened. I continued to help out around the greenhouses and borders of their market garden but began to take notice of what I was doing. It was strange for me to be part of a family. Tom's parents were much older than my mother; from a different generation. The clothes Mary wore and the TV they watched I considered old-fashioned. But they were pleasant people and I enjoyed their company and tried to forget the idyllic existence I'd shared with Mother.

As my mental state improved I craved my time with Lizzie, but had to put up with stolen moments. She tried to see me when she could but had to sneak out of the house. She said it was becoming more and more difficult. Every time she tried to leave other than for university, somebody stopped her. As for visiting the Manor I could not go there because it was linked to the Gate House. It was as if a part of my life had been severed from me.

Once when Lizzie had been obstructed in getting away she sent Gracie over in her place with a letter and an apology. I had watched the figure approach from the lane and my heart lurched when I discovered it was not Lizzie. It had been a horrible afternoon. Gracie was not good at conversation and I imagined her head was so overloaded with her own demons; she could not speak for fear they would spill out unchecked. Occasionally the silence was interrupted by Tom or Mary making small talk which only emphasised the awkwardness.

The next time I saw Lizzie she said, 'It feels as if I'm a prisoner, only nobody's told me what my crime is. I think they might be trying to split us up.' She regarded me with her determined expression; her chin tilted forward, her eyes defiant. 'But it's not going to work.' She grabbed my hand, squeezing so hard I could feel her nails digging into my flesh. Our intertwined fingers resembled a knot of tendons. Nothing could break the bond we had.

What Remains 4

My left hand, dangling uselessly at the side of the chair, suddenly felt damp, I glanced down to see Barklay trying to attract my attention, licking my fingers.

'Hal, Hal,' there was an echo from a great distance away. I could still feel the imprint of Lizzie's fingernails on my hand. It comforted me as I remembered our bond. Lizzie had promised never to leave me.

'Hal, Hal,' the echo continued. Then I was aware of Gracie. 'Are you alright?'

Deja vu. Here was Gracie's concerned face peering at me.

'It's wonderful that the Gate House is yours,' she continued brightly, 'You'll be a proper neighbour now.'

'Mother, died.' Those were the only two words I could string together.

It took several moments for my whispered words to sink in.

'Oh, Hal, God I'm so sorry. I'd forgotten. Let me get you something to drink.'

Instead of the cup of tea I expected, she returned with a cut glass tumbler half filled with brandy. I drank it down in one gulp, appreciating the burning sensation.

'Thank you,' I managed to say. 'And I'm sorry, but I don't think I want to visit the Gate House, let alone live there.'

'Well, there's no hurry, is there? It's yours to do what you want with. But if you decide you do want to go in, I'll go with you. Just ask.'

'What's all this then?' The booming tone of Nigel came near. 'Well Hal, you're a man of property now.' He slapped me on the back, Barklay made a small protective gesture towards him. And I thought I heard him growl.

'Bet you can't wait to get yourself moved in there?'

Gracie coughed and said quietly, 'That's where Hal's mother died, Nigel. I don't think Hal's happy about the inheritance.'

'Well, that was a long time ago, wasn't it? The cottage could be really pretty again, like it was in the old days.'

I tried to recall the taste of brandy in my mouth so I would remain calm but only detected bile.

Nigel pressed on, 'Don't you want a cup of tea? Come and meet some people. Annie's made her legendary chocolate cake.'

I presumed he left the room as Gracie apologised. 'Sorry about that. He's not the most sensitive soul.'

With Nigel though I always had the notion he knew exactly what he was doing.

'Would you like tea and cake?'

I made my excuses and left quickly before I was dragged into polite chat, dissecting the last will and testament of Charles Maurice Manning.

Once outside the insidious atmosphere of the Manor, I was able to take a deep cleansing breath. The sky was a perfect blue and I could glimpse the main gate. The trees at the end of the drive which hid the Gate House were moving gently like soft green feathers swaying in the breeze. I took another deep breath as I made my decision and with Barklay beside me I strode down the drive before I could change my mind. It took several minutes to reach the Gate House and by the time I got there my palms were clammy and my heart racing. But I found if I took regular gulps of air I was able to stop and look at the cottage. Up close I could see the place was not in the complete state of dereliction I had assumed when Annie had driven me passed two days before. Green slime obscured most of the roof, dimming the red tiles but there were only a couple missing. One of the diamond panes in the leaded windows was cracked and the wooden sills were rotting. But it was not as bad as I expected. The cherry red paint of the door was faded and peeling and the door itself appeared to sag like a downturned mouth. I could not help but feel sad for the place.

We didn't linger for long, but with each step on the paths of Leverbridge village to Tom's house, I decided perhaps I would take on my inheritance.

As I made my way down the hill towards the centre of the village I smelt cooking. The pub was open; two men sat outside smoking cigarettes and laughing. The aroma of food, beer and cigarettes was so familiar I didn't realise I'd decided to go in until I was facing the smiling features of a barmaid asking what she could get me. I ordered a pint of draught bitter, and sipped it slowly, enjoying the taste as I took in the surroundings. Though I hadn't been in The Huntsman for over a decade nothing appeared to have changed. The area was dim, the bar a dark wood square with two openings, one facing the lounge side and the other accessing the public bar. The lone barmaid stood in a small island. I knew the door behind her led to a storage space and entrance area with steps down to a cellar below and stairs up to living quarters above. The layout was familiar to me as I'd spent some days and evenings in the back waiting for Mother to finish her shift. The barmaid was pretty but not like Mother, who had stood like Venus rising from her shell in the centre of the pub with the flow of customers lapping around her waiting for a smile or kind word from her perfect mouth.

The barmaid put another pint in front of me and I was jolted from my reverie. 'Just visiting, are you luv?' she asked. A name badge identified her as 'Bev'.

I nodded, 'I grew up here though.'

'Wow, has it changed much?'

'Not at all.' But as I said it I realised beneath its unchanged surface everything had altered. 'Except the pub sign,' I continued.

'Oh that. That was done in honour of Mr Manning. I think it's a good likeness.'

'Yes, I recognised him.'

'So sad he died. He was good for the village.'

I nodded and sipped my beer. However much I personally disliked Maurice I could understand he was seen as a great asset to Leverbridge. I'd noticed a number of signs indicating how much money Maurice and his family had gifted various village projects, like the Garden Centre. There was even a road named after them, 'Manning Way'.

Bev continued, 'It was so unexpected as well. Of course he'd just turned eighty, but even so he looked as fit as a fiddle when he came in here.'

'So what did he die of?' I asked, having made the assumption it had simply been old age.

'Well, apparently he'd been ill for a few days,' she leant across the bar. I could feel the warmth of breath on my forehead as she whispered, 'then according to my friend who works there,' she clicked her fingers, 'suddenly, heart gives out, just like that.'

There were various posters along the bar for local events, the quiz-nite, an open mike evening, Leverbridge summer fayre and a smaller hand written flyer announcing a fete on Saturday at The Bowers residential home. It sounded familiar. But it was only as my pint glass reduced to half full; I remembered The Bowers was where Tom's dad had gone to live after his mother died. I wondered if he was still alive. Tom hadn't mentioned his death to me. As I sipped the last trickle of foam and beer from the glass I decided I might go to the fete on Saturday and see Tom's dad, just for old times' sake.

The weather remained kind for the rest of the week, Barklay and I took our walks further afield and I felt myself getting stronger. The limp, which for a year or two after my accident had always been so noticeable, had levelled out. Only occasionally did I become aware of it, on rough unfamiliar ground or when I was tired. I positively strode along the byways of my youth, visiting local villages and public houses I vaguely remembered. Some had gone but others been given facelifts or diversified into other businesses. It didn't matter. I walked and where possible had a pint and sandwich and found a bowl of water for Barklay.

Saturday dawned in cloudless perfection and momentarily I considered heading out again with Barklay rather than visiting The Bowers fete. Firstly though, I decided to take Barklay for a short walk into the village. As I strolled down the hill towards the centre of Leverbridge, a new poster had been placed in the stand outside the newsagents. The criss-cross of wire hemmed in the paper but could not constrain the words written in black.

'Bones at Manor are Alicia.'

I wobbled, suddenly aware of my missing foot, as if the prosthesis had been removed. Pain shot through me. As I leant against the wall Barklay gave me a quizzical look. I wasn't sure where the pain arose from, but my whole body was engulfed by it.

'It's alright, boy', I told Barklay, patting him; 'We'll go on in a minute.'

I closed my eyes feeling the weight of stone wall behind me, wringing my hands. Alicia was dead. Had been dead for a long time. Buried in the grounds of Leverbridge Manor.

'Are you alright?' a voice asked. When it repeated, I realised I was the one being addressed and I opened my eyes. A woman was looking at me with concern. I must look a state, I thought, and managed to reply, 'I'll be fine, thanks.' She nodded and went into the shop.

It took some time to regain my senses. The woman had smiled at me again on her way out of the shop and I'd lifted a hand to assure her I was okay. Finally, I managed to go inside and buy a local paper with its awful headline.

I made my way back home with Barklay. He wanted to run ahead, obviously feeling short changed by the brevity of the walk but my energy had been sapped.

Closing the front door of the house I flopped onto the sofa and did not move for a long time.

Gradually, I regained feeling and went to make myself a drink. I left the newspaper on the breakfast bar, incapable of reading more. It remained folded, but the edges of the headline were visible and I could hear the printed words, sounding in my brain like drums.

Time was moving on and I was aware The Bowers fete would be opening soon. I wondered whether to stay put but the decision I'd made in the pub was like a promise; I wanted to visit Tom's dad because I had never really thanked him for taking care of me when Mother died. With memories of Mother and Alicia so fresh in my mind I realised time might be running out to do so.

Balloons and streamers told me I was at the correct venue. Everybody was outside sipping cold drinks in the garden. The lawn was square, covered with rather yellow grass and enclosed by a wall of red brick against which roses and evergreens trailed. The borders were bright with yellow, pale blue and shots of red.

Groups of people stood around chatting but it wasn't the smooth, modulated conversation I'd expect at a garden party but a chaotic mix of voices with the occasional shout or cry and then a whisper, as if everybody was simply talking to themselves.

A woman with a name badge came over, 'Good afternoon, I'm Mrs Farrow, Manager. Welcome.' She held out her hand. I shook it. Her hand was pudgy and warm.

'Does Mr George Sheldon still live here?' I asked.

'Yes,' she replied. 'Are you a relative? I was expecting his son and grandchildren to pop in today.'

'Actually, I'm a friend of Tom's, he's on holiday this week, but I've known Mr Sheldon for many years, I'm staying in the area and just thought I'd drop in.'

'Well, that's lovely of you. George is sitting under that tree.' She indicated a large beech tree in the corner. There were several elderly men and women sitting in armchairs in its shade but as I made my way over I could recognise Tom's dad without difficulty.

'Hello George,' I said, touching his arm.

He looked up and smiled, 'Well, well if it isn't young Hal? Fancy you coming to see me.' I was about to remark how good his memory must be to recognise me so quickly but he was continuing to speak, 'Is Tom with you? You two are never apart, are you?' He turned to the woman beside him and said, 'Tom and Hal, never apart, the best of friends they are.'

He continued to tell the woman, 'Like another son is our Hal,' even though she didn't appear to be listening but was looking up into the beech branches above.

He asked me, 'Have you been making a camp up at the Big House then?'

It was then I realised time for George had been contracted and he was seeing me as a young boy. 'You can sit on the grass, can't you, Boy? We'll wait for Tom to come along.'

'Tom's on holiday,' I said. 'He can't get here today.' George ignored my comment.

'Oh, well he'll be along later, wanting his tea.' He laughed. I remembered him saying something similar many years ago. 'Tom'll be wanting his tea. Always hungry that boy.' It was so strong in my mind it was like an echo.

Bending down to talk to George was becoming uncomfortable, I could see no seat free, so I did as he'd suggested and sat on the grass beside his chair.

'So how's the camp going?' he asked. 'And how's your mum?' He patted my shoulder and then the top of my head.

I didn't know whether to tell him Mother was dead, or whether it would confuse him further.

'Beautiful woman your mother.'

There was silence for a moment as I desperately tried to think of something to say to this confused old man, who still looked like George Sheldon but was really just a husk masquerading as him.

'How's the camp going?' he repeated, 'Lovely weather this year, not like when little Alicia went missing.'

The mention of Alicia's name seemed to cause a rustle of the beech above us and shadows rippled across the people sitting beneath, emphasising the creases of age on each face and the bluish shadowed eyes. I shuddered.

'They won't find her.' He obviously hadn't heard the bones had been uncovered at the Big House.

The woman in the next seat turned and said to us. 'They found those bones didn't they? It was in the paper this morning.'

I nodded. 'Yes, unfortunately they did. At least we know where she is now.'

George's neighbour continued, 'But what can have happened to her? They don't seem to have a clue.'

George smiled and shook his head, 'They won't find her,' he stated as if having not heard the intervening conversation, 'Poor little girl. Never be found.'

The odd exchange perplexed me; I tried to move the conversation away from Alicia towards more mundane subjects. 'Are you doing any gardening then?'

'Oh, yes, I help out when I can. They like me to help.'

'I went up to the garden centre the other day. It's almost unrecognisable from when you used to live there.'

I looked up at George and felt terrible as I realised a tear was running down his face. What a fool to be so tactless and mention how his home had been changed. But then he said, 'Poor little girl, they'll never find her.' And he was shaking his head and the tears continued to meander down the lines of his face.

I got up and found the matron.

'Don't worry,' she said when I told her I'd upset him, 'Our residents often get confused with time. Sometimes they get stuck in a loop of sad memories; then again sometimes they remember nice things. It generally balances out. He obviously remembered you so that was nice for him. Come again, I'm sure he'd appreciate it.'

I promised I would try, if I stayed in the area. I bought some raffle tickets and headed off.

Walking home I took the back roads, avoiding crossing the centre square and passing the newsagents. The sun continued to shine, there was no breeze. Nobody seemed to be about and it was unnaturally quiet. The birds were silent and sheep appeared to have given up bleating. Looking at the brambles clawing their way along the hedgerows I was reminded of the story of sleeping beauty. Leverbridge might have been affected by a similar enchantment.

When I neared Tom's house something else seemed odd. It took me a moment to realise it was the Range Rover sitting opposite. As I got to the front door the driver leapt out and Gracie shouted, 'Hal, thank God you're here.'

I unlocked the door and went inside. Barklay wagged his tail and licked me in greeting. I was wondering if I was still in some enchanted world; never before had I been so in demand.

'Come in, I'll put the kettle on.'

Gracie followed me into the kitchen and sat on a stool at the breakfast counter. She put her head in her hands and began to sob. This was not my comfort zone. I made two mugs of tea and put some sugar in both. Sitting on a stool opposite, I pushed Gracie's tea toward her.

'Have some tea whilst it's hot.' I said, sounding like somebody else but not knowing what to say or think with Gracie weeping in front of me.

'I'm sorry,' she said finally looking up, her eyes ringed with smudges of mascara. She placed her hand on the folded newspaper. 'You've seen this then?'

I nodded.

'I can't believe it, can't believe it. Poor Alicia, I feel so guilty.'

I still had no idea what to say so placed my hand over Gracie's, aware of my reddened chapped skin against her smooth manicured fingers.

'What can have happened? What the hell did we do?'

'I don't know,' I replied, feeling hollowed by my impotence. The sense of guilt was mutual, somehow those of us there that night had been responsible. Now we were as culpable of Alicia's death as of her disappearance.

'The house feels horrible. I couldn't stay there, and I took Eliza to stay at a friend's house, it's not healthy up there.' Gracie continued, 'Grandmama is moving from room to room as if there's a fire following her, Annie Taylor is polishing the silver like she's trying to conjure up a genie and then every time I look out of the window someone from the press is skulking about just waiting to pounce. Of course, Nigel's going about as if nothing's happened.'

'Have you moved into The Manor?' I asked, aware at one time Gracie had refused to live there.

'Yes, just for now, to support Grace Elizabeth. But you never know, we might stay.'

'I thought you hated it there?'

'I did, but things change. For one thing I'm older and married, and Grandmama is all alone.' She looked down at her feet, kicking her toe against the breakfast bar. 'And Grandpapa is dead.' She said it without sorrow, more with a sense of finality.

'You don't seem that upset.'

Gracie shrugged. 'To be honest he was a bully. I'm not going to miss him.'

I wasn't about to disagree with her. For a few moments I listened to the rhythmic thud of her shoe hitting the table.

'So what's Nigel doing?'

'He said he was going to golf, just like he always does on Saturday, as if Alicia's disappearance had nothing to do with him.' She paused for a breath then continued quietly, 'I blame him most of all. He made up that stupid dare.'

I didn't like Nigel, but found myself defending him which felt strange. I said, 'We were all to blame for that. If any one of us had any sense we wouldn't have let her go off on her own.'

'But Nigel brought the wine didn't he?'

I couldn't argue with that, but again I could have said we didn't have to drink it. At the time I knew it would not have been an option.

Under my hand I could feel Gracie's fingers trembling. Looking at her I was aware it was just a symptom of her general state. Her whole body was quaking, even her eyes looked ready to shatter. I wondered if this was the beginning of a breakdown.

'Are you alright, Gracie? Do you need to take something?' I asked. I was not prepared for her response. She stood up and threw the paper at me.

'No, I'm not alright!' she screamed. 'I've just found out my little cousin has been buried in the family garden for years and years and I'm to blame.'

I lifted my palms in surrender. 'Sorry. But why are you taking all this blame on yourself? We played a stupid game. A child's game. We didn't kill her.'

The look Gracie gave me was one which might turn you to stone. 'If that's what you want to believe, fine, but you know as well as I do, there's more to it than that.'

She walked out of the kitchen.

'Gracie, please don't go like this. Stay, talk to me. We need each other.' I had not expected to say that, but I knew the words were true. Gracie and I were usually on our own. Once we had both shared Lizzie, she had kept us sane. And now we existed as rogue satellites drifting in space unable to communicate.

Gracie did not stop, but at the front door hesitated and turned to me. She shrugged. 'You're right. And I'm sorry to lose it like that. Put the kettle on again and I'll stay.'

Barklay accompanied her back to the kitchen. Once we had fresh cups of tea we speculated about the night of Alicia's disappearance.

'I thought she'd been abducted. I imagined her being kidnapped and sold to a rich couple who weren't able to have children,' she paused and took a deep breath, 'I know that's impossible, but it was a hope I could cling onto. Now I don't even have that. I keep thinking of how she could have ended up in that unmarked hollow. It makes no sense. If she had wandered off, even if she had fallen anywhere in the grounds, the police would have found her the next day. We searched so thoroughly as well.'

'And there were the dogs too,' I reminded her. 'And they searched the lake.'

'So the only conclusion is, she must have come to some harm and somebody was involved in hiding her body?'

I didn't want to admit it but could think of no other explanation.

'And who? Who would harm Alicia; she wasn't a threat to anybody. She was a six year old girl for goodness sake.'

'Perhaps she disturbed somebody?' It was the only thing I could think of. 'Do you get poachers on your land? Could she have got in their way?'

'I never heard of poachers on the estate, and I'm sure people would have come forward with information like that when a girl had gone missing.'

Another thought was niggling me, one of those uncomfortable ideas that persist; I scratched my hand to relieve the irritation.

Gracie looked at me and said what I had been thinking. 'There was that man with your mother. Could Alicia have disturbed them?'

It was my turn to be angry. It took me a moment to respond to her accusation. 'What! And their reaction would have been to kill her, hide her and then dump her? Thanks, but Mother wasn't like that. I'm not even sure I believe there was a man with her anyway. You just made that up.' I wished I didn't sound so much like the child from that night; the tremble in my voice took me back there more than the previous discussion.

Gracie continued to look at me with a steady gaze, made all the more uncomfortable because of the dark smudges of make-up around her eyes, like a Halloween ghoul.

'It wasn't a lie, Hal. Of course I'm not suggesting your mother would have harmed Alicia, but the man might have, if he shouldn't have been there.'

'What do you mean? Mother was a free agent; she was allowed to have a boyfriend, a lover even.'

'Hal, I'm sorry to tell you this,' she paused and for some reason I grabbed the edge of the breakfast bar, I knew I wasn't going to like what Gracie said. 'Your mother wasn't a saint. Of course she was a free agent, but from what I know she didn't have one boyfriend or one lover, she might have had several. And many of those would have been married and wouldn't have wanted to be discovered *in flagrante.*'

I couldn't speak; my grip on the table edge tightened.

'Hal, I'm not saying this to hurt you, but it's the truth.'

I moved so quickly that Barklay yelped at my feet. I went over to the kitchen door and put my palms on two small squares of glass. The combination of the moulded glass and the heat outside disfigured the garden, as if seen through a hall of mirrors. Nausea engulfed me. The only noise was the hum of the fridge resonating with the throbbing in my head.

Sometimes we know things. We don't admit them, but we know. I knew my mother liked the company of men. I had heard her often enough, flirting at the bar in the pub. I'd regarded it as part of her job although I knew it was more than that. I had even been aware of the laughing and lovemaking in the cottage late at night. And I knew the label the village gave her. All of my life I had managed to disregard it.

The fridge vibrated like a lewd man suppressing laughter, I nearly turned and hit it but my palms were glued to the back door.

After a long time Gracie said, 'I'm sorry Hal; I didn't mean to hurt you.'

'No, you're right.' I took my place at the breakfast bar again. 'I don't think she would have had anything to do with Alicia though. I really don't. If she knew anything she'd have told the police.'

Gracie gave a nod of sympathy. She turned and pulled a bottle of wine from a rack; it had a screw top and was quickly poured. But she did something else. Beside the wine was a bottle of champagne. Around its foil wrapped cork a tag dangled. Gracie must have noticed this. She frowned at it, removed it and dropped it in the waste bin. It was only later I thought about how strange her action was and retrieved the tag from the bin.

'Cheers,' Gracie said without any joy in her voice as we clinked our glasses together.

Our conversation moved on, but always came back to Alicia.

I asked about Eliza, hoping it would change the subject but that was worse. Gracie said, 'You see that's why I think finding Alicia has hit me so badly. Eliza is about the same age as Alicia was when she went missing. I sort of understand it more. I imagine what it would be like if Eliza disappeared. I would die. I would do anything to protect my daughter. Anything.' She stood up to make the point. 'You can't possibly understand that. When I think of how she might be harmed it makes my blood boil. That's how it makes me feel. Like I could kill somebody.'

Gracie's fingers around her glass tightened so much I thought it might shatter. It was only then with the way she held her glass and the light on her skin I was aware of thin scars on her wrists.

'You're not thinking of doing anything...' I asked. Not wanting to mention her previous suicide attempts but worried.

'No.' Gracie recognised the direction of my gaze and shifted her arm so the sleeve of her shirt covered her wrist. 'I'm not suicidal, if that's what you mean. I've got Eliza now. I have to stay well for her. I recognise the signs of depression and head to my doctor if I need.'

'Good, I'm glad you've got it under control.' In some ways I felt envious of Gracie. She seemed able to face her demons, I was not certain I had achieved a similar state.

What Was Taken 4

It had not always been the same. Gracie's illness was the trigger point for an alteration to my life; at the time it was wonderful but in hindsight was just a harbinger of the most terrible one.

I'd never known what exactly initiated Gracie's depression. On the surface she should have been happy. A pretty teenager from a wealthy family, private schooling and advantages most others would envy. Of course, she had lost her parents at a young age, but had been taken in by her grandparents who loved her.

Looking back it's easier to see clues. She had lost weight, thin anyway she began to look like a walking skeleton. Each time I saw her she had dyed her hair a different shade; from black to red to ash blonde and back again. Her demeanour changed as well, she'd either be quiet or extremely gregarious, never in between. Sometimes Lizzie said Gracie shut herself up in her room for days and didn't come out. Though Lizzie worried about her, we put it down to the trials of being sixteen. This was the consensus of any adult we approached. Lizzie did mention it to Grace Elizabeth who told her it was just a phase and Annie Taylor and Mother told me sixteen could be a difficult age for a female. I was a fifteen year old boy and agreed with this diagnosis, not equipped to suggest another.

It was the start of the Easter holidays when it began. Why Lizzie came to ask me to accompany her to the hospital, I don't know. At that time we were friends. I had never visited a hospital or dealt with illness. Still, there she was one spring morning standing on my doorstep.

Opening the door to her I had to catch my breath, she looked like a fairy creature. Her long hair coiled round her shoulders, little wisps of it catching the light as if she had been flying. Her eyes were large and wild with a film of moisture in them causing them to glisten. She was dressed in a loose gold dress, and beneath the outstretched branches of the budding beech trees around us, could have been a gift from the wood.

'Hal, are you listening?' I finally realised she'd been speaking.

'Sorry, what?'

'Gracie's in hospital!' That brought me round.

'Why, what's happened?'

'I'll tell you on the way.'

'You want me to come with you?'

'Yes. Gracie needs us. Come on.'

I grabbed a jacket from the coat rack, slipped trainers on, called a goodbye to Mother and followed Lizzie down the driveway.

I was surprised it was Annie Taylor who drove us to the hospital. We did not head for the Bainsford General, a huddle of mismatched rectangles on the outskirts of the town, which had been added to in a chaotic manner when the previous buildings were no longer adequate for the increase in population. We headed in another direction, to a place I had always known as the Sanatorium, if I was being polite. The Sanatorium was actually a private hospital; the central building was a grand house similar to Leverbridge Manor which had been extended with two low modern wings to each side. The driveway was cut short to make room for a large parking area which was half full. Annie's little Renault looked out of place beside the expensive models parked there; I could see none bearing a number plate over a year in age.

'I'll wait here for you,' said Annie. Lizzie made no comment. I continued to follow obediently.

Before we got to the oak panelled doors indicating the entrance I did suggest, 'You'd better tell me what's going on?' I felt so nervous my palms were sweating.

'Gracie tried to kill herself.'

'What...Why..?' I gabbled.

'She cut her wrists. Thank God I found her. I got back early and had that feeling, you know...?'

I didn't know but accepted the fact that as identical twins they had a bond stronger than other siblings and might well have some telepathic powers.

'Thanks for coming,' she said. I could see she had tears in her eyes; her hand was on my arm. 'I hate hospitals.'

I could feel her shivering through my jacket.

'It reminds me of when Mum and Dad died.' She paused, then said, 'You don't have to come in, if you don't want to.'

Though not a fan of hospitals myself, I liked the sensation of supporting Lizzie's trembling hand on my arm. I took a deep breath and told her, 'No, I'll come with you.' I added, 'I'll be fine,' for my benefit.

We were greeted by a nurse and after Lizzie had introduced herself, were shown down an airy corridor.

'This is Gracie's room,' the nurse indicated, 'Best she just has two visitors.'

Lizzie frowned. The nurse explained, 'There's already somebody with her.'

Lizzie let out a little 'Oh?' sound, as if she might suggest the nurse was mistaken. She was obviously not expecting anybody else to be with her sister at this time.

'Wait for me here, Hal,' she instructed.

I nodded, but was curious to see what was going on. So as Lizzie opened the door I looked in. My view was obscured by the broad shoulders of a man. He had a dark blue coat on and from his voice I could tell it was Maurice Manning. 'Now you hurry up and get better, little lady, the place isn't the same without you around,' he was telling her.

It was odd though, because at the moment the door had opened his voice had lifted into a jolly one. I suspected seconds before his words had been of a firmer less pleasant tone, as if he had been telling Gracie to pull herself together. But the idea may simply have been because of my previous exchanges with Maurice.

Gracie looked up as Lizzie entered. I could just glimpse her lying against the pillows. Her head seemed tiny, almost swallowed up by the cushioned bulk around her head. One arm was lying on the bedclothes, wrapped from the fingers to elbow in white bandage. As Lizzie went in the unhappy expression on Gracie's face changed to a smile and she looked less corpse-like, more like the old Gracie.

Maurice turned as he became aware of Lizzie, 'Oh, good you're here, Gracie's been waiting to see you. I was just leaving. Could I have a word,' and he grasped Lizzie's arm and came into the corridor with her. He looked in my direction but gave no expression of having noticed me. 'Now please don't upset Gracie by asking a lot of questions about what she did or why she did it. We've engaged a psychiatrist to do that. She just needs company and a normal chat for now. Is that understood?' There was no way of refusing his request; I nodded madly in mute acquiescence. Lizzie responded with a slightly less enthusiastic, 'Alright.'

We both went into the room this time. Though it was quite large I felt awkward, as if I didn't belong. Lizzie gave her sister a hug and I moved from foot to foot not knowing if I should make physical contact with Gracie as well. Finally I stepped forward and touched her fingers which were the only visible bit of her hand. They felt cold and I concentrated on their bluish lifelessness and did not look at Gracie as she said, 'Hi, Hal. Thanks for coming.'

I wondered what to say then. The obvious things I wanted to ask had been forbidden by Maurice. Lizzie was more adept and after a minute began telling Gracie about what had been happening at home and school. I sat in an armchair and looked out of the window onto a lawn which stretched away into the distance. A weak reflection of myself looked back, appearing uncomfortable. With the rise and fall of conversation in the background, I started a silent exchange with my reflected counterpart. What would drive a sixteen year old to cut their wrists? What would be so terrible to make me attempt such a thing, and would I have the courage? My reflection remained silent and I realised the chat behind me was similarly one-sided. Lizzie was speaking without taking breath as if afraid the forbidden question might creep in.

I was glad to leave. It felt like escape as we walked into the fresh afternoon air from the claustrophobia of Gracie's sick room. Back in the car Annie asked after Gracie and Lizzie answered crossly, 'As well as can be expected.' Annie took the hint and drove us back to Leverbridge in silence. Lizzie did not speak to me even to say goodbye as I was dropped out at the Gate House. I wondered if I'd done something to upset her. I was dwelling on this as I opened the door and was glancing over my shoulder at Annie's car making its way down the drive. My contemplations were interrupted by laughter. The noise was so unexpected I jumped.

'Oh, Ssh. Hal's home.' Then a giggle.

Mother came out of her bedroom, closed the door and smoothed her hair. 'Hello Hal, wasn't expecting you back just yet.'

The bedroom door opened again, and there was George. He coughed.

'Oh, George here's been helping me out making plans for the garden,' Mother said, 'I thought it would be nice to have a rambling rose trailing along beneath my bedroom window. What do you think?'

'I'm sure it would be lovely,' I answered, puzzled at being asked my opinion on roses, and aware of George's red face, convincing me Mother was covering up for something else entirely.

I went to my room feeling nauseous about the whole afternoon; first Gracie, then Lizzie's silence and now

George's presence in my home. My stomach rumbled and I realised I had not eaten since breakfast; I was hungry but unable to move from my room because of George.

I heard them go into the back garden and discuss flowers and planting schemes. I presumed this charade was purely for my benefit. Finally he left and I made toast in the kitchen. Mother didn't come in and I was relieved she wasn't going to continue lying to me.

The next afternoon Lizzie was again knocking at my door.

'Hal, I'm going to visit Gracie again. You'll come with me won't you?' In truth it was less of a question, more foregone conclusion; a Manning directive. I went and got my jacket and accompanied her out to Annie's waiting car.

I smiled and greeted Annie as I climbed into the back seat, then I watched the countryside move past in a muted stream of greenness as we headed towards the hospital. Nobody spoke.

It was a similar scenario in the hospital room. Lizzie spoke to Gracie and I sat in the armchair watching my reflection in the glass of the window with an addition to the conundrum posed the previous day, 'Why had Lizzie requested my company again when I served no purpose here?'

We followed the same process over the next week. Lizzie visited her sister frequently and always asked me to accompany her. I don't recall her visiting without me and besides greeting Gracie with a handshake I never joined in the conversation. I was aware though, over those initial days that Gracie's colour improved and she had gained a little weight and reciprocated Lizzie's chat.

In the first days Lizzie and I rarely spoke about Gracie's situation but gradually our conversation increased. Lizzie would tell Annie about Gracie's progress and I would occasionally chip in with a comment when asked. The weather had been pleasant, so one afternoon we'd strolled around the grounds, Gracie and Lizzie walked a couple of strides ahead of me and I maintained a respectful distance behind. I noticed the season changing and felt a similar stirring. Daffodils frilled the lawn edges. Beech trees stretched up to a spring blue sky and I was filled with the kind of hope nature can bestow when she is benign. It was exactly a month until my sixteenth birthday on the fourth of May. Whether it was simply the scent of spring turning to summer or the perfume and sway of the two young women walking in front of me suddenly I was aware of a strength in my body which had not been present even a week ago. Something had changed; a step across the chasm of puberty. Being included in Gracie's rehabilitation made me feel as if I had grown up. Lizzie stopped and turned, 'Guess what?' she said, smiling. 'Gracie might be allowed home for the weekend'.

'Fantastic,' I agreed, but Gracie didn't smile, she looked down and kicked her foot against a tuft of grass.

Lizzie ignored her and continued in an over-bright voice. 'Everybody's coming for the Easter weekend. Tara and Nigel. You like them, don't you?'

Gracie shrugged. 'Will Uncle Victor be there?'

'Probably.'

Gracie kicked at the grass again. This time a clump flew up in the air.

It was that same afternoon that Lizzie got out of the car with me at the Gate House and said she wanted some air and would walk to the Manor later. 'I'll have a cup of tea with you Hal,' she said, and then followed the statement with a quick, 'If that's alright.'

After being confronted with Mother and George, I was now more wary of entering the cottage but I nodded to Lizzie and took my time unlocking the front door, making more noise than was necessary to give warning if they were there. I needn't have worried, the cottage was empty. I showed Lizzie into the sitting room and went to put the kettle on and made tea.

Because it was Lizzie I ignored the usual mugs and teabags and poured water into the teapot and took a tray through with our china cups and saucers on. These were rarely used and I had to wipe dust off with the dishcloth before using them. The crockery rattled as I carried the tray through to the sitting room where Lizzie stood looking out of the window.

I poured the tea into the cups and added a dash of milk from a milk bottle; I couldn't find the milk jug.

'Do you take sugar?' I asked, like a proper servant.

Lizzie turned to me, and shook her head. 'No, thanks,' she said, and looked surprised. 'I don't drink tea really.' It was my turn to look confused.

'I thought you said you wanted tea.'

'I did, but I really need to talk to you about Gracie. I'm worried about her.'

She came and sat near me, in the armchair beside the fireplace, the chair faced the hearth and she did not look at me. 'I'm really worried about her.'

I had picked up my cup and a little tea slopped onto the saucer. The china was too delicate for my hands. Seconds of silence passed, and my cup clattered back onto its saucer. I needed to say something to break the quiet. 'I thought she was looking better today.'

'Yes, but the news about coming home should have made her happy and it didn't. There's something she's not telling me.'

The clock on the mantelpiece sounded each second. It was not an ornate clock but was suddenly the most conspicuous thing in the room.

'I don't know how to make her talk to me.'

'I don't understand,' I said, feeling out of my depth, aware of the twin-ship between Gracie and Lizzie and mindful of my single child status.

'It's as if she wants to tell me but can't.'

'Perhaps if you were alone. Perhaps I shouldn't come with you.'

I waited for her to say that would be a good idea and she didn't know why she'd invited me anyway. But instead she finally turned towards me. I was aware of her eyes on me, their golden gaze burning my skin so I could sense the blush on my face.

'No, Hal. I want you there. I need you there.'

I was so hypnotised by those beautiful eyes it took me a moment to stutter out, 'Why?'

I wasn't even sure my mouth formed the words but Lizzie heard the question either physically or telepathically.

'Because we're the same.'

I said nothing but again my thoughts formed a statement, Lizzie and I were nothing like each other.

She continued to answer me, 'We're the support, the framework for delicate but beautiful flowers. You have your mother and I have Gracie, without us they couldn't survive. We're stronger you see.'

I didn't really see. I didn't usually feel strong. However, I understood sitting beside Lizzie made me want to be that iron man.

'I ought to go,' she said eventually and I realised we had been sitting staring at each other for some time. The tea in my cup was cold.

'We'll visit tomorrow then,' she instructed.

So the following day, again we rumbled off towards the hospital. A light rain was falling and my view from the back of the car was distorted through the collection of raindrops across the glass. As we went into the building I said to Lizzie, 'Perhaps I should wait out here for a while, see if Gracie wants to say something to you without me hearing.'

She agreed but I had to promise to wait outside Gracie's room. From this part of the corridor I had a view of the car park. A dark cedar protected the path to the central porch. I watched cars coming and going and people hurrying from them with umbrellas to the shelter of the hospital. Opposite me I could see the other wing, it was signed, 'The Fellowship Wing', but was known in the district as 'The Loony Bin'. During the last war the main house had been a sanatorium and convalescent home. Now the new wing remained as a retreat for those with enough money to overcome their mental illnesses in privacy. I imagined I could see shadows wandering behind the darkened glass and wondered if I looked similar to anybody watching from over there. Rain was falling harder, tapping against the pane with increased tempo, and I could hear Lizzie and Gracie's voices in the room gradually getting louder as if in competition. There was a disturbing crescendo and then Gracie screamed.

'Get out! I'm not going home, you hear me. I'm never going home!'

The room became quiet. I heard the hurried footsteps of a nurse come towards me, she looked at me with a frown but did not ask me anything. I put my hands up in a gesture of submission, denying any involvement.

She pushed the door and I could see Lizzie hunched over the bed. Gracie was sitting beside the bed, looking as if a draped cloth had been discarded on the bedside chair; a straggle of hair suggesting it was a person. Sobbing was audible. Then the door was closed on me firmly.

A couple of minutes passed and Lizzie came out, her eyes red. She simply walked towards me not stopping until our bodies met. I had no other option than to wrap my arms around her and hug her. At that time we were a similar height and her face rested against my shoulder. I let her weep; great shuddering sobs which were so strong they made me tremble in sympathy. Whether it was human instinct or something I'd learnt from Mother, I found myself stroking Lizzie's hair and whispering, 'It'll be alright.'

Finally, Lizzie's weeping subsided to sniffles and she stood away from me. 'Thanks,' she murmured and smiled at me, a tiny gesture but at that moment I knew I would do anything, go anywhere, for Lizzie Manning.

Annie realised something was wrong when Lizzie got into the back of the car, climbing in before me. As I followed I shook my head at Annie, hoping it would be enough to prevent her asking questions, and added, 'Gracie was pretty upset today.' Annie took the hint and drove in silence.

The raindrops running down the pane mirrored my thoughts as they merged into one another creating an unfathomable web. I was in a similar frame of mind, not understanding what had gone on at the hospital either with Gracie's distress or Lizzie's intimacy. It did not become any clearer when I felt Lizzie's fingers reach for my hand. She clung to it for the rest of the journey. I wondered if she would get out at the Gate House with me again, but she did not. I don't even recall her saying 'Goodbye.'

But instead of feeling abandoned I felt wonderful. The effect of our hug and the warmth of Lizzie's body against mine remained. I watched the car as it retreated to the Big House not caring I was getting wet.

I wasn't summoned to visit the hospital over the Easter weekend. A lot of cars came and I presumed there had been a party of some kind. On the Monday morning Mother left for work in the pub and I was alone dreaming of Lizzie, wondering when she might call again. Finally I decided to go for a walk in the hopes of glimpsing her somewhere.

I didn't bother with a jacket, the weather looked fine and I wore my best shirt and washed jeans just in case I should come across Lizzie. Once I was reasonably happy with my hair reflected in the hall mirror, I left and took the path through the trees alongside the boundary wall. I wasn't concentrating on my surroundings, just hoping Lizzie would emerge dryad-like from between the tree trunks.

After about twenty minutes I approached the prominence which overlooked the whole Manning estate. It was only as I came through the last of the trees that I realised somebody was on the bench and appeared to be attacking it. I ran forwards ready to confront the hooded thug trying to prise the plaque from the wood, but when I was close the figure looked at me and I stopped.

'What on earth are you doing?' I asked Gracie.

She looked terrible, with the wild eyed glare of an escaped convict. Under the hood I could see strands of unwashed hair which she'd dyed black. Her hands holding a screw driver were dirty.

'Don't try and stop me Hal,' she shouted, whilst brandishing the screw driver towards me. I had no doubt if I got too close she would use it.

'Should you be out of hospital?' I asked thinking she might have run away.

'I didn't want to come back,' she answered, and continued to chip away at the plaque.

'Where's Lizzie?'

'I don't need a babysitter,' she said, then added, 'She's out riding with Tara.' She emphasised the T as if it was a swearword. I wondered whether she was cross Lizzie had gone riding without her or perhaps she hadn't been invited to join them.

As if she'd read my mind, she said. 'I'm no longer acceptable company.' And to prove it she spat on the ground.

I didn't know what to do. Below me the view was one of natural loveliness. I turned from Gracie trying to ignore her wildness and breathed in the serenity. The area was a bowl of greenness, protected by the arms of the distant hills. The Manor looked at its best from here, the blemishes on its white stonework unnoticeable. The balance of the main house to the stables and outbuildings was ideal rather than the cluttered effect experienced if you stood in the yard. The brilliance of the lake was untarnished by the straggle of bushes and mud which were noticeable close up. I was thinking how wonderful it must be to own all this. In fact it looked perfect and I said so.

'It's an illusion Hal,' Gracie said, her voice soft and sad behind me.

I turned back to her; she appeared to be making progress with her vandalism.

'There!' she said as the metal finally came away.

I sighed as I sat down beside her. She smelt slightly of urine and I wondered how they had let her remain so unwashed and unkempt. It crossed my mind she may not have been discharged from hospital and was sleeping rough.

'Do you want to come up to the cottage for some food and a wash?' I offered.

'That bad am I?' she said, shrugging. 'No. I don't want to go anywhere with anybody.'

She put the screw driver in her pocket and placed the plaque on the ground and began kicking her foot against it. My support of Lizzie had made me over bold and I grasped Gracie's hands thinking I could comfort her. However, they were so cold, and the skin so red and rough, it gave me the sensation of handling raw meat. She felt nothing like Lizzie and I dropped them. Her sleeves were long and covered her wrists but I imagined the red wheals there. It made me feel nauseous and I looked down at the ground. The metal of the plaque glinted in the sunshine.

'But it was in remembrance of your mother,' I said, my memory jolted, and I put my foot on a corner of the metal so she couldn't kick it any longer. It had been placed on the bench after the car accident which had killed Lizzie and Gracie's parents more than ten years ago.

'I know, and it's a lie.' She bent down and picked up the plaque. 'Here, you keep it.' And she thrust it at me. I read the simple inscription; *For Caro, who loved this place.'*

'She was a victim.'

'What do you mean?' I questioned, looking at the vista before me and feeling only envy.

'She was a victim,' Gracie repeated, and still I did not understand.

'Are you saying it wasn't an accident?'

'Maybe.' She stood up.

I heard her say, 'Goodbye Hal,' but because she was moving away from me I couldn't judge her tone. Only later I wondered whether I should have taken it as a warning.

I sat for some time thinking about Gracie and her action. The plaque became warm in my hands as I turned it. I contemplated the words as if it might be a riddle, which when answered, would explain Gracie's strange action. Finally, having got nowhere, I stuffed it in my back pocket and continued my stroll. As I made my way down to the lake I saw two figures fishing from the bank. Nigel and Leo. I immediately took a diversion and headed further away to the pasture stretching behind the house.

A narrow track along the edge of fields led to a junction with a bridle way. I took the track without much thought. I had walked some way and could see the stable buildings on my right coming into view. Once I had passed those it would be another thirty minutes to complete the circuit back up to the cottage. A couple of pigeons were startled at my approach and cooed and flapped belligerently. Then I heard my name called.

'Hal, hey, Hal. Wait up!' I looked back to see two horses approach, a grey which Lizzie rode and a chestnut carrying Tara. They made a striking picture with the sun behind them.

I have never been comfortable around horses. This is one area in which I must have been a disappointment to

Mother; although I blame her for introducing me to them when I was so young they were monsters to my infant eyes. I held my ground as the riders approached.

'We're just heading back. Do you want to join us?' Lizzie asked.

For some reason Tara made me nervous. I had always been in awe of her. She was four years older than me and had always been taller. She was staring at me with the dismissive glare I remembered. From the height of the horse she looked even more intimidating. The horse was ill at ease and paced and turned. Tara tapped it with her heels. But the horse reminded me of Tara. It was a thoroughbred with long muscular limbs and haughty features and could easily be spooked.

Watching her reminded me of the time I had spied on her. Aware of her eyes on me, I wondered if she had seen me that day when I had accidentally disturbed her at the lake's edge. It must have been over a year ago, one summer morning when I had been woken early by noises from Mother's room. Last summer there had frequently been voices, laughter and activity which I didn't want to think about. I certainly didn't want to meet a stranger on their way to the bathroom so I had taken to slipping out of the house early and wandering about the estate.

That particular morning I had walked down towards the lake. The water shimmered in the early morning light like a smooth silver plate. I was still some distance away when I realised it was not completely still. There was an arrow of water moving from the centre to the edge.

It stopped in the shallows and a figure started to rise. A golden creature climbed out of the water in a movement so fluid it was difficult to understand the transition from liquid to land. Her nakedness did not surprise me; it would have been a travesty against nature for her to have been clothed. But as Tara stood up I was mesmerised by her beauty. She was tall and slender with a perfect balance to her limbs. Her breasts were the exact counterweight to the buttocks creating the most wonderful curves. The dawn sunlight illuminated her in a spotlight, emphasising her honey coloured skin and hair as if trying to turn her into its own creature. It would not have surprised me if she had been beamed to some other world and disappeared leaving only the sparkle of gold dust spiralling in the place where she had been.

Having stopped to drink in the vision I crept closer to see more. She leant down and began to shake her damp hair like a dog might, creating an arc of droplets. It was then I realised she was not alone. From behind the bushes a man's voice shouted and tossed her a towel. She was laughing now and rubbing her hair with the towel. The man's hand reached forward and grabbed her ankle. It was a strong arm with well-defined muscles but the skin was pale and freckled. He was laughing and now Tara was squealing. 'Let go, let go,' she was saying playfully whilst jigging about ineffectively, her leg still clamped. Finally she collapsed in a heap on top of the concealed figure. From the noise which followed I supposed they were kissing.

I thought I'd better not stay and turned back towards the cottage. From this angle the Big House looked different, the proportions grand and symmetry unspoiled. The bay of the architecture swelled from the centre of the building. I admired it for a moment. That's when I noticed the movement of the curtain in an upper window. I couldn't be sure but I had the sensation somebody else was watching the whole scene; Tara swimming, cavorting with that man and probably me, sneaking about the grounds. As I half ran back to the Gate House I tried to work out the plan of the house in my head, because I thought the bay fronted room was Grace Elizabeth's and it was her figure I had seen, a Peeping Tom. Just like me.

Tara's horse stamped the ground bringing me back to the present. Tara was a groom at the stables and lived in the stable rooms. It was the job Mother had once done.

'No, better get back,' I told them. Had it been Lizzie on her own I would have stayed and told her about Gracie's odd behaviour. I nearly changed my mind but then the moment passed and they had moved on. It was too late.

I didn't see either Lizzie or Gracie through the following week, but on the Saturday morning there was a light knock at the cottage door and my heart lifted. Both Lizzie and Gracie stood there, Lizzie smiling, Gracie with a grimace. They didn't look identical anymore. More like the bad fairy and the good fairy. Gracie was pale, her black hair straggly. At least it looked washed and her clothes were clean. She was dressed in leggings and a sagging black top which emphasised the prominence of her bones and the wan skin. Lizzie on the other hand looked glowing beside her.

I invited them in and made them drinks. I sat beside Gracie on the sofa and Lizzie wandered around the room picking up ornaments and looking at the pictures we had displayed. There weren't many, so when she'd seen them all she did another circuit. It was distracting. Occasionally she would say, 'This is nice,' but I wondered what she really thought of our trinkets. They were of little value compared to the treasures contained in the Manor. One thing she came back to several times was a bronze horse on the mantel piece. It was one of those objects people were instinctively drawn to, especially if they liked horses. The sculpture caught the movement of the horse, in the way the mane and tail flicked out. Lizzie really did seem to like it. I imagined how the bronze felt under her fingers, the way the surface gradually warmed as it was held. 'Is this your mother's?' she asked.

'Yes, it's her favourite. It was a present.' I wasn't sure who had given her the ornament only that it was the thing she would save if there was a fire.

Gracie said nothing but shifted on the sofa and sighed as if she was bored.

I had been so desperate to see Lizzie through the week and now she was here. Watching her glide about the room I was finding speech difficult. Eventually I said, 'Are you back to school next week then?', knowing their private school terms were different than mine.

'No, we've a few more days,' Lizzie answered. Gracie said nothing but made a huffing sound as if I'd said something stupid. I looked at her; she was holding her coffee cup and regarding the liquid as though it had offended her. She had not taken a sip.

'Shall we go for a walk?' I suggested, thinking the atmosphere might be easier outside. Gracie made the huffing sound again.

'Thanks Hal, but I think we'd better go,' Lizzie said. I thought her look towards Gracie wasn't entirely approving.

'But I've hardly seen you,' I blurted out. I think Gracie sniggered.

Lizzie said nothing but made her way out of the room, Gracie followed. I showed them out, lingering on the doorstep. Before they walked away, Lizzie touched my hand, 'I'll see you soon, Hal,' she said with what I interpreted as an apologetic smile. It was enough to make me wake with hope each morning, thinking I might see her each day. However, I was back at school and I did not see her for two weeks. And when we did meet again it was not as expected.

What Remains 5

Before she left Gracie asked me when Tom was returning. He would be back at the end of the week and I told her I wasn't certain what I'd do then.

'I'll probably just head back to Milton Keynes,' I said, because it was the simplest solution.

'What about the Gate House then. Are you just going to leave it?'

I didn't want to disturb the Gate House and all the memories it held, yet I wasn't sure if I could leave straight away; so much had been stirred up just by being back in Leverbridge.

'You're not going to run away are you Hal? Please don't do that.'

Had Gracie not been present I might have left Leverbridge the following day, before Tom's return. I would learn to leave the past where it belonged, where it had been for over ten years.

'There'll be loads of paperwork to sort out. I don't know if I can be bothered.'

'I can take you over to Bainsford on Monday to do that. I won't take no for an answer.'

She didn't give me a chance to reply. Just got up, leaving me with my mouth open trying to think up an excuse. Yet my usual deference to the Manning's demands had kicked in, and I couldn't think of a way to decline.

'I'll be here at nine,' she called as she closed the front door.

It was only when I heard the click of the latch I realised there was no reason I could not have driven over myself had I wanted. My mini remained sitting in the drive. But somehow I'd acquiesced to Gracie's offer.

So on Monday morning there I was waiting for her as I'd been instructed. Barklay had been walked and watered and I'd spent Sunday tidying things up for the return of Tom and his family.

Whilst Gracie drove, I argued silently with myself. Why was I doing this? I could have slipped away in the middle of the night; I doubted anyone would bother to find me. However, I felt as if I was caught in a whirl pool, unable to resist the current taking me deeper into places part of me did not want to venture.

Gracie swerved up into one of the parking places outside Woodhouse and Partners. Slightly dazed I followed her into the offices, which smelt of fresh paint. A large bouquet of flowers failed to make an impression against the stronger odour.

The receptionist welcomed us and told us Mr Woodhouse would see us in a moment.

My whole morning could have been part of a somnambulist dream, so distant did I feel from the process. I signed papers, picked up keys and thought I was done.

'Do you want to take the portrait now or would you like us to deliver it?' asked Mr Woodhouse.

I had forgotten about the painting.

'We could easily fit it in the car,' said Gracie, helpfully.

I nodded and before long we were driving out of Bainsford with a spectral shadow of Mother, wrapped in brown paper, behind us.

The painting obviously excited Gracie because she kept on about it the whole way back to Leverbridge.

'Have you ever seen the picture?'

'No, have you?'

'No, I wonder what it's like though. She was so beautiful. I wonder if they've done her justice?'

That was what was worrying me most of all, that somebody would have daubed paint across a canvas and not captured her likeness.

'I wonder where it's been all this time. I was surprised there's a portrait of her. Perhaps it was a special gift? Lizzie and I had ours done on our sixteenth birthdays.'

I remembered those portraits; they were displayed with the rest of the family in the reception area and stairway of the Manor. In them Lizzie and Gracie were at their most different, Lizzie golden and happy, Gracie pale and skeletal with her hair dyed black. They looked like depictions of separate seasons, summer and winter. However, the paintings had been done well and captured more than simply their features. I hoped the same artist had been employed for Mother. Where Mother's painting had been hanging all this time I had no idea.

'Shall we go straight to the cottage, whilst I've got you captive?' Gracie laughed.

It was too close to the truth, so I made a point of saying, 'I'd like to check on Barklay first. I thought I might walk up with him later.'

'Alright, I'll leave the painting by the door for you, then you'll have to go up. I'll try and pop in later on; you'll probably want some cleaning stuff and bin bags.'

I did not argue, but was relieved to have some time on my own with Barklay, whose needs were uncomplicated and easily met.

It would have been easy to remain where I was, but Gracie was right about the portrait waiting for me outside the cottage. It still did not look like rain but I couldn't risk the picture being damaged.

So later in the afternoon Barklay and I made our way across the village to the Gate House. The weight of the cottage keys in my pocket was heavy against my thigh and I became aware of my limp again. I walked slowly; Barklay kept turning and checking on my progress, impatient as usual.

The main gates were locked shut, presumably against press intrusion since the discovery of Alicia's remains.

There was a key pad but I hadn't thought to ask for the code which would automatically swing the gates open. I recalled an old gateway and walked there. The door was set back into the brickwork and partially hidden by a curtain of ivy. I thought it might also be locked but it finally gave with a groan as it opened, as if it was annoyed about the intrusion. Strands of ivy snagged me as I walked through. Once inside, I took the narrow path alongside the wall just inside the grounds' perimeter.

It was cool and dark in this space with leaf mould still rotting by the base of the wall. Barklay snuffled through it and I breathed in the smell and remembered walking this path as if in an alternate lifetime.

Coming this way created an optical illusion. The cottage appeared to be on a slant. If anybody was in the house they wouldn't see you. It was a good way of returning if I'd been out late. I had to push through a gap in the garden hedge but then I could slip in through the back door and sneak into my room before Mother noticed I'd come in at a later hour than arranged. Today though I decided to go through the front door. Gracie had done as she'd promised and the brown package was waiting there. The old-fashioned door fastenings had been replaced years ago with Yale locks and the key slipped in and turned without a problem. Somewhere in the back of my mind I'd been hoping I'd been given the wrong key or the lock had seized up but it was not to be. I took a deep breath before going in. Barklay was beside me, interested in this new place. He nudged the door with his nose and then waited whilst I tentatively pushed it fully open. The first thing I noticed was the smell. The damp had crept in and the cottage had a forest filled air as if it was simply becoming an extension of the wood. A thick layer of dust covered everything but I could still make out the unmistakable smell I associated with home. Wood smoke, damp leaves and Mother's perfume.

The cottage appeared to have shrunk in my absence. It looked tiny. I didn't investigate further down the narrow corridor but went straight into the sitting room.

The furnishings had been left; somebody had thrown dust sheets over them so it was like a gathering of ghosts. There were boxes on the floor with random papers and books spilling from them. Cobwebs were strung between the ornaments on the mantel piece as if linking them together in an intricate puzzle. The carriage clock in the centre had stopped. I sneezed and the force shifted a puff of dust. There had been little movement here for a decade and the disturbance of the air made the room quiver. At the noise Barklay responded with a small yap and wagged his tail, brushing more dust off the covers and creating mini clouds. I sneezed again. Barklay headed for the fire place which was a brick recess with a wide grate. He looked up the chimney and barked again. I wondered if a bird had fallen down into the grate as he was so excited, yapping and wagging his tail.

I went over; my fingers left deep marks in the mantel dust as I held it and leant down to peer inside. There was nothing except old soot and a few ashes which were now disturbed by Barklay's movement and spilt onto the rug edge leaving a rim of grey against the red fabric like stubble over lips.

'Come away,' I instructed Barklay, but he didn't shift. He simply sat staring up at the hole of the chimney, his tail swishing debris across the rug.

I went and got the painting from outside, brought it in and placed it by the wall. I lifted a corner of dust sheet and perched on the edge of the sofa and looked at the package. Barklay continued his vigil over the fireplace and I contemplated the portrait and whether I dared look at it. Our musings were interrupted by Gracie calling, 'You got here then? What sort of state is it in?' She answered herself with, 'Oh, that bad. Have you only just got here? You don't seem to have got very far?'

'It's a question of knowing where to start,' I told her.

She didn't hesitate but went to open other doors. I leapt up after her. I wasn't sure I wanted her barging into things. She opened the door to what had been Mother's bedroom; again I was aware of shrouded shapes behind the door. For a moment the notes of Mother's perfume were strong, as if she had simply wandered from the room quite recently. The sudden sense of loss it stimulated made my head hurt. Gracie marched across the room, 'You need some air in here,' she said and opened the latch on the window frame. It creaked as she pushed it open. Outside the air was still, the atmosphere in the room remained heavy.

One of the drapes had slipped revealing part of a mirror. It was an oval glass on a small mahogany wardrobe. The movement of her reflection across the glass caught Gracie's attention and before I could stop her she had opened the door.

'I wonder what they did with all her clothes?'

'They went to the charity shop I expect,' I intoned, my head still aching.

'Wow! Look at this.'

Gracie retrieved an object from the back of the wardrobe, a long crinkled garment reminiscent of an insect's discarded skin.

'It's gorgeous,' Gracie said holding it against herself. 'What a beautiful colour.' The dress below the cellophane of the dry cleaning cover was a rich lilac. It rustled and sparkled as Gracie twirled in front of the mirror. Now the air shifted but it was like the dredging of a stagnant river bed. I felt dizzy and sat on the bed.

Gracie's reflected face looked at me with concern. She stopped moving. 'I'm sorry Hal, I shouldn't have done that.'

She smoothed the dress and replaced it inside the wardrobe.

'Come on, let's go.'

I followed Gracie out into the corridor, thinking we might sit in the lounge but she continued to the next door.

It was the kitchen. As the door opened another odour stirred my senses. It wasn't exactly unpleasant, just of things being preserved. My bedroom was next. It seemed smaller than I remembered, and surprising a bed could fit in there. Gracie turned and put her hand on the next door knob.

'No!' I shouted and she jumped back frowning. 'Not the bathroom!'

Gracie looked around, gave me a quizzical look and then ignoring my instruction turned the handle. I heard the door creak open and saw the white enamel of the bath, a cast iron leg curled to a claw, but then I had to turn away. My brain had created the image of Mother's foot dangling over the edge, a bloodless foot. And red pooling as blood leaked from her white arm and followed the lines of the wood flooring.

I sank down in the width of the corridor and put my head to my knees.

'What's the matter, Hal?' Gracie had closed the bathroom door and came over to me.

'That's where they found her,' I mumbled, speaking into the fabric of my jeans.

'Your mother died in there?'

'That's what they said.'

'Oh God, I'm sorry Hal. No wonder you didn't want me going in there.' She took a couple of steps away from me back towards the bathroom; I watched her heels tap against the wood. 'At least it's done now. The door's been opened. She's not there now. She's at peace. You know that.' She was beside me again, her fingers on my shoulder.

She was right, the door had been opened but it had not given me closure, simply flooded me with sights I had not seen but were the worse for being imagined.

Gracie's steps moved away, she opened the loo door and asked if I had the key to the back door. I reached in my jacket pocket. 'I think it's one of these,' and handed her the bunch.

I stood up and joined Gracie at the back door, looking out into the garden. It had once been pretty with neat hedging and a central circular border which had been planted with bright flowers in the summer. Standing in the middle was a wooden bird table, the type with a shelter on the top. This was hardly visible now as ivy choked the post and writhed through the openings. The border had been engulfed by grass so was indistinguishable from the lawn and the hedges were no longer neat but spilt over as if trying to submerge the space. The wood around enclosed it in a bough ridged bubble like the upturned hull of a boat and the astringent smell of elder surrounded us. Though the summer had been so dry, the back garden retained a damp air as if removed from the real world.

As we went out a blackbird shrieked from the hedge, alarmed its solitude had been disturbed. Barklay attempted to follow, running towards the bushes. He quickly tired of the game and came to sit beside me and then returned into the cottage.

'I don't think I want to be here,' I told Gracie and I followed Barklay inside. Back in the sitting room Barklay positioned himself in front of the fire place, whining.

'What is it, boy?' I asked, patting him, he looked at me with wise eyes but I couldn't understand.

I heard the clip, clip of Gracie's heels along the corridor and she came to the doorway. 'Well, it needs to be cleared up and sorted. Then you can sell it on.' She said this as if giving me no choice in the matter.

'Are you ready to leave?' she asked.

'No, I'll sit for a few minutes,' I said. I wasn't certain how long my legs would support me.

'I'll give a front door key to Annie and see if she'll pop in and make a start on the cleaning some time.'

She didn't wait for my reply, but I could hear her removing a key from the fob, then calling 'Goodbye,' as she shut the front door.

I sat down on the sofa, my mind taken over by memories, chasing like shadows. Some dark, but one bright light piercing through. The bronze horse was still on the mantel piece. I recalled Lizzie standing there holding that horse, stroking it with her slender hands as if she was grooming it.

I could not help but be transported back to the day of my sixteenth birthday.

What Was Taken 5

Mother and I had discussed the bronze horse a week before my sixteenth birthday, shortly after Lizzie and Gracie's visit to me. We had been discussing plans. That year my birthday fell on a Saturday, which should have been a good day for a party, but it was not going to happen.

We were in the sitting room, me on the sofa, Mother standing by the fire place. I didn't think her attention was really on me or my plans as she kept turning and stroking the bronze horse.

'I got this for my sixteenth birthday,' she said, and for a moment appeared to be in a dream. 'I couldn't admit it was my sixteenth birthday of course as I'd lied about my age to the Mannings in order to get the job. I'd said I was already sixteen when it was still two months away.'

She wasn't looking at me but having the conversation with the horse. Gazing into its blind eyes as if it might give her the answer to some inaudible question.

'So who gave it to you?' I asked. Mother didn't respond but continued her monologue with the ornament. 'It was perfect really because it was the night of the ball. I really felt special, as if it was a celebration just for me. Everything was perfect.'

Suddenly she stopped as if something had jolted her out of her trance. Turning to me she said, 'But we need to sort out something for you, to make your birthday special. Would you like a party?'

I shook my head.

'What about bowling or something like that?'

Again I shook my head. I felt I didn't have enough good friends to make a party or outing worthwhile.

'You have to do something,' she said.

'Maybe I'll just go out with Tom, go into town and see a film.' But in the back of my mind I was wondering whether I had the nerve to invite Lizzie out rather than Tom.

'That's not very exciting,' she replied.

'I know, but I don't want a fuss.'

So the day of my birthday dawned and I had no celebration to look forward to. I had not seen Lizzie to invite her anywhere and I hadn't plucked up the courage to write to her or visit her. Somehow, even without plans to mark my birthday, I expected to feel different. At the start everything followed its usual pattern. I awoke with bleary eyes and climbed into jeans and a T shirt, the same as I did each Saturday. Mother was going to be working most of the weekend; she'd said if I didn't want a party then she may as well work. I lay in longer than usual in the hope she would bring me breakfast on a tray and a birthday present. She did not. Later, I heard her call 'Bye,' as she left and I wondered about my gift. There was nothing waiting for me as I went into the sitting room and kitchen. She had probably postponed it and would tell me she'd take me to town to buy new clothes. I realised Mother had taken me at my word about 'no fuss,' and I felt irritated. Teenagers are the only group who can 'mooch about,' and I did so for a while. At some point I was vaguely aware of a siren in the distance. At the time it didn't encroach on my bad mood. I banged the crockery around as I made tea, toast and eggs for brunch, which did nothing to improve my demeanour.

At first, I was not conscious of the tapping. Then I realised it was not some irritant noise but somebody at the door.

As I opened the door I began to smile. It was Lizzie. She had come to say 'Happy Birthday,' and bring me a present. She was empty handed and did not smile back.

She stood there swaying slightly. Today the vision was dishevelled and tearful. She stumbled into my arms and I had to squeeze her to stop her from falling. I staggered backwards still holding her. She did not speak but sobbed as I held her. It was sometime before Lizzie had recovered enough to be led into the sitting room. She sat on the sofa and I moved beside her. I had no idea what to do but she looked as if she was in need of comfort. She was crying, tears running down her face. Her hands looked discarded on her lap; they were pale, mottled blue. I reached out and held them. My fingers tended always to be cold but were warm in contrast to the marble of hers.

'What's the matter?' I finally asked.

'Gracie,' was her short answer. Then her head was against my shoulder. I felt her warm mouth talk against my shirt. 'She tried again.'

'What happened?'

The words were muffled but I made out, 'Sleeping tablets and alcohol this time. They've taken her to hospital.'

I recalled hearing the siren earlier and realised what it signified.

Lizzie's sobbing against my shoulder continued and her voice was so quiet I don't know if I heard correctly. 'They don't know if she'll li.i..ve.' The last word choked out.

I imagined Gracie lying in a coma, oblivious to the pain she had generated, like the epicentre of an earthquake which ripples out. Her melancholy presence was there in this room, pressing us down. Bringing us together. A damp patch was forming on my shoulder, but rather than discomfort I felt only delight at Lizzie's closeness.

It hardly seemed any distance from the warm wetness of her lips against my shoulder to our mouths meeting. Lizzie's mouth was sweet but I could also taste the salt from her tears. The kiss was so wonderful I thought my body must have been lying dormant and had suddenly been resurrected. I had kissed before but not like this; this desperate search for meaning. We continued our exploration, removing clothing, our lips still fixed and then momentarily parting to look in each other's eyes. I saw every nuance of Lizzie's irises, the gold and green flecks, the pupil darkening and widening. I could imagine my image inverted on her retina and her brain absorbing each part of me as I was visualising her. Our bodies moved together in some known dance, a pre-existing understanding deep within us. We became molten, pouring ourselves into one another. There were moments of clumsiness but though we said nothing we weren't awkward with each other. Wordlessly, we made love.

Afterwards we rested on the carpet in front of the fireplace. From there I could see the sky crisscrossed with tree branches moving outside. The canopy of young leaves fluttered, turning the room's interior green. Then a ray of sun shone in. After my new experience I was overwhelmed by what my body was capable of, I felt so powerful I wondered if I had conjured the beam of light. Because now it followed my command. It moved around Lizzie, accentuating her beauty, caressing her outstretched limbs, outlining her with a glow turning her to gold. It also caught the bronze ornament on the mantelpiece. The horse appeared to flick its mane and stare with silent eyes.

Lizzie leaned over me and started to trace my face with her finger. 'You're so beautiful, Hal,' she said. I was unable to speak. Living in the reflection of my mother's loveliness I had never considered myself remotely handsome. How could anybody feel beautiful in the presence of her radiance?

And teenagers in general don't consider themselves attractive. They dwell on their imperfections. So it was strange how Lizzie appeared to like the features I despaired of most. She marked a line down my nose stopping momentarily on the bump I had always found awkward and said it made me look distinguished. Then she traced my mouth which I thought a little thick, 'Perfect,' she said and kissed it. Her fingertip continued round my pointed chin and across my cheek bones. 'I want to remember you, just in case I never see you again,' she said, and then proceeded to cover my face with soft kisses marking the places her finger had been. At that moment the idea was alien. With sunlight bathing us and our bodies touching, if you had asked, I would have told you, 'Lizzie and I will be together for ever!' There was no doubt in my mind. We had not only shared our bodies; but something so fundamental had altered within me that I imagined ourselves part of each other, like some belated Siamese conjunction. We talked. Though I don't think the conversation was lengthy, I believe I have never known somebody as truly as I knew Lizzie. How long we remained there I don't know. To me time was irrelevant.

It was Lizzie who moved first. I didn't want to let her go but held her wrist tightly and made her promise she would not be gone long. 'I do have to go to Gracie,' she said finally and I loosened my grip. 'I'll come by later and tell you what's happening.'

I watched her whilst she dressed; aching with each moment she moved further away from me. But I had to let her go. We parted with a lingering kiss at the door. 'Come back soon,' I told her.

I followed her out to the centre of the drive so I would be able to see her walk all the way to the Manor. I watched her move away, lost her in the dip by the trees and then saw her reappear as a distant figure at the Manor door. 'Look back,' I willed her, raising my hand to blow her a kiss; I had no doubt she would turn to look at me. She did not. That was a thing I was never able to control.

Only then was I aware of the cold rough ground beneath my bare feet.

I tidied the house so when Mother returned for her break around six o'clock she was surprised.

'Are you expecting visitors?' she asked.

'No, just thought I'd tidy a bit.'

She raised her eyebrows in an expression of doubt.

'Anyway, it's a nice thought. Perhaps you could tidy up a little more often.' She laughed. 'Now, did you get my present?'

I shook my head, reminding myself I should be feeling cross with her for not remembering.

'I left it out for you,' she said, then groaned as she went into her bedroom. 'Sorry, sorry,' she apologised, coming back into the sitting room with a wrapped package. 'I didn't put it out, and now you think I'm a terrible mother for leaving you on your birthday with no present.' She hugged me, saying, 'Sorry, sorry,' over and over again and ruffling my hair as if I was a young kid. But I didn't feel like a youngster any more so I twisted away from her. 'Don't be cross with me,' she pleaded.

'I'm not. But I'm sixteen now, and I don't like my hair ruffled.'

'Ooh. We have grown up all of a sudden.' She laughed again, having no idea of the cause of my abrupt evolution. 'I have got a treat for you anyway'.

At that moment there was a knock on the door. My heart literally jumped in my chest. Lizzie was at the door. I brushed my hair with my hands. If Mother noticed my sudden sprucing she didn't say. I went to the door, my hand shaking as I turned the handle.

'Happy Birthday to you, Happy Birthday to you...' sang Tom. 'Sorry, is my singing that bad?' he said, when I can't have given him my normal grin in response.

'Sorry,' I said, 'Come in.'

He was holding a present out to me.

'Come in Tom, so glad you could make it,' Mother said, and I realised there had been some conspiracy.

'Who else have you invited?' I asked in a panic.

'Nobody else, I promise,' said Mum.

Once Tom and I were in the sitting room Mother went back to the kitchen and brought a cake through. It was alight with, I presumed, sixteen candles. 'How childish,' was my thought as I blew the candles out. My wish was full of images of Lizzie and me together forever.

Then I was forced to open my presents. Tom's was wrapped in a bag. The stupid faces on the cover grinned at me, 'Dumb and Dumber.' We had watched it at the cinema last year and laughed all the way through. Looking at it in my hands, I wondered what had made it so hilarious.

'You'll be able to watch that tonight,' suggested Mother.

Mother's present was more difficult to unwrap. Inside the intricate wrapping of gold paper was a small box. In it, a wristwatch. 'Look at the engraving,' she said excitedly.

To my darling Hal, it said on the back. It was a handsome watch and I went over and kissed her. 'Thanks.' In other circumstances I would have been happy with their presents and company. Now, nothing matched up to Lizzie.

Mother had to return to work for the evening session.

'Don't wait up,' she said, 'Oh, and there's food in the fridge and some shandy.'

She smiled indulgently as if it were a great treat. I knew I should be more grateful but could barely raise a smile and a 'Thank you.' All I wanted was for Lizzie to be there.

Mother left and Tom went outside and collected some cans he had hidden behind the cottage. He pulled one open and handed it to me and then put on the Video. I didn't respond, I was wondering whether Lizzie would visit after all. I was barely aware of the taste of lager in my mouth.

'Are you alright, mate?' Tom finally asked when I still said nothing. I was not the most talkative person but usually with Tom we chatted and laughed.

'No, everything's fine,' 'except Lizzie's not here', I wanted to add, 'It's just not been much of a birthday.' That wasn't true and I felt bad lying to Tom. We were usually honest with each other, but I felt I had to make some excuse for my distracted mood.

'Dumb and Dumber' were just singing Mockingbird in their car and after two cans of lager I had mellowed a little and was joining in, when there was a knock on the door.

'Oh, who's that?' Tom complained, putting the Video on pause. I tried to keep my cool as I walked towards the door, but my heart was sounding in my chest so loudly I thought it might pull me over.

Had it not been Lizzie I think I would have cried, but there she was, standing under the porch lamp which created a halo of light above her angelic face.

She kissed me. I wasn't sure how long we stayed there but suddenly Tom yelled, 'Who is it?'

His voice returned me from my dream and I took Lizzie through to the sitting room.

'Hi,' said Tom and I noticed his face flush and his awkward movements at Lizzie's arrival.

Lizzie accepted a can and the film was switched on again.

There was no more singing along with the film, we all watched in silence. Even Tom didn't laugh out loud. I just wanted it to finish so Lizzie and I could be alone. I wasn't even that interested in what she had to say about Gracie. I presumed Gracie was going to live otherwise Lizzie would already have said something.

The credits played and Tom took the hint and said he'd be off. I went to the door and thanked him for coming over.

Returning to Lizzie, I asked, 'So how is she?' restraining myself from kissing her again.

'They've pumped her stomach and she's regained consciousness but she'll be in hospital for a while. In the psychiatric wing this time.'

She began to cry and I held her, kissing her and stroking her. 'I love you,' I said, surprising myself. The words had bubbled up from my sub-conscience. But she replied, 'I love you too, Hal,' and though I had never before understood the term, 'my heart sang,' that was the only way to describe the sensation.

By the time Mother returned from work Lizzie had gone. I was sitting in a warm haze, dreaming of Lizzie, unable to stir myself to get ready for bed. Mother came into the sitting room and said, 'Tom's gone then?'

She must have smelt Lizzie's perfume in the air because she went on, 'Has a girl been here?'

'Yes, Lizzie,' I said and smiled, just saying her name made my heart flutter. I thought Mother would be pleased Lizzie was my friend so I was unprepared for what happened next.

'Hal, I meant it when I said you shouldn't get involved with the Manning girls.'

Indeed, she had told me this several times, and I always replied, 'But they're just my friends,' thinking she would repeat the usual refrain, that we were an inferior species to the Mannings.

But today she grabbed my upper arms and was squeezing them. 'Ow, you're hurting me!' I complained. Never before had she struck me or hurt me. Then her face was in front of mine, and for the first time she didn't look beautiful. Her eyes were hard and I could see furrowed lines on her forehead. She hadn't applied her lipstick properly and as she shouted at me her mouth was distorted. She shook me. 'You must not get involved with Lizzie Manning. Those girls are bad news. Do you hear me! Do you understand?'

What Remains 6

I could taste salt on my lips and realised it was my own tears I was detecting. Looking at me through a net of cobwebs was the bronze horse. It had lost something of its lustre but still appeared to read my thoughts.

I locked the cottage and headed back to Tom's house. It was pleasant to be back in the modern building. It was bright and square without the nooks and crannies of the cottage, nor did it have ghosts lurking in shadowy corners.

As I made myself a cup of tea I noticed the red light flashing on the answer machine. A press of a button and Tom's voice filled the room.

'Hi Hal, hope you're getting on alright. We're having a fab time but it's coming to an end. We'll be back by Thursday afternoon. Don't feel you've got to leave straight away, it would be nice to catch up.'

I spent the evening watching TV. It was the summer of the world cup and I watched various football teams I had no interest in, running around as aimlessly as my thoughts. I had retrieved the gift tag Gracie had discarded, from the kitchen bin and occasionally looked at it. On it was simply written, *'I did it! Thank You, Tom. Enjoy your holiday...and don't worry! Love G. xx'*. I wondered what Gracie had done and why she was thanking Tom alone. And surely he didn't have to worry about a holiday he'd won. I couldn't understand why she'd removed the tag. Perhaps Mandy wasn't meant to see it. It was another riddle that I was not party to.

Barklay rested at my feet and I occasionally stroked him, gaining comfort from his presence. Perhaps it was time to go back to Milton Keynes. I could leave the clearing of the cottage to Annie Taylor with Gracie overseeing it and I would never have to think about it again or all that had passed there. Yet something held me back.

When I thought of home I did not think of my flat in Milton Keynes. I still thought of Leverbridge. A place that had memories. Even with all the horrible recollections, the happy times I had spent with Mother and Tom were here. And, of course, those sublime days with Lizzie.

What Was Taken 6

Gracie's depression hung like a cloud the summer after my birthday, but it remained distant to the joy of my relationship with Lizzie.

We would make use of the cottage when Mother was at work and spent a lot of time squeezed into my bed together.

Because of Mother's previous reaction, I became secretive about our relationship. I made her think I was a friend of Lizzie's, as perhaps an equerry might be, offering her support and companionship when she visited Gracie.

It made those moments cocooned with Lizzie even sweeter. I was now a player in the game Mother had always played. The one in which her assignations and relationships were unknown to me. A game like Cluedo, where my father's name was sealed away and about which Mother gave me no information. The guilt which I normally felt if I told Mother a lie did not trouble me. The competition was now even.

Lizzie and I visited Gracie regularly. She was the first to know of our relationship. And we made her promise to keep the information to herself. We hadn't discussed keeping it concealed but instinctively we were both secretive about it.

It was different when we went to see Gracie. We'd often walk in the extensive grounds. On these walks Gracie would behave quite normally. She looked tidy and had put on weight. Whilst we walked the perimeter of the grounds I wondered whether she needed to be there at all.

Lizzie would hold my hand. The first time she did this Gracie laughed and said, 'I knew something was going on with you two.'

I thought she might be jealous or upset by our happiness, but she appeared pleased for us.

119

'It's good that one of the Mannings can have a normal relationship,' she said. I didn't know what she meant, I wasn't aware of Gracie having had a relationship and Grace Elizabeth and Maurice had been married for many years. Gracie's parents Caro and Hugh had been killed in the car accident but I thought they were happily married. My knowledge of relationships was so limited I could not think of what Gracie was referring to. And anyway, I wasn't sure Lizzie and my liaison was all that normal, otherwise we would be open to everybody about it.

She linked her arm in mine and said, 'Hal, you'll have me to answer to if you hurt my sister. Understand?' And she made a gun shape with two fingers and pointed it at my temple. Then she skipped away, laughing. I stopped walking and must have looked worried because Lizzie kissed me and said, 'Ignore her, she's only teasing you.'

Those days of summer stretched out delightfully. Lizzie and I picnicked in the grounds of Leverbridge Manor and sometimes if I thought Mother could disturb us at the cottage we might make love in the folly in the glade. It was not a comfortable building but at least it had a roof. We took blankets down. The musty smell of neglect quickly vanished when Lizzie was in my arms. It must have been the end of August when things changed.

'What are you two doing here?'

Lizzie and I pulled away from each other and gathered our discarded clothing around us. Tara was standing in the doorway, blocking the light. She said nothing more but the force of the glare from those grey eyes terrified me. By the time I had fumbled into my jeans, Tara had gone.

Lizzie was staring silently at the door, her face stricken to the colour of stone so she resembled the statue in the glade outside.

'Do you think she'll tell anyone?' I asked.

Lizzie didn't answer straightaway. 'I don't know,' she said. 'Does it matter if she does? We're not doing anything wrong.'

I guessed she was saying that as much to convince herself as me, because though we were not doing anything illegal, I didn't think the Mannings would be happy about our union. And when Lizzie came round to visit me, Mother appeared uncomfortable. Sometimes she would say, 'You should be going out with friends from school, Hal. It's not healthy to be around Lizzie and Gracie all the time. They live in a different world to us. I don't want you getting involved with them.'

She was always polite if Lizzie visited but if she knew our relationship was sexual I don't think she'd have been at all pleased.

Each of the following days I awoke in the morning expecting our tryst to be common knowledge and went to sleep each night relieved it had not yet come to light.

On the Saturday before the school term started I met Lizzie and she invited me in to the Manor kitchen for tea.

Annie was there pottering about fetching us scones. 'Lucky you, I made a fresh batch today. You can test them.'

They were still warm. Annie went out for a moment and Lizzie whispered to me, 'I spoke to Tara, I pleaded with her not to say anything.'

My mouth was stuffed with scone and jam and I could not respond.

'She says she won't. I think she was just shocked finding us there.'

I mumbled through the crumbs that it was good news.

'I've promised we won't go there again, or anywhere else on the estate. She said if Maurice had found us he'd probably have killed us.'

I thought this an exaggeration but understood her point. I doubt if any grandfather would have been happy finding his granddaughter in the clutches of a boy in an out

121

building. I chuckled at the thought of Maurice's furious face if he had found us, and then choked as a scone crumb caught in my throat.

Annie came back in and wanted to join in the joke. 'What's so funny then?' she asked, getting me a glass of water. When the sip of liquid had cleared my throat, I said, 'Just something Lizzie said.' Lizzie scowled at me. 'I don't think it was meant to be funny though,' I added.

September and school returned too quickly. Lizzie would turn seventeen in October and she was hoping to persuade Gracie to come home for their joint birthday. 'You'll help persuade her it's for the best, won't you Hal?' I promised her I would, but was uncertain I would be the person Gracie would listen to.

Gracie, though still pale and thin, appeared so contented I did wonder why she was still residing at the Sanatorium. In her room was a pile of books and she mentioned the tutor appointed to teach her several times. I guessed she had a crush on him. 'Gavin says I can take my A' level early if I keep working hard. We're studying Hamlet. Is that what you're doing, Hal?' She didn't give me time to reply. 'We had an amazing discussion about the Oedipus complex; how important it is within Hamlet's relationships. Don't you think it sheds light on the development of our own family connections? What do you think Hal?' Now she did wait for a reply. She was watching me as a black bird might study a worm before impaling it. Any gold in her eyes was harsh yellow, set in the surrounding shadowy hollows. It was as if she was deliberately trying to make me uncomfortable.

At school I had also been studying Hamlet, but the Oedipus complex had barely been mentioned. Gracie's question disconcerted me. I wondered what she was getting at. My mother's presence hovered in the room like an unseen cloud. Instead of replying to Gracie's question I diverted the conversation.

'What about your birthday. Why don't you come home?' I asked more bluntly than I would usually. She blinked. Then her eyes widened as if it were taking time for the words to filter through.

'I'm never going back there, Hal. It is not my home. Ask Lizzie.'

I looked at Lizzie, asking the question with a shrug. She shook her head, 'Not now, Hal. I'll tell you later.' But she didn't look at me and I realised for the first time she was keeping something from me.

The room was quiet and I felt nauseous at the thought Lizzie might lie to me.

'Now, our birthday!' said Lizzie a little too brightly. 'I want a party.'

'If we arranged a party would you come?' I asked Gracie.

'I might,' she said. She picked up one of her books and flicked through the pages as if she was searching for a quote. 'In fact, I do want to leave here, but I don't know where to go.'

Later, when I asked Lizzie what Gracie had meant when she said the Manor was not her home, Lizzie ignored my question and said, 'What if we sorted out a place for Gracie to live in Leverbridge for her birthday, a flat or something?'

'We don't have that kind of money,' I said, and was cross Lizzie hadn't answered me.

'We'll have to ask Grandmama for help.' So that was the ruling.

The following day I found myself climbing the steep back stairs to the first floor of Leverbridge Manor. I hadn't often been upstairs. The last time must have been the year Alicia went missing and I had looked out from the twins' playroom on the top floor. The corridor was dark, lined with oil paintings for its entire length. In other circumstances I might have stopped and looked but felt I had to keep up with Lizzie.

'Wait here,' Lizzie instructed me. She turned and knocked on a door. 'Come in,' Grace Elizabeth's firm voice responded. I thought I would follow Lizzie in but she turned and put her hand on my shoulder, 'No, wait here,' she told me again. She vanished into the room but left the door ajar.

I did as I was asked, looking from the dimly lit corridor into the brightness of Grace Elizabeth's study. I imagined the room with its wide windows overlooking the back of the estate and down to the lake.

Paintings hung each side of the door frame, one a landscape with figures in riding apparel crossing the scene in the foreground. The other was a portrait of a man who looked at me with disdain. His eyes were almost black and he had thick lips which seemed to move as light fanned through the gaping study door, causing his mouth to sneer. I would not have been surprised if he had said, 'Why are you sneaking about here?' because it was then I realised I was eavesdropping on the conversation within the room.

'So you think Gracie would come home but not to the Manor?' Grace Elizabeth's voice said.

'Yes, I'm sure she would. If there was somewhere else for her to stay. Maybe one of the stable rooms?'

'No, not the stables,' came the curt response. 'But...' There was a pause in which I imagined Grace Elizabeth looking down to the lake, standing erect her hands behind her back. 'There is the worker's cottage. Though it's not been lived in for many years.'

'You mean the building next to Annie's?'

'That's the one. Do you want to have a look, see if it might be suitable? Then we'll need to find out what work needs to be carried out to make it habitable. See if Annie's about, to fetch the keys for you, then you can have a look.' Moments later Lizzie emerged from the room, smiling.

Grace Elizabeth's parting words of, 'Let me know how you get on,' floated after her.

Lizzie led the way back down the stairs and with Annie's assistance the keys to the cottage were found.

'I'm not sure this is a good idea,' Annie told us as she fumbled in the key cabinet. 'That house is a mess. Gracie'll not want to live there.'

Lizzie ignored her complaints. As we headed down the rutted bridleway towards the house at the edge of the estate, Lizzie told me it had once been the home of Fraser, a farm manager. It was a name which sounded familiar. He had once been a regular visitor at the Gate House. I had been too young to remember him well but I did recollect the exhilarating sensation of being lifted by strong arms and swung around like an aeroplane. The exact reason for his leaving I did not know but he had left suddenly due to some disagreement with the Mannings. As I tried to recall what he'd looked like Lizzie continued, 'I don't think Annie's happy about having a neighbour again.' Then she laughed. It was a cruel sound, which resonated with the seagull calls as they followed the furrows of the fields.

The workers' cottages were a semi-detached building of two connected properties in the basic brickwork of the sixties. They looked anaemic against the rich red brown of the adjoining arable land. It was an isolated place, though close to the back lane which crossed the countryside joining up hamlets and farmsteads.

Annie had lived here for years and her side was tidy with a paved front garden populated with individual pots and several fairy ornaments. Again Lizzie laughed and made some comment about the 'twee' display. I thought she was being mean but didn't tell her.

Annie's garden was bounded by a neat wicket fence. The garden next door had been tidied but still looked unkempt with wisps of long grass straining to escape the boundary.

I followed Lizzie up the path; it was cracked, with patches of yellow algae like melted cheese. They were the only feature which imbued any sense of warmth, otherwise the place was colourless.

I was surprised at the cleanliness of the house as we went in. There was just a hint of polish in the air and I suspected Annie actually kept an eye on the place. The main feature was the wallpaper, which was in swirls of psychedelic orange and purple as if left from a sixties rave. There was a main lounge-diner, which was unfurnished and covered the full length of the house extending from the front to rear. Outside, the back garden was an impenetrable mass of weeds and brambles.

Off the hall was the rather grey kitchen with basic fittings and a sticky linoleum floor. The upstairs was divided into two bedrooms, one larger at the front and a box room beside the bathroom at the back. There was a strange odour of fish and I wondered whether it was fertiliser drifting from the open fields beyond.

Lizzie kept saying, 'This is great, this will do,' each time we opened another door. In the bathroom she turned taps on and, after a moment of gurgling, water splashed out. 'Yes, this is great,' she said, putting her hand under the stream as though it were a novelty.

We finished our tour and Lizzie was grinning. 'Well, that's settled,' she told me. 'All it needs is some decoration and the electrics checking and it will be superb.' She looked beautiful when she was happy and I couldn't help but wrap my arms around her and try to kiss her, but she pushed me away. 'Not now Hal, we've got things to do.' Pushing passed me, she hurried out, and I followed.

As we walked she said, 'You'll help with the re-decorating, won't you?'

Of course I agreed, which was why over the next week every evening was spent down at the house painting everything a uniform white.

'I think Gracie will prefer that, then she can decorate how she wants,' was Lizzie's argument. After Lizzie had given me instructions for painting, I didn't see her for the entire week. One day I went in to find a note saying, 'I think the skirting boards in the bedroom need a second coat.' And then in a scribble I could hardly read, an afterthought, 'Keep up the good work.' I screwed the paper up and shoved it in the black bin liner. Still, I did repaint the skirting.

It was obvious other people attended during the day. I arrived one evening to find the kitchen had been completely refurbished. I stood looking at it with envy for several minutes, as I thought how much the kitchen in the Gate House needed updating. Another time new settees covered in plastic were sitting in the middle of the lounge. One evening George's truck was parked outside, and as I went into Gracie's, George emerged from Annie's front door. He nodded a, 'Hello, lad,' in my direction whilst brushing cake crumbs from his overalls. He had obviously been busy in the back garden of Gracie's house because more light filtered into the lounge, with the accompanying smell of crushed vegetation. Sometimes Annie would come round. She might bring a flask of tea or soup and chat for a while. Unlike George, I was never invited to her house, but I wondered what her home looked like. Too much chintz and lace I envisaged, with photographs of the Manning family everywhere.

Annie would point out the bits of painting I had missed, more often though she would restate, 'I don't think this is a good idea. Gracie's not fit to live on her own, she's fragile.'

I didn't disagree but said, 'At least she's got you next door.'

'I suppose, but I'm not a nursemaid, I can't be expected to be at her beck and call.'

Her tone echoed that of Mother. Every night I returned home, the first thing she said was, 'Gracie Manning can't live on her own. The girl's unstable. And you're being used as slave labour. Who do they think they are, getting you to do the painting?' She would come over to me and wipe spots of paint from my face or hair. 'And anyway, why would anybody who had the chance to live in a beautiful mansion choose to live in a hovel like that?'

Once the re-decorating was completed, Lizzie finally came down. 'It looks great, Hal. Thank you.' I kissed her then and felt my chores had been worthwhile.

On the morning of October the twenty-fifth I found myself blowing up balloons in Gracie's new house. As I had left the Gate House, Mother had again repeated her warning, 'No good will come of this. Gracie should not live alone.'

So between balloons I asked Lizzie, 'Do you really think it's sensible to let Gracie live on her own, after what she's been through?'

'That's about the hundredth time you've asked me, Hal. The answer is still, 'I don't know'. But I know it's got to be better than her staying in the Sanatorium and she won't consider going back to the Manor.'

I stopped blowing the balloon I was holding and it made a sound of deflation; a comical sound, which might have amused in other circumstances.

'But why not?' Lizzie did her usual eye-aversion tactic to this question. There was something she wasn't telling me.

She waited long enough, until I was blowing the balloon up again to say, 'It's to do with Mum and Dad. Gracie finds she remembers things about them when she's there, and it pulls her down. She'll be better with a fresh start.'

My breath inflated the balloon. Through its red film Lizzie and the room looked distorted, her story didn't ring true.

'I could always make up a bed in here so I can stay.' I guessed from Lizzie's tone it was the end of the discussion and the ringing of the doorbell made it final.

Lizzie answered the door and came back in with Annie, somebody else hovering behind them. 'This is so lovely isn't it?' Annie said, 'Just right for Gracie.' Considering her concern, on her previous conversations with me, I guessed her change of opinion must be for the benefit of Lizzie. I wouldn't say anything but I was starting to agree with Mother because, even with the painting and furnishings, I thought it looked sparse compared to the opulence of the Manor.

'Now you mustn't worry about Gracie,' Annie told Lizzie, 'I'll be looking out for her and I suppose you'll be here some of the time as well, won't you?' Lizzie nodded.

A voice saying my name made me turn to the doorway. Tara said, 'Hal, we need to get the drink out of the car.' She passed me a set of car keys.

My cheeks felt strained from blowing up balloons and my head dizzy but I went out to the front to collect the drink as ordered. The Manning Land Rover was parked outside and I unlocked it and started the process of bringing boxes of wine and beer in. Nobody assisted me. Each time I went out I was aware of hushed conversation behind me, when I returned the talking stopped. I knew I wasn't of enough interest to warrant being talked about so I could only assume it was Gracie they discussed. Probably posing the same question I had asked, 'Was this a sensible idea?'

When I'd finished lugging drink in and handed Tara back her keys, Lizzie said, 'Hal, could you collect the food from next door. That's alright is it, Annie?'

I thought Annie might have hesitated momentarily before she nodded and handed me a key. 'It's all in the kitchen,' she said.

Annie's house smelt strange; there was the perfume of furniture polish but also of something less pleasant. The air was very still as if time had been caught in a capsule and was slowly turning rancid. Looking into the lounge confirmed my expectation of a space filled with clutter, frills and ornamentation. A Mills and Boon novel lay on a side table. Everything looked ordered and polished but it was a front, masking a room distended with unmet desires. Over the electric fire where a fireplace would originally have been, were two portraits, one of Maurice Manning, the other of Grace Elizabeth. On the other walls were photographs in frames of Gracie, Lizzie and a couple I recognised only slightly. Caro and Hugh, their parents. There was also a photograph of my mother. I couldn't move from it. Mother was dressed in a floral frock which made her look very young. She was leaning against a tree looking up at the camera as if she had been disturbed from a daydream. It could have been taken on the estate but I couldn't work out where.

'What on earth are you doing in here?' Annie almost shouted making me jump. She pushed past me and straightened the portrait of Maurice as if I had disturbed it. 'You shouldn't be in here. This is my home. You have no right.' She adjusted an antimacassar and chided me out as if she were herding me. I had never seen her so agitated and felt guilty about my intrusion. I might have reacted in a similar way if somebody had entered my room uninvited and was looking at my things.

'I'm really sorry, Annie, I didn't think.' When she didn't respond I again repeated, 'I'm so sorry Annie.'

This time she huffed a reply and said, 'We need to get the food next door.'

After a couple of journeys with Annie watching me carefully, so I didn't leave the official route, all the trays had been delivered.

They were put on a table still under cling film at the front of the room. The two settees had been placed facing each other in the centre. Even with the balloons and Welcome Home Banner I thought the place looked uninviting.

I think it was Tara who decided to drive Lizzie back to the Manor to get changed. I was not invited and they left me to walk back to the Gate House. Annie ignored me as she hurried next door.

We gathered at the house later, waiting for Gracie to arrive. The room was crowded; there were too many people in the small space. I felt claustrophobic. Nigel was present and the Manning family relatives; Uncle Victor, Aunt Eleanor and Uncle James with Leo and Tara. Uncle Charles alone. He had separated from Alicia's mother some time ago. I went into the kitchen and had started to sort out glasses for drinks when he came in. He didn't speak to me but went over to the back door and opened it. It was drizzling outside with enough breeze to blow the damp into the room. He took out cigarettes and lit one, hunching beside the door in an attempt to blow smoke outside and keep protected from the weather. It didn't work and smoke was blown back inside. Of course we had all aged since Alicia's disappearance six years ago, but Charles more than the rest of us. In the dull light his skin was grey and wrinkled; his eyes behind spectacles red-rimmed, as though he drank too much.

'Any chance of a drink then?' he asked, I was about to say we were waiting for Gracie to arrive but he was already uncorking a bottle of red saying, 'This needs to breathe,' and then pouring a large glassful. He returned to the door and looked at the gardens behind the houses. Annie's plot was a flourishing mass of evergreen shrubs interspersed with colourful autumnal foliage; Gracie's side was all spikey stalks and brambles where they had been chopped back. It was bounded by a barbed wire fence turning to rust.

Suddenly I heard Lizzie shout, 'She's here!' so I made my way back to the lounge. Charles did not follow me.

Maurice came into the room first, followed by Tara and then Grace Elizabeth, 'Welcome to your new home,' she said as Gracie finally stepped into the lounge. We awaited Gracie's reaction like an audience waiting for a play to begin and concerned the actor had forgotten her lines, because at first Gracie just stood there. Then she started to turn around spreading her arms out and spinning faster and faster causing a draught, enough to flutter the 'welcome' banner and nudge the balloons hanging in the corners of the room. 'Mine. This is all mine,' she said.

She hugged everybody in the room, ending with Grace Elizabeth.

'I'm so glad you like it, darling,' Grace Elizabeth said, smoothing Gracie's hair where it had flicked up after all the hugging. 'I must admit I had a moment of inspiration. Lizzie said something and I suddenly thought Gracie might come home if she could live in the little worker's house. We've just given it a very basic spruce up, but it's all yours and you can decorate it however you want.'

Everybody started clapping, everybody except me. I was speechless. I hadn't expected to be thanked for the work I had put in, but for Grace Elizabeth to take credit for the idea was despicable. I tried to see Lizzie's expression but she looked thrilled. I was making my way back to the kitchen when Grace Elizabeth said, 'There's a birthday surprise for you too, Lizzie.'

Grace Elizabeth and Maurice invited her outside, the crowd of us followed behind. There, parked a little way off was a small red car. Grace Elizabeth handed Lizzie the keys. Lizzie jumped up and down and hugged her grandparents.

'I'll take you for a drive,' offered Tara.

'Come for a drive with me, Gracie?' said Lizzie, and Gracie pushed through the group and climbed in the back.

I waited for my invitation, tried to catch Lizzie's eye, but she was too taken up with her new car and her sister being home. The rest of us returned to the house and people started helping themselves to food and drink. I joined Charles in the kitchen and swigged a bottle of beer.

Even when Lizzie and Gracie reappeared a short time later I remained where I was, wondering if she would eventually miss me.

Various people visited the kitchen, but not Lizzie. 'Having your own party in here?' Nigel commented as he came to collect more bottles. Charles turned from his post at the door and stared at him blankly.

Later Eleanor came in and told her brother, 'Us oldies are going to head back, leave the young ones to it.' She went over to Charles and linked arms with him. 'It's time to go, dear,' chivvying him as if he were a very old man who had lost his senses.

Still I stayed in my retreat until I heard the sound of the doorbell and Tom's voice. Walking into the lounge my feet stopped, as if I had hit an invisible wall. I had a sense of deja vu. The smell of cucumber and chicken tikka mingled, making me nauseous. Now dark outside, lamps had been switched on making a ring of shadows circle the walls. Tara must have gone to the loo, because now, in the centre were the same faces that had been present on the night of Alicia's disappearance and Tom's arrival accentuated the vision. Even when Tara returned, her presence was not enough to dispel the sensation.

'Are you alright, Hal?' It was Gracie who asked. I was going to blurt out what I had been reminded of, but then I thought better of it and answered, 'Yes, I just need a beer.'

Tom set up some music and we drank and talked. The two sofas had been filled so I sat on the floor at Lizzie's feet. Nigel sat between Gracie and Lizzie behind me; I didn't turn to look at him as I suspected his arms were stretched out around their shoulders. In the middle of the sofa across from me sat Tara, her long legs primly placed, knees together. Her hair was very short and blonde, with a longer sweep of fringe. She was wearing a black shift dress, which clung to her and fell softly, skimming the top of her thighs. Her shoes were black with multiple straps and very high, I found myself following the line from the heel, up the smoothness of her legs, over her knees, to the dark crevice formed between her thighs and the edge of her dress. She noticed me looking and gave me a secretive smile and let her knees move apart slightly. I had the distinct feeling she was not wearing underwear. Behind me Nigel said, 'Bloody hell, Tara, you're giving me a hard on.'

Tara giggled, sweeping her hair from her eyes and I wondered if she had been flirting with Nigel and not me at all. Nigel leaned over, offering a cigarette to Tara; he got up and lit it for her then sat back down, not offering the cigarettes around. Though I was not a smoker I had the desire to blow smoke rings and appear cool.

'Get some more beer somebody,' he demanded. Nobody moved in response, but I felt the nudge of Lizzie's knee in my back and knew it was my summons to serve. I got up and collected bottles from the kitchen, handed them out to everybody and took my place back on the floor. Nigel started to tell jokes and rude stories about university life. Leo added occasional comments and as the drink flowed the tales got more exaggerated. 'Let's dance,' somebody suggested as the latest Spice Girls tune played. All of us except Nigel, who lounged along the sofa smoking, got up. I managed to dance my way to Lizzie, though she twisted out of my grip when I wanted to hold her.

We'd been dancing for a while when Nigel suddenly got up. 'I've had enough of you jerks bopping about. Is this some sort of sixth form disco? Let's have some proper music. What you got on there, Tom?'

Tom went over and The Verve was selected. All of us except Tara sat down; I took her place on the sofa opposite Lizzie. The lyrics hovered around us, about drugs not working. Tara continued to dance. She moved awkwardly and not really to the music, but it was strangely attractive. I watched her mannequin limbs jolt and jerk and she looked at me and smiled, holding my gaze, her movements particularly her pelvis becoming more thrusting.

Whether Nigel had been aware of this exchange I couldn't tell, but he got up and started dancing with Tara, mirroring her moves. He handed her his cigarette and she took a drag on it and passed it back, her eyes locked with his now.

'Let's have the dance music on again,' Gracie asked as a Radiohead track began. But Nigel, ignoring the fact he was in her house, for her party, said, 'No, this is great.' As Thom York's voice pierced the room Nigel commented, 'This is my favourite song.'

He started moving away from Tara and stopped in front of Gracie. Leaning down he joined in with words from the track; 'Paranoid.' Shouting them out. 'Android.' He repeated the words, his face getting so close to Gracie's his lips were almost touching hers. He shouted louder as the song reached its climax. 'Panic...Vomit!' I was surprised Gracie remained so still. Then he pushed away from her and fell into the space beside me, laughing. The last bars of music drifted away and the room was quiet as if the smoke had finally damped out sound.

Nigel was lying back in his seat obviously pleased with himself and the effect he'd had on the rest of us. I think he was unprepared for Gracie's reaction as she stomped over to him. She took his current cigarette and stubbed it out in the ashtray. 'This is a no smoking house. If you don't like it, go somewhere else.'

Nigel reached over and grabbed her wrist. His fist looked huge holding her twig-like arm. For a minute they didn't move, staring each other down. Finally Nigel pulled her arm towards him and kissed the back of her hand with an exaggerated smacking sound.

'Alright, alright,' he said, 'You only had to say.'

After that exchange, the party never really got started again and we all left. I told Lizzie I'd walk her home, but she said she'd stay over and go back in the morning.

Nigel and Leo strode away leaving me to walk with Tom. He turned off before me and I wandered back to the Gate House alone, feeling sorry for myself.

I was glad when the weekend was over and I was back at school. I didn't see Lizzie the whole week, but on the following Saturday there was a knock at the door and Lizzie was standing there, smiling. 'I'm taking you out for the day,' she said, 'No arguments.' Though I had been brooding all week about her treatment of me and had been making up conversations in which she would have to apologise for ignoring me at the party, now I said nothing. Instead, I kissed her and forgave her.

That day, we did not venture far. Lizzie took my hand and led me to woods on the far side of the estate. She had a picnic basket with her. We spread a rug on the ground and ate sandwiches and strawberries. We talked and giggled. At that time, there was always laughter with Lizzie.

It was a glorious autumnal day, and the sun beamed through the thinning canopy of leaves, illuminating everything with an amber glow. It transformed the tree trunks into precious metals with its touch. One slender birch looked as if it had been cast in silver. From it, I pulled a strip of bark. Then, I kissed each of Lizzie's fingertips and tied the silvery band around her ring finger.

'You know what this means?' I said.

'No,' she shook her head.

'It means we have made a solemn promise to marry. It cannot be broken.'

She did not say anything for a few moments. But then she giggled, and began to dance around the tree. She twisted her wrist to and fro, posing her hand, as if she was trying the fit of a ring from Tiffany's.

Finally, she stopped dancing and faced me. 'I love it!' she said. 'You are so sweet and silly, Henry Bennett.' We kissed for a long time, warm within the golden wood.

Christmas came and went. With time spent at Gracie's house and Lizzie passing her driving test we had a new sense of freedom.

It was around my seventeenth birthday everything changed.

Visiting Gracie at the beginning of April she told me, 'We're going to have a party here for your birthday, Hal.' I didn't want a party, I would be happy with just her and Lizzie for company I told her. But she was having none of that. 'It's going to be great,' she said, and I wondered if she was aware of my lack of friends. In the end what I feared came to pass. I arrived to a room full of people, most of whom I didn't know.

The party was unremarkable and unremembered. The night was not.

Gracie had wanted us to stay after the party so we had sorted the cushions from the sofas into a makeshift double bed on the floor of the lounge. It was only midnight by the time we said goodnight, proving the mediocrity of the party. I snuggled under the duvet with Lizzie and didn't mind that the party had finished so early.

'I need to tell you something, Hal' Lizzie whispered.

'That sounds serious,' I joked.

'It is,' she responded and I felt scared. I moved away from her trying to make a distance from the dreadful thing she was about to say. I shivered.

'I'm pregnant.' For a moment I felt relieved. I thought she was going to tell me she was leaving, dying or something else that would take her away from me. Then the significance of the statement reached me.

'Say something,' she pleaded.

'It's going to be alright,' I told her, pulling her towards me, thinking about the thing growing inside her, not at all certain I was ready for this.

I couldn't think what to say. My emotions were jumbled. I was scared but beneath that sensation I trembled with excitement. We had created a new life. Putting my hand against Lizzie's stomach I imagined the burst of growth inside her and forgot my fear. 'It's wonderful,' I said. Hugging Lizzie with our little bud between us I felt warm, as if we were encircled by a huge hand. A family. However much love there was between Mother and me, the two of us were never a true family unit. Now I had achieved something. A family was three; mother, father, child. With that comforting thought in my head, and listening to Lizzie's even breathing, I fell asleep.

Lizzie was not beside me when I awoke and I wondered if I had dreamt last night's conversation. She brought me a mug of tea. 'Do you still feel the same?' she asked, 'about my news?'

I nodded. 'Does anybody else know?'

'Well, only Gracie.'

So Gracie knew before me. 'We'll need to work out who we're going to tell and when. Perhaps we should keep it to ourselves for now and work out a strategy,' I said. 'You shouldn't have told Gracie'.

My plan would be not to say anything to anybody and roll with the consequences when it was obvious and too late to stop.

'I wanted Gracie to know.'

I hadn't time to elaborate because Gracie walked in.

'Wanted me to know what?'

'About me being pregnant.'

'It's fantastic,' Gracie said, 'How is Mummy-to-be feeling this morning?' she asked Lizzie and hugged her.

I had never knowingly felt jealous of Gracie but I did now. I could feel a green flush spilling over me. Lizzie was mine. The baby was mine. Nobody else needed to know or share that.

'We're not telling anybody else just yet,' I almost shouted to interrupt their embrace, 'Not everybody is going to see it as such a good thing.'

Gracie looked at me; I was still lying on the floor in the makeshift bed and felt at a disadvantage, 'Sure it's not you who doesn't think it's a good thing?' Gracie said.

'I'm fine with it,' I told her, but not feeling as certain as I had earlier. I continued my point, 'But you know how Grace Elizabeth and Maurice will take it.'

'Maybe,' she shrugged.

Another month passed with Lizzie looking lovelier each time I saw her. Looking at her, there was no physical evidence she was pregnant, but to me she glowed.

I was delighted when July arrived and Mother said she was staying over at a friend's house for the weekend. I didn't question her about her plans, just thought Lizzie and I would have the cottage to ourselves.

The wonderful weekend I had planned was to start with a romantic night on the Friday. I had chosen what I thought was a fairly simple recipe. Following a cook book carefully I prepared a salmon salad and I'd bought a cheesecake for dessert. The table was set with candles and a carnation in a small vase.

I had told Mother, lied to Mother to be accurate, that I had invited over a girl from school. She was delighted. 'That's good,' she said. 'I was getting worried you were spending too much time with Lizzie and Gracie Manning. I don't like to say this,' she dropped her voice to a whisper, 'But there's something unhealthy about that pair.' I wanted to make a comment to protect the name of my beloved and her sister but I couldn't think of what to say without disclosing my secret. The cutlery made a ringing noise as I dropped it on the table. Mother came over and straightened a knife and moved a napkin. 'Am I going to meet this mystery girl then?' she asked, 'Does she have a name?'

'She's called,' I hesitated, 'Ophelia,' I fibbed. Mother frowned at me, 'Unusual name?'

'Yes, her parents are Shakespeare geeks.' Why I continued the dreadful lie, I don't know. Mother shook her head and shrugged, 'Well, have a good time and don't you two be getting up to mischief while I'm away.' She came over and hugged me. 'You've grown up so quickly,' she murmured. 'You know you can always talk to me about anything, don't you? Anything at all.' For a fraction of a second, I thought I could tell her my girlfriend was pregnant and ask what I should do. After all she might understand, she'd had me when she was sixteen. I had opened my mouth and was about to form the words when the blaring of a car horn sounded and Mother sprang away, 'That's for me,' she said. And so the moment vanished.

Lizzie arrived and we sat down to eat. The question about who we told and when, must have been on Lizzie's mind as well.

We were half way through the salad when she said, 'I think we should start telling people, Hal.'

'No,' I said more firmly than I meant to, 'I'm not ready.'

'We have to think about other people now; I'm going to start showing soon.'

I crunched a piece of watercress between my teeth. When I didn't reply she said, 'They might not take it as badly as you think.'

The watercress tasted bitter. I continued to munch my way through the salad, trying to work out my thoughts.

'Hal, talk to me.' Lizzie had put her knife and fork down. Her words had an exasperated edge to them. 'We need to make a decision about this.'

'I've told you, I'm not ready. Can't you let it be at that?' I shovelled another piece of greenery into my mouth, realising it wasn't particularly appetising.

'I'm also going to have to go to the doctors and hospital for check-ups and scans. Grandmama would help with those.'

I paused, a lettuce leaf half eaten, whilst I worked out the meaning of what she'd said.

'So the local GP and general hospital isn't going to be good enough for Lizzie Manning. Is that it?'

'You know that's not what I meant,' she started, but I cut her off,

'Well, I'm sorry I won't be able to afford to keep you in your former life style, perhaps you should have thought about that before you got involved with me.'

'Hal, don't get cross about it. This hasn't got to do with you and me; it's to do with whatever's best for the baby now.'

But for me, that wasn't it. As soon as the Mannings knew they would engulf Lizzie and take over. I would be on the side-lines of my newly forged family, my life. I couldn't find the words to explain it to Lizzie so said, 'I'm still just the servant boy to you, aren't I?' My chair squealed against the floor as I pushed it back. I removed our still full plates back to the kitchen.

In silence I cleared the table and washed up leaving Lizzie in the sitting room.

When I returned she had put the TV on and was watching a game show. We didn't say a word for the rest of the evening. It was still early when she said she was going to bed. I gave her an hour hoping she would be asleep by the time I got in, but I could tell she wasn't as I squeezed beside her. We did not say goodnight.

It must have been early morning when I was awakened by the sound of water running in the bathroom next door. I found I could stretch out; Lizzie must have gone to wash.

As I stretched my fingers to the space where her body had been they felt sticky. I threw back the bedding. In the dim rays of early morning I could see a black pit in the centre of the bed. In my still sleepy brain it took me several moments to realise it was not a hole but a spread of dark liquid. I stumbled into the bathroom, squeezing in behind Lizzie who was at the sink. Her face reflected in the mirror was so still and so pale it looked as if she was captured under ice. I put my arms around her, she felt cold.

We stayed locked in our tragedy for a long time. Finally she said to my reflection in the mirror, 'I guess we don't need to argue about telling people anymore.' She looked down at the sink and began washing her hands. 'There's nothing to tell.'

I watched the water rotate down the plughole, within it was a ribbon of blood and as it disappeared my stomach felt hollow with loss.

As I changed the bedding, folding the soiled sheet into a bin bag I thought about the stain. It had become darker as it dried and resembled a black hole pulling everything towards it. It had the same significance to my life as the death of a star because, with our loss, I think Lizzie was lost to me also.

What Remains 7

The TV was muted and the only sound was an unsettling scraping like the rasp of sandpaper. I looked down at my fingernails grating across the back of my hand. Darkness had crept over the room. The light from the silent television played shadow games. Across the room a photo of Tom's children showed two brown haired, brown-eyed, smiling boys. I wondered what my baby would have looked like, pale skinned and black haired or golden like Lizzie. What a terrible waste. I wasn't yet old but it felt as though I had lost the only opportunity I'd have to be a father.

Words came to me from a distance as if a character off the TV was talking to me. Lizzie's voice. It reminded me of a real conversation we'd had weeks after the miscarriage.

'They say miscarriages often mean there was something wrong with the baby.'

'Do they?' I had responded, not wanting to further the conversation.

'You know identical twins are supposed to be a mutation?'

'No, what are you talking about?'

'Yes, fraternal twins are supposedly hereditary but identical twins like Gracie and me are a blip.'

'Lizzie, don't be daft.' The conversation made me uneasy.

'No, that's what people say. I'm a mutant.'

'Lizzie, don't say such a thing.' I reached over and held her hands and tried to make her look at me. 'If you're a mutant, you're a perfect mutant.' But she stared into the middle distance, her eyes glassy with tears.

'I'm a mutant. That's why I lost my baby.'

My hands were raw when I woke the following morning; I applied more antiseptic cream from the bathroom cabinet, unable to ignore the diabetic syringes and wondering how Tom must feel injecting himself each day.

I took Barklay out for a long walk, trying to steady my thoughts about the baby. Besides the mutant conversation, Lizzie and I barely mentioned the event. The power of memories made me unsteady and I found myself sitting on the bench overlooking the Manning estate. If I had difficulty accepting the loss of the baby, after all this time, then had Lizzie ever been able to come to terms with it.

The dry weather had continued, parching the land around the Manor, and it resembled desiccating bone in the middle of its bowl, like debris caught in a sink. I remembered bloody water draining away in the cottage bathroom and again reflected that perhaps that was the moment I lost Lizzie. Because although we appeared content in our continued relationship, there was always a shadow at my shoulder.

When I got back to the house I busied myself with tidying, ready for the return of Tom. It served to keep me distracted.

Thursday arrived. I went to buy groceries at the shop and when I returned there was Tom's estate sitting outside the house. Barklay barked with excitement as we arrived at the door, and I felt dismayed as I realised he was delighted his real family was back.

I knocked at the door.

'Hi Hal! Come in. come in!' I was once again the guest. Tom's sons looked at me with curiosity. And after an awkward hug Tom introduced me to them.

The house seemed small. It had been ideal for one man and a dog, but adding a family of four made the walls compress.

As I sat with Mandy and Tom in the evening Tom assured me it would be fine for me to stay. 'That's alright isn't it, Mandy?'

'Of course,' she replied sweetly. I knew she sort of meant it, though it would mean the boys sharing a bedroom. 'Stay as long as you like.'

I asked them about their holiday. 'It's really great you won the holiday. What sort of competition was it?' Tom said nothing but appeared to be concentrating on the TV listings in the paper.

'What?' Mandy replied. She looked puzzled. 'We didn't win a holiday, Hal. What on earth made you think that?'

I was the one confused. I was sure Tom had told me they'd won the holiday in a competition. Now I doubted myself, our phone conversation seemed so long ago. However I answered, 'I'm sure Tom said you'd won a competition.' I looked over at Tom but he was still engrossed in the paper.

'No, I think you've got the wrong idea, Gracie paid for us to go.'

'Gracie?' I said sounding dumb.

'What's wrong with that?' Tom suddenly demanded. 'I told you on the phone we'd been lucky, we were going to Florida, but I never said we'd won it. You must be imaging things.'

I was sure I wasn't but I didn't want to antagonise Tom. I remained quiet. He clicked the TV on and a film soundtrack swept into the room.

So what was the bottle of champagne about then and why on earth had Gracie sent them on holiday? Foolishly I forgot about not antagonising Tom and asked him.

He snapped back at me, 'Because we're friends. Because I've done loads of extra hours re-designing the garden at her house. Because Mandy helps look after Eliza.' He slammed the paper onto the coffee table. 'Is that enough reasons for you, Hal? Or do you want to have it in writing?'

'I'm sorry, I was just confused by what you said before.' Watching Tom's expression, I changed my words, 'by what

I *thought* you'd said. I must have been mistaken though. I'm sorry,' I added.

'Yes, you should be. Especially as it was Gracie who suggested you for house sitting.'

Why on earth would Gracie want me back in Leverbridge? It seemed odd she would even think of me.

It finally dawned on me just how Tom's life must have changed. Alterations I had no conception of. Sometimes old friends, when they haven't seen each other for a long time, say, 'Everything fell into place. It was as if we'd seen each other yesterday.' It wasn't like that for me and Tom.

For a while we watched a film. I suspect none of us had a clue as to the story line. However, there was a scene where a lone person attended a funeral service in a huge church.

'I went to Maurice's funeral,' I said. 'The church was packed.'

Tom shrugged; either he didn't hear me, didn't care or was actually interested in the film.

But after several minutes he said, 'I'm surprised you'd want to go back to that church.'

I didn't feel able to tell him I had not wanted to, but I had thought I might see Lizzie. At some point I needed to ask him why he hadn't told me Lizzie had been pronounced dead. But now did not seem like the right time.

'You shouldn't scratch your hand like that, Hal, you'll make it sore.' Mandy said. I pressed my palms together as if praying; it was the only way to stop the movement. I was concentrating on my hands when Tom asked,

'Was anything said at the funeral?'

I wasn't sure what he meant. 'Well, there were the usual readings and a tribute.'

'No, I mean about the way he died?'

'No,'

'So nobody thought his death was suspicious?' Tom asked.

'No.' I was taken aback by the question, there had been no suggestion Maurice had died from anything other than natural causes after a short illness. 'No,' I repeated, 'Why would you think that?' Tom looked at me and shrugged. 'It was just a question, Hal,' he said, annoyed again. He continued to glare at me so I decided to move on.'I was invited to the will reading though. He left me the Gate House.'

'What?' said Tom, obviously astonished. 'Why would he do that?' I had no answer to that question so said nothing.

Mandy said, 'Wow, that's wonderful. Now you'll be able to stay in Leverbridge.'

'I'm not sure I want to stay in Leverbridge, it's got some pretty bad memories for me. Anyway, the cottage is a mess. It could take months to sort.'

With the memories I associated with the cottage, I was certain it could never feel like home.

The following morning I was woken early by the sounds of children arguing and running down the stairs. Barklay yapped with excitement and Tom's voice shouted, 'Hey you two, less noise, we've got a guest remember?'

Having been master of the house for a week I felt displaced. I didn't fit here.

'Look, why don't we take a walk over to the cottage today?' suggested Tom. 'See what needs doing.' Tom clipped Barklay's lead and I followed the pair out of the house.

I decided to ask him about his diabetes but felt unsure how to broach the subject so reverted to the banter of years before. 'What's with the pharmacy in your cabinet?' I said with a laugh.

Tom said nothing for a few moments but gradually reduced his pace until he had come to a halt. He looked at the ground and said, 'What do you mean?'

'The diabetic stuff.'

147

'Well I guess it means I have diabetes.' His answer was loaded with sarcasm. I realised how insensitive I had been.

'Sorry,' I mumbled.

'Look, it's crap. I have to test myself, inject myself, be careful what I eat and drink. That's the extent of it. And I don't want to talk about it, okay.'

'Okay,' I responded, recognising the subject was closed.

Again I was aware of the distance between us, of our friendship in the past and the strangers we appeared to be now. We walked in silence until we reached the village shop, our attention drawn to the news board outside. Bold black letters stated:

'Twist in Leverbridge Manor Tale.'

'What does that mean?' Tom asked.

'Should have said something before,' I said. I wasn't looking at him but mumbling at my shoes.

'What?'

'They found Alicia's bones buried at the Manor.'

Tom stopped walking and stared at the board as if trying to decipher the story within those five words. 'Alicia. They found Alicia? Shit.'

I left him outside and went in to buy a paper. The story was on the front page. Alicia's inquest had been held the previous day. I walked back out aware of the warmth and light after the dim interior of the shop. Tom looked like a statue, he had not moved. Barklay waited at his side.

'Some information's been leaked. The police are treating it as a murder investigation,' I told him.

'Why?'

I skimmed the first paragraphs of the article. 'It says the hyoid bone was broken, which suggests strangulation.'

Tom didn't turn to look at me but said, 'And they have no idea who did it?'

'Nope. Her disappearance had remained an open case, now it's officially a murder investigation.' There was no more information, just a photograph of Leverbridge

Manor. I folded the newspaper and walked onwards. Tom followed reluctantly as if he had difficulty tearing himself away from the words on the news board. He didn't speak until we were outside the cottage.

'We were all there that night. We gave her that stupid dare.'

'Yes,' I said as I turned the key in the lock. We entered the house and I was surprised by how tidy it was. Obviously Annie had been in and thoroughly cleaned it. Instead of the previous musty odour of disuse there was perfume hanging in the air rather than cobwebs. The dust sheets had been removed and although several cardboard boxes still remained, it looked quite homely. The mantelpiece had been dusted and Annie must have wound the clock—it was ticking again, keeping the correct time.

'I thought you said it was a mess?' said Tom, as Barklay crossed the sitting room and whined at the chimney breast. 'This is a great place. You jammy bastard, inheriting from Maurice Manning.'

I could hear the tinge of envy in his voice.

'It was a mess, but Annie Taylor must have been in to clear up. Gracie said she would ask her.'

'You saw Gracie?' again I thought I detected a hint of resentment.

'Yes, at Maurice's funeral and then after the reading of the will she came back to help me here.'

'What's that?' he indicated, noticing the brown package leaning against the wall.

'It's a portrait of Mother. I inherited that as well.'

'Why don't you open it?'

'Don't think I'm quite ready to face her just yet.'

Tom shrugged, not understanding my reluctance. He sat in the armchair by the fireplace, Barklay at his feet still watching the chimney anxiously.

'Tell me what's been going on whilst I've been away Hal.'

So I filled him in, from Maurice's funeral to the finding of Alicia's bones, then the reading of the will and Gracie helping me to return to the cottage.

Tom did not interrupt. I finished but he remained silent, looking away from me. And as he didn't comment on what I'd just said, I told him I'd been to see his Dad.

Finally, I'd provoked a response. He turned his head sharply and asked, 'Why?'

'There was an Open Day and I thought it would be nice to see him.'

'I would have told you about the Open Day if I'd wanted you to visit him. He's an old man and gets confused. You had no reason to go bothering him.'

Tom's reaction surprised me.

'What did he say?'

'He was just expecting you to turn up because I had. He thought we were kids again.'

'He gets confused,' Tom repeated. 'And upset, especially if you mention the Manor.'

'I know.' So my good intention to visit George had been an error. I remembered the tear wriggling down George's face. 'I'm sorry,' I thought I ought to let Tom know the extent of my mistake. 'I do think I upset him. He said something about Alicia, about how they'd never find her.'

Tom stood up and pointed at me, 'You see,' he shouted, 'He gets confused.'

'I know that, Tom, I know.' Tom's temper was unexpected. In the short time I'd been here he'd been more bad tempered than I had ever known. Perhaps having diabetes did that to you. And I wondered if the holiday had really been such a success. He had seemed tense since his return.

'Was the holiday really alright?'

'Yes, the holiday was fine. It's always the coming back.' He turned to look at me and I wondered whether he was going to lose his temper again. I waited for angry words.

'Look Hal, things haven't been going very well for me lately. A couple of months ago, Maurice sacked me. No reason, just dumped.' Tom raked his fingers through his hair so tufts stood up. 'Bloody bastard. And don't say anything to Mandy, she doesn't know.'

'What about now?' I asked, 'Now he's dead.'

'Well, hopefully I'll get my job back, before the contract company he took on, ruin all my landscaping.'

He was scratching his head again. 'You really are jammy, inheriting this place.'

Tom just didn't get it. How desolate these walls and all the things associated with them made me feel.

'Now it's tidy, you can move in here. Can't you?'

'Well really, I'd prefer to stay at yours a while longer.'

'Truthfully, it's a bit of a squash, and Mandy feels awkward with you around. She can't relax.'

I didn't know what to say, I was upset by the false words of welcome. At the time they had appeared genuine. I was certain I hadn't misread Mandy's invitation for me to stay as long as I wanted. Tom continued, 'Anyway you've got this place now. No reason you can't move in here.'

Tom was a practical man, I couldn't bring myself to tell him it wasn't my physical comfort that bothered me, but all the things you couldn't see in this cottage, which made me not want to stay here. The past seeped into the wood of the furnishings, running with the water in the plumbing and held within the sooty remains up the chimney.

I tried to keep my reply as composed as possible.

'Look Tom, I'll move back here, but you need to understand it holds bad memories for me.'

I could tell from his expression he had no idea what I meant.

Barklay's tail shifting on the hearth rug caught my attention, it gave me an idea. 'Could I borrow Barklay for a few days? We got on pretty well whilst you were away, and I could use some company.'

'You'll have to ask Mandy, but if it gets you out from under her feet, I don't see why not,' replied Tom.

His response disturbed me. I may have been paranoid but I got the impression it was Tom trying to get rid of me. Or perhaps the diabetes affected his mood. I thought I might have read that somewhere.

'Let me show you the garden,' I suggested, feeling the need to get out.

Once he'd had a good look round we made our way back to the village, stopping off at The Huntsman on the way. Tom's usual pleasant mood had returned and we joked with the barmaid whilst we drank our beer.

'You'll be coming to the Summer Fayre, won't you?' she asked, 'We're setting up a beer tent there and the bar skittles.'

'Wouldn't miss it, Bev,' Tom replied, 'The kids will want to go, and Mandy usually enters something for the flower arrangements. Hope you've been tending her flowers whilst we've been away, Hal, so we've got a prize-winner. She might forgive you then.'

What had I done to require forgiveness? I had thought I was the perfect house sitter. Also, because of the hosepipe ban, I hadn't watered the garden. I hadn't even taken a watering can to the borders.

Returning to the house, I felt awkward, but Mandy greeted me happily.

Tom told her, 'Hal's going to move into the cottage. I've said he can borrow Barklay for a few days so he's not lonesome.'

He said it as a done deal. Mandy didn't appear worried. 'That's fine, he seems very happy. You've done a good job of looking after him.'

My suspicion it was Tom who wanted rid of me increased, especially when on discussing the Summer Fayre Mandy said, 'I don't think the flower arranging competition will be up to much this year, with the drought affecting everything.'

Relieved at the thought I hadn't deliberately ruined her chances, I gave Tom a quizzical look which he chose to ignore.

So in the afternoon I packed up my mini. I included food and bedding for Barklay and some gardening tools, then I drove the mile and a half to the Gate House. The small car fitted the space outside the cottage perfectly.

A letter was waiting for me on the door mat. I recognised the black scrolled lettering as the same that had been on the Will summons. The contents of this were slightly different, though they were still an order of sorts from Grace Elizabeth. It was quite brief.

Henry,

I'm sure you won't want to remain at the Gate House. I hope we can discuss a sale and come to a mutually beneficial agreement.

She signed it *Mrs G.E Manning,* making it rather formal. I spent some time sitting and tapping it on the table and then against my teeth as if divining its authenticity.

Tom walked up with Barklay later. I offered him a beer but he made his way to the back garden and started to clip bushes with force. I wanted to ask if I'd upset him; he was clipping with such brutality, but couldn't work out how to pose the question. I left him for a while and then took him a can. 'Is something up?' I finally said.

He paused to take a slug of lager. He wiped his mouth on his sleeve and then using the secateurs as a pointer he demarcated the garden and the house. 'Well look at this, it doesn't seem fair.' The point of the secateurs came to rest at my chest level, 'Why should good things happen to you. Why should you be left a house?'

For several moments I could not respond. A blackbird flew from the hedge making a chattering sound. It bore a resemblance to what I wanted to say. How could Tom suggest that anything good happened to me? After all he

153

had just been on a free holiday. I told him this whilst watching the sharp implement in front of me wavering slightly.

'It's not the same,' he said. 'And you're so miserable about it, as well. You're rubbing my nose in it.' He took another swig of lager.

'I'm sorry,' I said, 'It's just bad things have happened here.'

He moved the secateurs in front of me like a wagging finger. 'Look I'm sorry your mother died, but my mum is dead too. Died in her bed. Shit like that happens.'

I felt captive whilst he talked to me at knife point. I couldn't tell him his mum's death didn't compare to the tragedy of my mother's suicide. He also didn't know about the loss of my unborn baby in the cottage.

'I'm sorry,' was the best I could come up with.

It seemed to be enough. 'Look Hal, I don't want to argue. Let's get this garden tidied.'

Tom continued to work on the garden through the evening, and following his instructions I helped out. We chatted a bit but left the subject of inheritance alone. It was on my mind though. I was adding up all the bad things that had happened to me, of which there seemed many measured against the good, and comparing them against Tom's lot. At one point I nearly called to Tom to remind him how his parents had also benefitted from Maurice Manning's benevolence; because from simple gardener and cleaner George and Mary had suddenly been elevated to market garden owners. It was only a rumour I'd heard from Mother and must have been twenty years ago, when Tom and I were just kids. On the imaginary balance sheet I was creating it seemed significant. Maurice had also put money in to further improve it later on; I'd seen the plaque at the Garden Centre.

'Hey Tom, didn't Maurice help your Mum and Dad move to the market garden?'

The anger in Tom's face as he turned to me was so absolute I thought he might run at me with the secateurs.

He remained still though and the tendons in his neck became prominent as he clenched his jaw, as if forcing himself not to take a swing at me. 'That was because my dad helped Maurice out all the time. He was a bloody good gardener; he could make something from nothing, much better than me.'

I didn't think that was true, Tom was equally as talented when it came to horticulture. However with the rumours still fluttering round my head like fallen leaves, I had to continue.

'He must have done something pretty special to be awarded that sort of reward.'

'I don't know. It happened ages ago when I was ten or eleven. It wasn't a bribe if that's what you're getting at.'

'I never said it was.' I shrugged and returned to weeding, but the more I thought about it the more I wondered just what George had done to earn himself a market garden.

We worked in silence a little longer but the light soon faded. Tom said we should call it a day. I was reluctant to leave the work as I realised the time was approaching when I would be left in the cottage alone overnight.

'Have another beer,' I said as we went inside. Tom refused.

'Got to go, mate,' he said, 'Mandy will be getting worried if I'm too late.'

'I'm sorry,' I told him as I saw him out. 'I'm nervous about staying here. I guess I took it out on you.'

'Not to worry,' he said, in the amiable way he used to, reminding me of the old Tom, 'I'll come by tomorrow.'

I set up a bed for Barklay on the hearth rug, he seemed to like that spot. I decided to sleep in Mother's room. The bathroom was next to my childhood bedroom and I could not consider lying in a bed where once I had heard Mother singing and splashing in the bath through the wall. Now all I could imagine was her corpse and my lost child.

In fact, when I went to wash before going to bed I got as far as turning the handle on the bathroom door. It shook under my grip and I didn't go further. Instead I washed and cleaned my teeth in the tiny sink in the toilet, relieved I could manage without facing the echoes in the bathroom.

There were no curtains at the window but the trees outside provided a screen of sorts, and though there was only a half-moon it was bright in the clear sky of summer. As I settled to sleep there was some familiarity in the creaks the cottage made and I was comforted. I imagined the trees surrounded me like a protective cage. It was an image I'd envisaged many times before and under its shielding effect I finally slept.

Warm breath on my face woke me. Barklay was whining at me, telling me it was time for his breakfast. I got up, let him out into the garden and made myself some toast.

Tom did come by the following day but couldn't stay long having family chores to do on a Saturday. However, I took his visit as some kind of truce.

'I'll see you tomorrow though,' he said, 'We'll pick you up on our way to the Fayre.'

Tom's family arrived at one thirty; he had never been good at time keeping so I knew it was Mandy's influence which meant we got there promptly. When the Fayre had been held in the grounds of the Manor it had seemed very grand. Now I was surprised at how small it was. The modern village hall had been built in 2000, for the Millennium celebrations and another plaque told of Maurice's generosity and funding. Bunting was threaded around and looked as if it had been in place since then. The faded triangles, which had once been brightly dancing, now hung limply as if weary of the heat.

Mandy and the boys made for the Bouncy Castle and Tom for the show marquee. Mandy had managed to scrape together an entry after all. I headed to the beer tent and was deciding whether to indulge in a sample tray of guest beers when there was a tap on my shoulder.

'Not surprised to find you in here. Mine's a white wine.'

I bought Tara a drink as directed, she already seemed unsteady on her feet but I suspected it was due to her high heels catching on the matting.

'Cheers,' I offered as I took a sip of beer.

'I'm not very cheery, really, Hal. I'm putting a brave face on; it's what Maurice would have wanted of course.'

She was dressed in black. She obviously noticed the quizzical look in my glance; I had to check she wasn't kidding. 'I'm still in mourning, Hal.' And I realised she was genuine. Her attitude to her Great-Uncle was different than mine. I would not wish bereavement on anybody but grief suited Tara. It gave her a vulnerability which softened her usual hard edge. She looked like an exotic flower, a black stem crowned with pale petals, marked with huge eyes. I moved closer to her and inhaled her heady perfume.

'He always opened the Fayre, even last year. It seems wrong somehow it's just Grace Elizabeth this time.' As if on cue the back ground music from a speaker stopped, then over the crackle of interference a voice spoke. 'Ladies and Gentleman the official opening of the Fayre is about to begin. Please make your way to the central plaza.'

'Come on,' I said.

'I'll wait here,' Tara replied and so I left her. As I exited the tent I turned back and saw her tip back the rest of her wine and turn to buy another.

'The Central Plaza' was rather a grand title for what was a makeshift raised dais against the wall of village hall. A swathe of pink material was wrapped around the base. On top, three chairs were arranged in a line. Gracie sat on one side of Grace Elizabeth and a councillor on the other. As I arrived at the rear of the crowd, Grace Elizabeth stood up; though short she cast her usual aura.

I tried to remember back to those earlier days of the Fayre when Maurice Manning had loomed on the stage. Afterwards he had always had a photo taken, his arms around Gracie and Lizzie, hugging them to him. Mother and I always bought the paper the next day to see the photograph printed, as if by living at the Gate House we received some reflected glory. Mother would spend a long time looking at the photo as if she wanted to be part of it. 'Don't they make a wonderful picture, Hal? Maurice is so handsome and he just adores those girls. They get prettier each year don't they?'

Indeed they did, and as the two girls had grown more beautiful in those photographs, each year the width of Maurice Manning's smile increased as he clasped them at his sides.

Mother's response gradually altered over the years as well. 'Those two girls will break some hearts. Don't you be getting involved with them, will you Hal? They're a different species to us.'

After the opening I went back to the beer tent but I couldn't find Tara. Aimlessly I wandered among the stalls and tents.

In the main marquee the heat was intense. The white canvas, instead of reflecting heat out, appeared to redirect it inwards. The items on display were visibly shrivelling against their white cloths. People were panting and fanning themselves with their programmes, attempting to cause a draught. It achieved nothing more than making eddies of heat, tainted by sweat and stale display objects.

I noticed Tom talking to a woman in a corner. It was only as she turned to move closer to Tom whispering something to him I realised it was Gracie. I had not known they were close but their body language betrayed them. Gracie's hand was on Tom's arm and their conversation looked furtive. Tom, seeing me, moved away indicating to Gracie somebody was approaching with a nod, emphasising the secretive nature of their meeting.

'Hi, you two,' I said, 'Hot isn't it?' but Tom had already turned to leave the tent.

'You two looked cosy,' I said to Gracie. She just smiled and said, 'He's done wonders for my garden at home and still manages some of the gardening at the Manor. We're friends.' But I noticed a flush spread across her chest and up her neck which the placid smile could not hide. 'Let's look at the flower arrangements,' she said and gripped my arm turning me back into the heat of the marquee. We moved beside a trestle table displaying various arrangements.

'What do you think?' she asked.

'I'm no expert but I don't think it's been much of a year.' We looked critically over the drooping flowers.

'Annie entered her cakes; shall we have a look at those?' I followed Gracie over to a table laden with cakes. The icing on many was congealing in droplets as it melted; however, I was delighted to see a winner's rosette on Annie's famous scones.

'I moved back to the cottage, you know?'

'That's wonderful, Hal.'

'Annie did a great job of cleaning up, and I've got Tom's dog to keep me company.'

'I'll come and help sort out some of the boxes if you like, once I've done my duties here.'

I told her I'd appreciate it. Delving into those boxes could unearth anything. Company would be good.

Nigel approached us, but before he could make his usual snide comment, I left and went to find Tom. He was waiting for his sons to finish yet another session on the Bouncy Castle. I watched their small legs spring from the mattress and wondered where they got the energy. Even when they reluctantly climbed off they went running down the playing field towards the park swings and slides. 'Don't you want to see the stalls?' called Tom but they were already in the distance.

'Do you remember when we were that energetic?' Tom asked me. Indeed I did. My muscles felt heavy with memory.

What Was Taken 7

The energy of young boys cannot be underestimated. I did not know when I had lost that youthful vigour, perhaps when it had been labelled as 'exercise' at school.

But I remembered the day of the hunt meet like it was yesterday. A residual memory touched a remote part of my brain and made my muscles weak. Even my missing foot throbbed.

Tom and I didn't ride horses, but we loved our bicycles. So on the 26th December 1986, we joined the crowd of people congregating for the Boxing Day Hunt. Mother had been up since dawn preparing the Manning horses. It was an extra special occasion this year she told me, 'Little Tara's doing her first hunt. I've got to make sure everything's perfect.'

I was six so Tara was ten. From Mother's stories I knew Tara was already an accomplished rider something Mother wanted for me. I had disappointed her in this ambition. I wasn't sure Mother approved of the limelight which surrounded Tara. For some time Tara had helped in the stables. Occasionally, Mother would come home saying, 'That young lady's a prima donna.'

Because Mother was so involved in Tara's debut I felt the pressure lift off me for once, which is why I asked if Tom and I could follow the hunt on our bikes. Mother hardly registered my request but said, 'Yes,' before rushing off on some Hunt related errand.

I could not imagine doing anything similar nowadays or Mandy allowing her boys to ride out trying to follow the hunt along the narrow lanes around Leverbridge. But I remember the day as one of the most exhilarating of my short life.

It was a Boxing Day meet, the sky above the village square like a cool blue ceiling, constraining the crowd below into a dense hub of excitement. It was cold but the sun shone, refreshing the usual dowdy grey brick surrounding the square. Tom's and my faces were already red cheeked by the time we pushed our bikes to the meeting point. There were so many people milling around with the horses and dogs at ground level, we created a warm mass. I worked out Tara's mount; it had the green ribbon of a novice on its tail. She sat upright, her blonde hair plaited and tied with a matching green ribbon hanging down her back. Next to her much broader, astride his hunter, the unmistakeable back of Maurice. His hair was still red at that time and formed a bright lip between the black of his collar and hat. The horse's flanks were so glossy they reflected the red of his coat like glowing coals. Victor was on her other side, a rather squat figure in comparison. He was in a plain black jacket indicating his inferior status when it came to riding, but even from here I could tell he was laughing and joking with the company. I preferred him to his brother Maurice. He sometimes came to the cottage asking for Mother as well but without the same demands. He would stand at the door winking and ask, 'I've come to take your Mum out, is she there?' He would sometimes ruffle my hair and ask how I was getting on at school, whereas Maurice would ignore me.

I'd attended the first summer camp that year and felt I knew Tara, Lizzie and Gracie a little. I had formed an admiration for Tara at the camp. Being the eldest she had bossed us all and we had followed her instructions. She had told us, 'I'm the groom at the stables.' I knew that was untrue, my mother was head groom at the Manor and Tara helped out as a stable hand in the evenings and weekends. But I did not question Tara's statement; she had spoken with such authority.

I didn't see Lizzie or Gracie that day. Victor was now handing round the stirrup cup. The bray of his laugh carried on the cold air. Though younger than Maurice he always appeared older, he was tubbier and looked shorter, and his hair was grey. I had asked Mother once why his hair was grey when Maurice's was red and she had answered by saying she thought it looked very distinguished. He wasn't quite the horseman his brother was, his horse was stepping in tight circles, swishing its tail. Even to my inexperienced eyes it looked agitated. Victor was tugging the reins first one way, then the other, trying to keep the cup steady.

I kept away from the horses. Their hooves cracked against the paving in the square with impatience. I liked the hounds better; they were friendlier and less intimidating. They came up and nuzzled my fingers. We all felt the thrill of anticipation that morning. The noise was at a higher level than me, shouts of greeting from horseback to horseback, words from the followers thrown upwards to the riders. And the gathering breath puffed out, like smoke after fire extinguished.

Then they were off and Tom and I followed on our bicycles, our legs pumping madly around like spinning comic book creations. I suspect it was in my thoughts, Hal the superhero, flying off on an adventure. I'd had a new bicycle bell from Santa, and George had fitted it that morning. Occasionally I'd twang it with my thumb and the ring would explode into the air and resonate around us.

Wisps of cloud scudded with us, giving the impression of wind. But there was no wind just our speed below the still sky.

At times of course we lost the pack but then heard the bugle call or a shout of 'Tally Ho,' carrying through the clear air and we were able to work out how to get near them. We flew down narrow lanes, the tyres making a rushing noise as we pedalled, accompanying us like a movie soundtrack of speed. We took pathways we knew to be short cuts and then bumped down bridle ways made firm by earlier frost.

We came through a stand of trees. The branches bare and black created a tunnel for us. At the edge we stopped at a gate. This led into a field we were unable to cross. But as we waited, panting with exertion, the bugle sounded again and from the dip below we could see the flap of the hounds' heads as they followed the trail towards us up the hill. We sat on the gate enthralled. Never before had we been so close to the action. Two huge trees drooped branches, making a frame for us to watch through as the picture unfolded before us.

'The fox. The fox,' Tom croaked, still out of breath. I didn't believe him. But there it was. A scrawny red creature losing ground to the approaching pack. They made short work of him. Bringing him down and then encircling him so we didn't see any tearing of flesh but simply heard the excited yapping and exultation of achievement.

The first horses arrived. One of the riders jumped down and pushed through the remaining dogs to collect the body in a sack. Others arrived, whooping. And then I made out the smaller figure of Tara looking up to Maurice and him leaning down saying something to her.

The remainder of the morning is like a film reel in my head. I'm uncertain how much of it I misinterpreted due to being exhausted from cycling, but when I scroll back this is what I see.

Firstly Maurice dismounted. He turned to Tara and held his hand out to her, she climbed down too.

Then Maurice collected the sack holding the fox. It happened so quickly we hardly noticed. He cut the tail off the fox.

Tom made a noise of disgust, 'What's he doing?' he whispered to me. I couldn't speak to reply, I was rigid with the anticipation of what might happen next.

Tara remained quite still as Maurice bent down to her, her face tilted up a little with either pride or determination or both. Then Maurice rubbed the fox brush against her cheeks leaving bloody streaks. Still Tara did not flinch; in fact I think she smiled. What was more extraordinary was what occurred next. My memories are in slow motion. Maurice dropped the fox brush; it twisted as it fell catching the light like a great red catkin falling from a tree. Maurice lifted his hands up; encased in black riding gloves they looked big and heavy. He dropped his hands on Tara's shoulders and I wondered if she would fall under the weight of them, but she stayed upright. I thought he was going to say something to her, perhaps officially welcome her to the hunt. His lips moved but he said nothing. His mouth moved closer to Tara's face. And he kissed her. Not a fleeting kiss, but a full kiss on her upturned mouth. There was disagreement between Tom and I how long their lips remained in contact. Tom says a couple of seconds, and I say at least thirty. In the end the extent of the kiss does not matter, it was just so weird. Even at six years of age, instinctively I recognised it as wrong.

The audience of dogs and horse and riders behind them were silent, the only hint of discomfit was a horse harrumphing and stamping the ground.

Surprisingly little was made of this spectacle in the following days, which is why I think I may have been mistaken in what I saw.

What Remains 8

After time with Tom's family and the hustle of the Fayre, I was glad to reach the cottage. It made me hopeful I could put the ghosts to rest. I was in such a positive frame of mind I decided to make a start on the boxes.

There did appear to be some method in the packing and I could see one box with the edges of folded newspapers in it. I would start there.

The papers were sepia tinted and smelt of mould. As I selected one from the box it felt brittle in my hands as if it might disintegrate. I gently unfolded it to see the date; December 12th 1985. Turning back the brown edges I found a central Christmas section with photos from local school nativity plays.

It took a while but finally I made out me and Tom side by side, with tea towels on our heads, supposedly as shepherds. It was strange seeing that little boy staring out at me, as if I didn't know him at all. He looked innocent with a faint smile; as if he believed his life would be uncomplicated.

There was too much history here for me to deal with after all. I refolded the paper; it left a trace of dust on my fingers.

A knock at the door. Barklay got up and I followed him down the corridor. Gracie stood there holding a plate of scones. Beside her Grace Elizabeth. 'We've come to welcome you to your new home, Hal,' Gracie said. 'Can we come in?'

'Of course,' I replied and held the door aside for them to enter. 'Let me take those and make some tea,' I said. 'Please go through into the sitting room and please excuse the mess.' I had become a bowing and scraping servant again in the presence of Grace Elizabeth.

After a few minutes I returned to the sitting room. I had discovered the best china and teapot packed in a box in the kitchen and quickly rinsed them. The crockery rattled on the tray as I carried it through, and then I fetched the plate of scones.

Gracie was sitting on the settee and was stroking Barklay as his usual position had been usurped. Grace Elizabeth was standing looking critically around the room. I noticed her eyes resting on the wrapped portrait and wondered if she'd want to see it. Had she asked, I knew I would have no option but to unwrap it. After handing her a cup of tea I sat beside Gracie and waited for a proclamation from Grace Elizabeth. She placed her cup on the mantelpiece before she began to speak.

'I know life at the Gate House has not always been easy for you, Henry,' she said with unexpected insight. 'But we hope you'll be happy here.'

She made no reference to the note she'd sent me. The letter was folded in my back pocket. As I moved it rustled as if it wanted to be revealed. I considered taking it out to look at it again to check I had not misunderstood but Grace Elizabeth was looking at me with a fixed smile and I did not dare. I stood up to thank her managing to tip scone crumbs onto the rug. Barklay made short work of them.

I held out my hand to shake hers. 'It was really a shock to inherit a house; I wondered if you knew why he left it to me?'

She smiled and managed to distance herself from me. She did not take my hand. I returned to my seat.

'Well,' she began, her fingertips pyramided in front of her. 'We both liked your mother. She was here for a long time.' Grace Elizabeth's eyes had become bright; she was staring at a distant point in front of her as if she was making a well prepared speech. 'In fact, we gave her the chance in life she needed.' I was aware of the clock ticking; Grace Elizabeth's metronomic diction matched it. 'She was very young when she came here; we were instrumental in the beautiful, accomplished woman she became.' She gave a small cough; it was a move I suspected she had been taught to make more impact of her final words. 'Her loyalty to us deserved recognition.' Her eyes were glassy now, whether through real emotion or simply at the effort of staring I was not sure. The tick of the clock was loud in my ears and I realised Grace Elizabeth's words had a similar empty echo. I wondered when she would ask me how much money I wanted to sell the cottage back.

I thanked her for her kind words and even found myself saying I would do what I could to make the Gate House lovely again. Still she said nothing about me selling up.

However, as I walked her to the door she said, 'We'll talk again Henry.' No smile accompanied the sentence and the words were spoken in a threatening way. I returned to Gracie in the sitting room. She gave me a funny smile.

'What?' I asked, shrugging. I thought I wouldn't mention Grace Elizabeth's offer or her manner a moment ago. I suspected she'd tell me I was being paranoid.

'You sycophant,' she said, 'cosying up to Grace Elizabeth. Perhaps I ought to warn you though, when we walked up here Grandmama was telling me how cross she was at having you move back to the Gate House. She told me she thought you'd never come back. In fact she was mad at me for encouraging you.'

'Why would she come and welcome me then?' Perhaps I should tell Gracie about Grace Elizabeth's note.

'Grandmama is very good at saying what she thinks should be said. I wouldn't be at all surprised if she doesn't have a plan for making you leave.'

I didn't reply, knowing the first steps of that plan had already been taken.

'You mustn't go though, Hal. You belong here in Leverbridge with us. This is your home.' She said it so firmly that for a moment I believed her.

'Have you made a start on the boxes?' Gracie asked, looking at the bland shapes cluttering the floor.

'Not really.' It was a half-truth.

'Well, why don't we start here?' Gracie indicated the box closest to her, the one I had approached earlier. 'Look there's newspapers. Your Mum must have kept these for a reason.'

I shuddered as Gracie took several of the newspapers out and piled them on the seat beside her. Debris fell from them. Though early evening, light still fell into the room divided into sections from the diamond shaped panes. Motes of dust swirled like minute typhoon clouds ready to pick things up and drop them without warning.

'June 1988, June 1989, June 1990, June 1991. These must be the Summer Fayre reports.' She began flicking through the papers. 'Look—me and Lizzie.'

She laid out the papers open on the floor with the coloured squares of Fayre photographs uppermost. I went round and knelt in front of them to see. Indeed there was the marked progression of beauty of Lizzie and Gracie Manning.

'Look at this one, Hal.' she said passing me another paper, 'I think you're in it.'

And there I was, slightly fuzzy in the back ground, my sulky teenage frame preserved for ever. Even in the washed out colour of the print I looked monochrome. I couldn't recall ever being so pale, though I did remember the fall of my greasy black hair. In the picture it swept across my brow like a bird's wing concealing one eye as if I was trying to hide. I was concentrating on the photo trying to remember the year. June 1993, I would have been thirteen.

Suddenly Gracie made a strange noise. I looked up. 'What is it?'

'This paper's from January 1986.'

'Yes, what of it?' I was wracking my brain, trying to recall if anything particular had occurred that year. It was the year of my first Manor summer camp, but that wasn't until July.

Gracie's hand was across her neck, her eyes were squeezed shut. 'Take it away,' she said softly, the sound of a sob in her voice. 'Just take it away.'

I stood up and took the offending object from her. This time it was the cover which held the story. 'Tragic accident.'

There was a photograph of a mangled BMW hanging off the side of a road. And now the memories flowed back. The death of Gracie's mother and father, Caro and Hugh. The article said they had found no underlying cause for the accident. Caro hadn't been drinking and no other vehicle had been involved.

Gracie was motionless on the sofa.

'Let me get you a drink,' I said, and realised I had no alcohol in the house. I went to the kitchen to fetch a glass of water.

By the time I had returned to the room Gracie was picking up sheets of newspaper and crunching them up or tearing them through.

Barklay thought it was a game and was chasing pieces of flying paper with excited yaps.

Gracie was ripping through any paper within reach, the ones of the Summer Fayres, the Christmas ones. Then she took the box and threw things out of it, letters and folders and photographs. We must have noticed the portrait still wrapped in brown paper leaning against the wall at the same time. It was simply asking to be torn. 'No, stop!' I shouted, slopping water as I put the glass down and moved towards Gracie.

Her fingers hesitated at the edge of brown paper. My fingers grasped her wrist too tightly. But she stopped. She turned to look at me, 'What's the problem, don't you want to see a portrait of your mother?'

'I'm not sure,' I replied, releasing her wrist now she was calmer. I had left red fingerprints on her skin, the white scar showed like a bolt of lightning.

Gracie stood up looking at the discarded papers around her. 'I'm sorry about the mess,' she finally said. 'I thought this sorting out might be fun.'

'Never mind, it was a shock, coming across the newspaper article like that.'

'I wonder why your Mum kept that one though; the other papers were nice mementoes.'

I hadn't thought of it like that, but it was a fair question. 'I suppose it was an important event. Even though it was about a horrible accident.'

Gracie's shoulders dropped and she sighed. 'It wasn't an accident though Hal. She meant to do it.'

My words were too loud when I spoke. 'You mean it was suicide?'

Gracie nodded. 'She tried to kill us all.'

'It wasn't just her and Hugh in the car?'

'No. All of us. I should have died as well.'

No wonder she had responded in such a way. Being suddenly reminded of a smashed car, in which her parents died, and in which she and Lizzie might have died.

'I didn't realise you and Lizzie were there as well.'

'Yes,' she sniffed, moving to the settee and finding a tissue in her handbag.

'What happened?'

'It was such an ordinary day. Mum said she'd take us out for a treat. We thought nothing of it. And we were driving along just the same as usual, except Mum was driving and Dad usually did that. I don't think I had much concept of speed then, because I couldn't remember her driving fast, but somebody said she must have been doing over seventy on that country lane. I don't know how they work these things out.' Gracie leaned over and picked up the glass of water. She held it as she continued, her fingers looking magnified against its wet surface. 'I had complete trust in Mum, she was a good driver. I only knew we had left the road because the car was light in the air, for a moment it was thrilling, like a fairground ride. It felt like flying. Then I realised we were going to crash. I can't remember if it was me or Lizzie who screamed, but there was a scream. And then a screech as the car twisted and slid over the ground. That's all I remember until the hospital. Lizzie's head was bandaged and her arm in a sling. I only had a few bruises.' She sipped the water.

'And you think it was suicide? Not just a terrible accident. And why would she try to end her life and yours?'

Gracie shook her head. 'Nobody knows. But it was so out of character. There must have been a reason for her to drive like that. Maybe I'm the only person to think she did it deliberately.'

I was aware of the tick, tock of the newly wound clock. It reminded me of counting seconds and minutes and years. The feelings of those events of childhood linked to the present by a series of tick, tocking. The sound seemed inadequate; it should not have been so innocuous.

Gracie put the glass down and began collecting pieces of paper.

'Don't do that,' I told her, 'I'll clear up later. Let me walk you back to the Manor.'

She didn't argue. She appeared drained and limp, as if by remembering the accident she had lost substance. I held her arm and propelled her out of the door, Barklay followed at my heels.

We got to the back door just as Nigel pulled up in his BMW and skidded to a halt on the gravel.

'Having a little stroll in the evening sunshine, are we? How nice.' He had a sarcastic smile stretched across his face.

He leaned in to give Gracie a kiss; she didn't look at him but let him brush her cheek with his lips. I expect he hadn't noticed her mood or the tear stains around her eyes.

But perhaps he had, as he continued, 'Come in, we'll see if Annie's around to make us some tea.'

I went inside; following them along the passageway passed the kitchen. For some reason Nigel took us into the dining room. Gracie said she'd be back in a minute and left. Nigel told me to take a seat and he'd sort some tea out.

I was alone in the big, blue room, sitting on a high backed dining chair. The surface of the table resembled the colour of a new conker, and was so glossy I could see my reflection in it. My pale skin was given a macabre sheen under the wood. My fingernails dug the back of my hand.

I didn't like this room, the ceiling was too high. It was the room where we first realised Alicia had gone missing. But the other occasion I had been here was when Mother and I had been invited to dine after the Boxing Day hunt. A wave of nausea spread over me, everything about the evening had been too rich, the laden table, the unfamiliar food, the noise from conversation I could not contribute to, the heat and something else, which at six years old I did not understand.

I had been so tired after our bike ride; I think I was nearly asleep when Mother dressed me for dinner at the Big House.

Mother was excited, 'It's not every day you have an invite to dinner with the Mannings,' she said, 'Come on, Hal, I need you to behave like a gentleman.'

'I'm too tired,' I whined, struggling from her grip as she fastened my shirt buttons. She wanted me to wear a tie.

'Look, we'll forget the tie, but you must promise you'll be well behaved and polite.'

I nodded feeling the weight of my heavy head which I would have preferred to be laying on my pillow.

Mother was wearing a long gown of iridescent violet, which made her eyes sparkle. I knew she had beautiful eyes but never before had I seen them resemble emeralds. She looked wonderful and smelt of flowers. I tried to hug her and close my eyes against the smooth fabric of her dress, but she pushed me away. 'Come on now, Henry Bennett, you're not a baby anymore. I don't want you clinging to me all night.'

'Can't I just stay here?'

'Of course not. Don't be so silly.'

Mother wasn't usually so sharp with me and I didn't argue further. I stepped out with her glad of the cold night air on my face to wake me up.

The Big House was alight as we walked down the drive. The fringe of mother's shawl tickled my wrist as I held her hand. A charm from her bracelet knocked the back of my hand with a regular rhythm as we walked.

'It looks so beautiful doesn't it,' Mother said, her voice soft with awe, 'It's like a great ship setting sail, filled with wonderful people in their gowns and suits, dancing.' Indeed the house with its lines of lights did look like a vessel floating on an ocean. Mother sighed as she sometimes did when she was telling me fairy tales, as though she had stepped across the boundary from reality to fiction and was inhabiting a magical world in her imagination. 'Like the Titanic.'

I knew what had happened to the Titanic and it felt odd that my mother should use it to describe the Manor.

Mother often became overwhelmed with emotion when it came to the Manor. If it was mentioned in conversation she would follow with, 'It's such a beautiful house,' with the same note of awe as some religions did after mentioning a holy name.

As we entered the dining room, I felt small. Everything around me appeared magnified. The portrait of Maurice on the wall oversaw everything with a regal gaze. I saw Tara, who looked to have grown since I had seen her earlier in the day. Even at ten she was tall but I guessed she was also wearing heels. There was something else about her this evening though, an aura which placed her on the borders of adulthood, as if somehow she was aware of the secrets of that strange land. She was dressed in red which suited her colouring. The fabric clung to her slender frame. Standing across the room from Mother they could have banded a rainbow. I bathed in the light between them but was aware Mother was looking at Tara without as much admiration as me. Then she bent down and whispered in my ear, 'That girl's a cunning little minx. You keep away from her, you hear.' She spoke so quietly I later wondered whether I had misheard. Mother wasn't a person who was often mean.

I was drawn to Tara in the way a moth is drawn to light. All evening I watched her across the table, glowing in the candlelight, flickering like flame each time she moved her head. I was sitting a few places away from Mother so it was unlikely she noticed my preoccupation with Tara. Now we were sitting at the table she was also creating her own pool of luminosity with her smiles and chatter. She was seated next to Victor who was obviously enjoying his place between Mother and another older woman with a generous cleavage. He spent most of the evening turning from one lady to the other, barking with laughter and winking. I was never sure if his wink was actually a tic he had no control over or whether he had overused the gesture so much it had become habit. He also allowed Mother and the other woman to feed him spoonfuls of food, sucking sauces off the silverware with a slurping noise and 'Ooh, that's delicious, darling.' I blushed as Mother reciprocated and licked a spoon he proffered to her. Nobody, especially Mother, noticed my unease.

The food was delicious. We ate through a starter of salmon with a cream sauce, then slabs of beef and vegetables. By the time I had finished a dessert of meringue my stomach was full and I felt sleepy again. The conversation around me became a soft hum like a lullaby in the background.

Then I was jolted awake, whether by an elbow or by my own drooping head I don't know. My serviette slid off my knee and I bent down to pick it up. It had glided right under the table and I pursued it into the dark world beneath. It was like a den, with three great tree trunks rising through the centre. These were carved into ovals with clawed feet gripping the ground. Looking around I could see the legs and feet of the guests. In the dimness, the fabrics were muted, which made them resemble leaves of a dense, impenetrable forest. Within the underworld I noticed movement, a rippling of cloth and limbs. I observed hands, a kicked off shoe, a white leg, hands again, a shoeless foot entwined with a dark leg, a hand on a thigh. It was as if the forest had become alive with a species of snake writhing about me. I screamed and tried to get out. I hit my head on the table and emerged dizzy.

'What on earth is the matter?' Mother hissed across the table at me. 'Please sit down and stop drawing attention to yourself.' I did as I was told, feeling embarrassed. Swaying faces glared at me through my giddiness. Gradually the room stopped moving. But my head hurt and I felt confused as I tried to work out what I had seen.

Coffee was served and guests either stayed seated, chatting and smoking, or stood up and mingled. Maurice lounged at the head of the table. He had undone his bow tie and his shirt was open at the neck. He sat back smoking a cigar. Two people stood at his side listening to him speak. I could see his mouth move. His lips would then pucker around the cigar. I thought of him kissing Tara. The people beside him looked on and laughed at his words. He reminded me of a picture I had seen of a roman emperor in a history book.

In contrast Grace Elizabeth moved around the room talking and smiling as if she were a wound-up mechanical toy. I felt out of place. Nigel came up to me at one point and made a remark but I ignored him. I needed a wee and left the dining room.

I thought I knew the house a little but I had not been there in the dark, and the corridors seemed longer, with dense shadows in the corners making everything unfamiliar. I started as a figure appeared but then I realised it was a plant on a stand, which had loomed at me like a savage with a spiky headdress. I turned down another corridor thinking it would bring me to the entrance hall but found myself in a maze of passages I did not recognise. These were narrower with dark wood panelling and black and white floor tiles. At another time I might have hopscotched over them but tonight they increased my sense of disorientation. Panic was disturbing my meal into a mixture of sickness curdling in my stomach. It weighed on my bladder and I felt a spot of dampness on my underwear.

A glow of light ebbed from under a door further away, I moved towards it. Then I heard a sound. I was about to yell but I recognised human voices beyond the door, and then a giggle. It was a woman's laugh, one which reminded me of Mother. It sounded familiar yet was distorted by the wood and tiles in this place.

Then footsteps sounded behind me, 'Henry Bennett, what on earth are you doing here?' It was Annie. 'I need the toilet,' I mumbled and started to cry, tears of relief that I had been found. From behind the door came loud moaning sounds and a gasp.

Annie pushed me into a closet below the stairs. 'Here you are,' she said, flicking a light. She had shoved me so roughly I thought she must be cross with me. The bulb lit a tiled space with an old fashioned toilet, its cistern high on the wall and a dangling chain. There was a strange cloying odour.

I kept the door ajar as I didn't want to be left alone in this strange echoing space. I was aware of Annie's footsteps outside, and then heard her knock on a door and say, 'I don't know who you are. I don't want to know. But you should be ashamed of yourselves.'

I finished my business. Annie walked me back to the dining room.

Some of the guests had cigars and the smoke made a dense pool of fug over the table. Above, wisps of bluer cigarette smoke spiralled like will-o-the-wisps.

Nigel came up to me and thumped my arm with unnecessary force and said, 'Look what I'm drinking.' His glass was half full of a blackcurrant coloured liquid. 'Wine,' he giggled at me, 'How cool is that?' I responded it was indeed 'cool', but my attention was not on him. I wanted to go home but couldn't make out Mother amongst the dreamlike shadows in the smog filled room.

The rattle of crockery made me look up. Annie entered the room and placed a tray on the table.

'Nigel asked me to bring tea for you.'

'Where's Gracie?'

'I've taken their tea upstairs. Gracie usually takes her afternoon tea with Grace Elizabeth. Grace Elizabeth's not been feeling too well these last few days.'

I did not tell her I'd seen Grace Elizabeth earlier and she had looked quite well. I realised I had been deserted. Barklay gave a sigh as well, as if he also felt the rebuff.

Getting up from the table I told Annie, 'I won't stay then, I can drink tea on my own at the cottage.'

'Look, why don't I bring this into the kitchen?' Annie suggested, 'Come and have tea with me.'

'That would be nice,' I said, grateful to get out of the uninviting dining room.

Sitting at the kitchen table felt more appropriate. I would always be an interloper in the 'Big House.' The kitchen was the limit of my welcome. I wondered how it would have been if I'd married Lizzie. I doubted I would have felt any more at home.

Annie asked how the sorting at the cottage was going.

'It's going to take a while,' I told her. 'To be honest I'm finding it difficult.'

She put her hand over mine. It was a hand which showed the many years of hard work with rough reddened skin, but it was warm and comforting on mine and was accompanied by a smile of understanding.

'I'll come and give you a hand tomorrow.'

The light was fading as I returned to the cottage. My legs felt heavy as though the memories I'd had of the cycling earlier remained with me. My stump ached, and my breathing was laboured as I made my way up the slope. The air was too warm for evening as if a cloud had settled over the Manor.

Even Barklay didn't roam but remained at my heel as we trudged back.

The cottage's cool interior welcomed me. Under the trees with its thick stone walls it was protected from the summer weather outside. After feeding Barklay and cooking beans on toast, I decided to investigate another box.

The one I selected had some Law books visible. It looked less malicious than the newspaper box. I presumed it contained the few belongings which had been returned from university. I lifted the books out but did not flick through them; I had no desire to recall my brief foray into university education. From underneath, I took out a pack of letters secured by an elastic band. It had corroded, and broke as I removed it, allowing the letters to slide onto the floor. Mother's handwriting squiggled across the front and I recognised my university address. Though I had been there so briefly it appeared she had sent me more letters than I remembered.

One stood out from the others, as it had remained unopened. It had been postmarked, so I suspected it must have been delivered when I had already left. The date on the envelope was too faded to make out. As I turned it in my hands it took on an added weight as I realised it must have been the last letter Mother sent me.

Before I could hesitate long enough to reject it, I tore the envelope away. Inside was a single sheet of paper.

Mother did not go in for the usual formalities of letter writing. No address or date. The missive was note-like even more so than her previous letters to me. Her hand-writing, never neat, was scrawled as if written in a hurry. I followed the words with dread.

Hal darling,
I felt I had to write this note. Something has happened which I think you should know. It's important for me and for you. I should have told you before but sometimes things are difficult to say. Things haven't worked out the way I expected or wanted. It is quite sensitive and I must talk to you face to face. Please don't worry. We will talk soon and I'll explain everything.

There were a few more lines of polite scribble but I disregarded them. It was these lines that held me. What on earth had happened to make her write such a thing? It could have been at either end of a spectrum, either joyful; she had met somebody special and was going to marry. Perhaps she had been dating them a while and felt she should have told me about the relationship before. Was it somebody I knew? Or the news could have been dreadful; she had been diagnosed with cancer and hadn't said anything because she'd passed a lump off as benign and now they'd told her it was terminal.

During the past eleven years letter writing had become almost obsolete. A written letter scribed by a hand holding a pen, wielding it with effort over the page, giving something of the writer in the way they formed each letter; that meant so much more. My mother's urgency in those words could not have been expressed more strongly if they'd been written in blood.

The letter slipped from my fingers. I leant forward and allowed my head to rest in my hands. Barklay came up and licked me. 'It's no good,' I told him, 'Everything here holds too much pain.'

I left the letter, the strewn envelopes, and ignored the ripped newspapers from earlier. I settled Barklay in his place by the hearth and went to bed.

Sleep didn't come. I couldn't stop wondering what Mother had wanted to tell me and whether it had any bearing on her death. It didn't sound like a typical suicide note but who knew what had been going on in her mind. Perhaps that is what it was.

The moonlight was bright in the room and glinted off the glass of the wardrobe. I remembered Mother's dress hanging there. I may have sleep walked because before I was aware of it I was standing in front of the wardrobe with the dress draped across my arms. The satin shushed like water released as I removed it from the protective cellophane wrapping. It was cool in my grip. The moonlight transformed the fabric into a pool of mother-of-pearl.

I carried it back to my bed and held it against me. If I was not already asleep I sank into a dream where rainbows shimmered over moonlit water.

I woke with a start. Barklay was growling. It was still dark outside and I thought I'd better check what the disturbance was. I didn't bother with my prosthetic foot or switch on the light; moonlight lit my way as I hopped into the sitting room.

'What is it boy?' I asked him. He was sitting by the front window, still growling. I went to him and looked out. Everything was still. In the distance was a glow of light from the lamp outside the front of the Manor. I was about to turn away when a movement caught my eye, just a shadow briefly interrupting the moonlight. Looking more closely, I could make out a figure walking past the cottage towards the Big House. There was enough light to make out a tall and slim silhouette, with hair gleaming like a halo under the moon.

'Lizzie,' I whispered. Then louder. 'Lizzie!' I tried to run to the front door but without my foot could only hobble. Barklay behind me gave an excited bark.

I went outside. The ground was cold under my one bare foot and I had to hold the door frame for support. The midnight air was cool on my exposed skin. Trees shushed and hushed above me like an audience settling before a performance. I could no longer see the figure and wondered if I had dreamt the whole thing. Had I seen a ghost? But Barklay had definitely alerted me to something. Would he bark at a ghost?

Then there was an interruption of lamplight near the Manor, indicating movement. The figure reappeared from the dip in the driveway. Identification was impossible even when I squinted. Then the figure was gone.

I returned to the cottage and made myself a coffee. One foot was cold and my stump throbbed. I sat in the lounge and talked the incident through with Barklay. He didn't reply but just curled back up on his bed now the excitement was over.

'Do you think it was a ghost, boy, or was it my imagination? You wouldn't growl unless it was flesh and blood would you?' Barklay snuffled as if I was interrupting his repose.

'Maybe it was Gracie, having a midnight stroll? You know Gracie though, don't you? No need to growl at her. Perhaps she disturbed you coming past the window.'

Barklay continued to ignore me. I knew now I would be unable to sleep. The sheet of paper I had read earlier glowed in the darkness. Switching on the table lamp I picked it up and read the words again. The message remained unfathomable.

The letter must have been written only days before she died. Could the information she was going to reveal have been so devastating for her to deal with that she decided to kill herself?

What Was Taken 9

When I think about Mother's inquest I recall it like watching a play. A play which I ought to know but had forgotten the lines. The actors involved had their script off pat, as if they had been practising for a long time. They knew the words, how loudly and in what direction to say them. They knew when they should move and to their exact positions.

I felt disorientated by Mother's life being displayed in this manner and challenging the woman I thought I knew. Thankfully Lizzie was there. She sat beside me the whole way through, occasionally squeezing my hand as if she was holding me down. Indeed there were moments when I wanted to stand up and shout.

It was quite an informal setting, in a room at the back of the main court buildings. The coroner was a pleasant looking middle aged woman dressed in a black suit and pink shirt. I had prepared a statement for the coroner to read out. As I took the oath my voice vibrated and I was glad I didn't have to say any more; my voice would have wavered and whined. The coroner had a nice voice, low and firm and she read out my statement in a measured way. It said how Mother was beautiful not only outside but inside as well. Like most mothers, she was sad at my leaving home for university but she had always been supportive of me. She had good friends around her and enjoyed her work at the pub. It finished by saying I had no idea why she would want to take her own life without leaving a message. The statement sounded strange being read by someone else who hadn't known Mother, and though she read well, the words didn't resonate with meaning the way I had written them.

The first witness on the stand was George Sheldon. He had found the body. It was early morning, and he'd been going to tidy the garden. He usually visited once a week, which was why my mother had given him a key so he could get in if she wasn't about. As he spoke I saw a flush spreading from his neck, creeping up his face. It occurred to me he was embarrassed speaking in front of the full room, or he was not telling the whole truth about his visits to the cottage. He had presumed she was out or asleep when nobody replied to his knock at the door.

He had shouted out, 'It's only me; George,' as he'd entered. In court he acted the words out as if he was able to remember the precise tone and expression he had used. I wondered if he'd practiced it over and over for days before the inquest. He continued to explain how the bathroom door was ajar and he'd seen a pool of water spreading into the corridor.

George was ashen as he spoke, 'I thought the bath had overflowed and rushed to the door. Then I saw her.' On the stand, he trembled, as though he might fall. Then he continued, 'I called the police from the cottage and waited.'

The police officer who took the stand next supported George's account of events, and then the doctor who'd arrived and confirmed death spoke. As the details were told I felt numb.

Dr Roberts, our usual GP, spoke as well. He gave me a smile, the paternalistic type I remembered when I had visited him for minor ailments as a child. I wasn't aware of it but Mother had been to see him and he had prescribed medication for anxiety. He confirmed she had consulted him following my departure to university.

Suddenly the room became airless. As Dr Roberts spoke I felt another burden of guilt press down on me. I had to concentrate on inhaling and exhaling, otherwise I think I would have ceased to breath.

Grace Elizabeth was the final person to appear. She looked straight at me throughout. 'We were terribly sad when we heard of Chantelle's tragic death,' she paused and took a deep breath. I could imagine it filling her tiny frame, satiating her before her next words, a little like a miniature bull before it charges.

'We were not surprised though. She thought she had lost the most precious thing in her life... her son.' Her eyes stared at me; it wasn't a look of warmth or sympathy but of ice. I was reminded of her words to me once long ago when I had dropped the snow globe. It was as if she had predicted this day.

The words tumbled across the surfaces of the court and in my ears I could hear a rumbling noise as menacing as the snow globe rolling across the Manning parquet all those years ago. I started to shake. Lizzie gripped my hand more tightly.

Grace Elizabeth was continuing. 'After her son Hal left for university, she confided in me how sad she was, how she disliked living alone, and how she wished he hadn't gone.'

She gave a little cough and then she turned to the coroner and, with a tilt of her head, her expression changed her to a meek older lady. 'I feel responsible in some way, I just didn't realise she had become so desperate and would consider doing something like this.'

After Grace Elizabeth had spoken the court became very quiet. The clamour in my head continued. I didn't hear the rest of the session. It washed over me like white noise, as statements were read and the coroner's verdict of suicide was issued. The next image I have is of Lizzie dragging me from the chair to a smoke-filled pub, where I downed several pints in quick succession.

What Remains 10

When dawn edged through the windows, it found me still sitting on the settee with the letter in my hands. I was in a state somewhere between sleep and wakefulness, a kind of waking death and I felt as if I could remain here, where I was protected from the world. But Barklay nudged me with his nose, a request which insisted life must go on, and he needed to be let out into the garden.

I got up, stumbled to the back door and let him out. Then I washed my face in the toilet sink and avoided looking at my haggard face which had suffered from lack of sleep.

The day began to unwind slowly; I got dressed, drank tea and took Barklay out for a short walk on the edge of the estate. I tried to recollect the vision of Lizzie or Gracie I'd seen during the night. My head was so heavy with unfulfilled sleepiness I felt drugged. It was possible I had dreamt the whole thing.

I returned to the cottage took one look at the boxes still to be sorted, and the mess of crumpled newspapers, and went to lie on the bed. Perhaps I dozed because Barklay's bark and the knocking on the door startled me. Wiping my face and smoothing my hair I unlocked the front door to Gracie. She stood in front of a police officer.

'Afternoon, Hal. You look dreadful. You've got a visitor.'

She pushed past me into the cottage, so I did not have the opportunity to ask if she had taken a midnight walk. I was left at the door looking at the police officer. He could have been as old as me but with his short brown hair fringing his rather round face, which did not appear to have obvious stubble, he had a youthfulness I knew I had lost. His greeting was more polite than Gracie's.

'Good afternoon, Sir, are you Mr Henry Bennett?' When I nodded he continued, 'I'm Officer Greg Barrow and I'm here to ask you some questions regarding the night of Alicia Manning's disappearance.'

He flashed an identity badge at me and I glanced at it. It showed a vague resemblance to the man in front of me. I stepped aside so he could enter. Gracie had already put the kettle on, calling to us from the kitchen, 'Can I get you both a cup of coffee?' Greg declined, I accepted.

I showed Greg into the sitting room and Gracie came in with a mug of coffee for me. 'I've already spoken to the officer. I've shown him where Alicia's bones were found and where we camped that year.' She made no move to leave and started picking up the newspapers she had flung around the day before.

'Right, Sir. As you probably know, Alicia's death is now being treated as a murder investigation. What can you tell me about the night she disappeared?' He had a pad of paper out and began writing quickly as I spoke. I told him everything I could. The memories came in waves, patches so clear I could have drawn the scene and then other parts vague. I told him about the dares, about Nigel and me going to collect the midnight feast and bringing wine as well. I looked towards Gracie, in case I had said something which she had kept quiet about but Greg said, 'Yes, both Mr and Mrs Phelps reported that as well.' He had already spoken with Nigel then.

'You must have been a little worse for wear as the evening progressed?'

'Yes, we all were. We didn't let Alicia have any wine,' I assured him. In hindsight, we supposed we were protecting Alicia from grownup things. Yet we hadn't protected her from death.

Guilt made my mouth feel dry. I sipped coffee keeping hold of the mug. Even though it was pleasant outside, the room hadn't warmed up and my fingers felt cool. The skin on the back of my hand prickled as the warmth from the coffee cup seeped through.

I continued my tale, about how we had only realised Alicia had disappeared the following morning and searching the grounds afterwards.

'Mrs Phelps tells me she saw a man with your mother that night. Do you know anything about that or who it might have been?'

I felt affronted by the question and angry at Gracie for mentioning it to the police. My reply was sharp. 'No.'

Gracie was still picking up papers and wouldn't look at me. Greg just waited for me to say more, his pen hovering above the page, unruffled.

I continued in a more regulated tone, 'Nobody was with her when I saw her the following morning. In fact, only Gracie saw this mystery man and it was a dare.' I wanted to throw doubt on Gracie's statement, though I knew of course it had been true.

'And Lizzie,' Gracie had turned around.

We were quiet for some moments, pondering the events of that night. I could hear the sound of Greg's pen scribbling on his pad, Barklay's breathing as he lay in front of the hearth and the ticking of the clock. I had put Mother's final note on the mantelpiece beside the clock and as the second hand moved round it seemed to point at the paper, drawing attention to it.

'What do you think happened to Alicia?' I finally asked, breaking the silence.

Greg seemed to be staring at the hearth, deep in thought. His pen tapped on the paper of his notebook. He replied slowly, 'I can't really comment on that at the moment, Mr Bennett.'

He continued to stare ahead seemingly fascinated with the exposed brickwork of the fireplace.

'We thought she must have been abducted, taken away. But that can't have been the case if she was found on the estate, can it?'

I don't know why I continued to question him, but I didn't like the quietness of the room. At any moment I thought a finger might point at me accompanied by the words, 'You are found guilty.'

Greg didn't look at me; he was finding the fireplace far too interesting. He spoke as though he was turning a thought over in his mind and had mistakenly said it out loud. 'We think Alicia must have been held somewhere on the estate, some place which wasn't searched.'

My eyes tried to follow his gaze to see what was so fascinating about the chimney place. Then he looked at me and said, 'Nice dog.'

Barklay, recognising he was being complimented, got up and allowed himself to be patted by Greg. 'I'd love a dog but, what with my working pattern, it wouldn't be fair,' Greg continued.

I was disorientated by the direction of the conversation. 'He's not mine really. My friend Tom lent him to me while I settle in.'

'Nothing like a dog to make you feel at home,' agreed Greg.

The tense atmosphere had been broken and Gracie said, 'Shall I make some more coffee?'

This time Greg accepted the offer.

Gracie took my empty mug from me and moved towards the kitchen. Perhaps it was Greg's manner with Barklay but another thought had occurred to me sitting there. I asked him, 'How difficult would it be to kill somebody and make it look like suicide?'

From the corner of my eye I saw Gracie drop my coffee mug. It cracked as it hit the floor; droplets of residual coffee flew out.

'I'm sorry, I'm sorry,' Gracie said, 'I'll get a cloth.'

'Not thinking of doing away with somebody are you, Sir?' Greg responded to my question, with a smile.

'No,' I said, wanting him to take me seriously, 'My mother was found in a bath with her wrists cut.' Greg's smile vanished, 'I'm sorry, Sir. And you don't think it was suicide?'

I shook my head.

Gracie came back into the room and proceeded to clean the broken cup away.

'Well,' Greg continued, 'I think if somebody's been depressed or had personal problems, it might be quite easy. The police are probably not going to look further than the obvious unless there's a strong suspicion of a motive for murder.'

'She didn't leave a note.'

'A lot of people don't.'

Gracie brought a tray of coffees into the room. I got up and showed Greg Mother's letter. 'I found this recently, I think it was the last letter she wrote.'

He took a few moments to scan it and said, 'Well, something was obviously troubling her. Perhaps she was overwhelmed by it before she had a chance to speak to you. Was she depressed?'

'Apparently she'd been to the doctor when I went away to Uni and had been prescribed some tablets for anxiety.'

'And can you think of a reason why somebody might want her dead?'

Gracie's head moved sharply, with a frown which questioned the direction of the conversation. Barklay moved over to me. As he laid his head on my lap he sighed. It echoed in my words as I admitted, 'No reason at all.'

'I think you've got your answer then.'

Gracie took the letter from Greg and read it. She made no comment but she put the letter down, came over to me and squeezed my shoulder.

Greg finished his coffee and left soon afterwards. I watched him leave. Barklay had accompanied me to the door, wagging his tail in goodbye. He returned to the chimney place and gave a yap before turning in circles on the hearth rug and settling.

'Something bothers him about the fire place,' I told Gracie. Since the conversation with Greg a strange idea had started forming. 'Look, this may be a daft idea but could Alicia have been hidden in the chimney before being moved?' My thoughts had not followed far enough to work out what it would mean if that had been the case, but I knew I would have to search.

'No, you're being paranoid again, Hal. There's probably a nest or something caught that's rustling. You should have a look if it bothers you.' She picked up her handbag and made to leave.

'And you shouldn't be making up conspiracy theories about your mother's suicide, it's not healthy. Next you'll be saying Maurice was murdered.' She laughed.

I recalled Tom enquiring whether anybody at the funeral had considered Maurice's death suspicious and now with Gracie mentioning the possibility of foul play it seemed to carry extra weight. Until that point I had assumed Maurice had died of natural causes. Gracie was right; I was paranoid. Because suddenly it sounded conceivable.

'Don't forget it's Alicia's memorial service tomorrow,' Gracie added as she left. I assured her I would be there.

Returning to the sitting room I could not relax. Now my thoughts had been set on the chimney I could not focus on anything else. I was reluctant to investigate because I had created an image of Alicia stuffed up that chimney. It was so real I was terrified of what I might find.

To avoid thinking about it further I took Barklay for a ramble. We covered several miles. I did not notice the surroundings as I walked; it was enough to feel solid ground beneath my feet. By the time we returned it was dusk. I went to bed early, physically and emotionally exhausted.

In the morning, as I collected Barklay from the sitting room to let him out, I realised the chimney and I could not remain in this stand off for ever.

At least it was daylight and the room was bright. I went to find a torch. It was rusted but threw out a feeble light. After moving Barklay out the way I peered up into the darkness of the chimney looking at the spots of light wavering over the brick work. The bricks gleamed amber where the light struck them and then merged into orange, red and finally black as I looked upwards. There was nothing obvious there and it was with relief I saw there was nowhere big enough for a body to be stored, not even a child's body.

A layer of bricks made a small rim around the chimney interior a little way up and I could see a square which was dense compared to the bricks surrounding it. A hole. I had to strain my shoulders around so I could reach my hand towards the space. My fingers gripped the ledge of brick and felt blindly into the opening. Old soot floated down, covering my shoulder and arm.

Then my fingers brushed something cold and smooth compared to the surrounding brick. 'There's something here,' I told Barklay, my words muffled by the brickwork. I tried to extend my reach by pushing my fingers further in. Whatever I was touching shifted a little so I could grasp a corner. I scrabbled some more and what felt like a box was dislodged. Suddenly it fell into my hands and I clung to it as a shower of soot and brick dust stung my eyes.

I swung out into the room unable to see, and put the box down, choking. It took me a moment to recover and then I looked at the treasure I had found. It was a tin box, ingrained with soot. I brushed some of the loose debris away and recognised it was an old biscuit tin with the remains of a country scene faintly visible on the lid.

Barklay was excited as well; he came over and sniffed the box, wagging his tail.

'Shall we look inside?' I asked him.

The lid of the box had corroded onto the base and it took time to remove. After several minutes of metal squeaking and flakes of rust, it came away. Inside was a book. I was still kneeling on the hearth as I picked it up in my stained hands. It appeared to have been well read, as the pages were bulky within it.

The cover and spine had no title but, as I opened it, it became clear it was not a novel but a diary. My mother's diary.

On the page was Mother's distinctive writing, perhaps more looping than in her letters to me. And the title confirmed the diary was indeed hers.

The start of my New Life. Chantelle Bennett.

I can't believe it. They gave me the job! I didn't think Mrs Manning liked me she said I had no experience with horses. I thought it was no good. But Mr Manning smiled at me and said he thought I had the right attitude and I'd probably pick it up quite quickly if I worked hard. I promised I would...several times I think. And in the end they both smiled and said alright then. .

I had to lie about my age and my parents but I called Miss. Thomas at the kid's home and she said she'll write a reference for me. She was pleased I'd phoned and that I was alright. I can't believe how everything is suddenly going so well...Hope it lasts!

I've got a room above the stables all to myself and a shelf where I can put my things without the risk of them being 'borrowed'.

The Manor is very grand. When I walked in the front door I felt like a Princess. I wish I could live in the Manor itself. But I suppose I must be grateful I've got this room.

There was a knock at the door. I put the diary down and got up to answer it. Annie stood there. 'Aren't you coming to the funeral? Gracie told me to call for you. She knew you'd forget.'

'I haven't forgotten,' I said, although of course I had, 'I just got side-tracked.'

'Exactly. Same old Henry Bennett.' She was shaking her head from side to side, her grey bun moving like a pendulum against her neck. 'And what have you been doing. You look like a chimney sweep.'

'I was just...' but I decided it was too complicated to explain to her.

'You've got about ten minutes to get yourself sorted,' she said, looking at her watch unnecessarily. We could both hear the church bell tolling. When I nodded she continued, 'I'll see you there.' She walked away shaking her head and tutting. I thought I heard her mutter, 'Some things never change.'

When I went to wash I realised why she had been so thrown by my appearance. In the mirror my face was smeared black with soot. My arms also had streaks of blackness. I stripped and washed the best I could. The basin remained soiled when I'd finished but I didn't have time to clean now. I threw on a t-shirt and pair of jeans and hurried to the church.

What Was Taken 10

As I was late, the church was already packed. There were so many people they were almost spilling out of the door. I joined the group of people standing at the back. Looking around I could see no sign of Annie but could make out Tom nearer the front; I couldn't catch his eye though.

The vicar introduced the service saying the death of a child was always desperately sad, but we should try and make it as joyous as possible, remembering the happy few years we had shared Alicia's life. As the organ started to play 'All things bright and beautiful,' I pushed my way out of the church into the open air.

The Manning crypt was easily identified. It was the largest most ornate grave in the churchyard. It was the size of a Wendy House with pillars etched onto the sides making it look Grecian. Between the pillars were figures of cherubs carrying garlands. Today it also had ribbon around it in preparation for Alicia's burial. Maurice's decomposing body was now lying there with all his ancestors. It made me shudder to think that Alicia would be joining them later. I was glad Mother had stipulated she wanted a cremation, and her ashes to be scattered in the woods around the Gate House.

I wandered the perimeter of the churchyard picking oxeye daisies and yellow flowers growing along the hedgerow. Then I placed them as near to the tomb as possible, saying what could be considered a prayer and an apology to Alicia.

It wasn't a long service and people soon started making their way down the path. I watched from a distance as the family completed the service beside the crypt.

Then I followed them down to the Manor for the wake.

Unlike Maurice's wake people were quiet, as if still shocked by the realisation that Alicia was indeed dead and had been buried so close to the house for such a long time.

The house was too warm, the guests giving off an odour of despair as if they were wondering what the point of it all was. I had no answer to that unspoken question so decided to go for a walk.

I strolled down to the lake. The water was low leaving a tide-line of sand and algae exposed like the edges of a grey ulcer. There was an unpleasant odour in the air and I left quickly, following the line of trees up to the fateful campsite of twenty years ago. Under the green leaf-cover which rustled in the gentle breeze it appeared benign.

Finally, I walked down to the stables, thinking it was the last action we knew Alicia had taken. Approaching the steps of what had once been the stable block, I saw I was not the only one to have the idea. On the top step Tara was seated. She was smoking and a grey cloud hung over her head as if she were the source, rather than the cigarette in her hand. She resembled a black stick insect in her mourning outfit. Her legs encased in patterned stockings were too long, dangling awkwardly over the steps. As I took the stairs up to her I saw she was holding a wine bottle in her other hand, from which she would take an occasional sip. Cigarette butts spotted the top step. As I brushed them aside and sat beside Tara, she did not greet me or look at me.

We sat in silence for a time, I was considering this was the last place Alicia had been alive. The stable block had been given a good make over with the paintwork fresh and the smell of horses long since gone. But I supposed this was the place where Alicia had placed the horse dung as dared. Tara finished her cigarette and ground it out with force on the space between us.

'I think I was the last one to see Alicia alive.' Tara's voice made me jump. Her words had broken into my thought stream about Alicia. I turned to face her, not absolutely certain of what she had said. I repeated her sentence back to her and when she nodded I asked, 'You mean you saw Alicia on the night she went missing?'

Tara nodded and took another slurp of wine. She held the bottle out to me which I declined.

'Why didn't you say anything?' I demanded.

Tara swayed in front of me, in dazed inebriation as if she was having trouble focusing on me. Her eyes were smudged with mascara giving her a wide-eyed innocent look. I demanded again, 'Why didn't you say anything? You could have said something. You could have said something the morning after, before we all went off searching for her.'

Tara lurched away from me, the bottle clanging against the railing. 'I couldn't.'

'What do you mean you couldn't? If you'd have said something she might have been found!'

My voice was becoming louder; in contrast Tara's reply was barely above a whisper. 'I would have got into trouble.'

I must have looked completely baffled, my brow twisting as my mind tried to form a question. Tara had turned back to the bottle and was concentrating on it so fully she might have forgotten I was there and was simply continuing her conversation with it.

'She found us together you see.'

I did not see. I regretted having downed two glasses of wine rather quickly. Its effect had been delayed but now my brain did not appear to be functioning.

'Was it a dare, the reason she came here?' It took me a moment to realise Tara had asked the question. I did not reply. The pathetic task we had set Alicia still made me cringe. I managed a nod.

'Alicia found us in bed. She saw us.'

What the hell was Tara saying? I couldn't make it out, my thoughts beginning to spin. Who was the 'us' she was referring to?

'We didn't see her at first. She'd come right into the room and was watching us. By the time I saw her it was too late. She didn't say anything, was just standing there with her mouth open in shock.'

'So what happened?' I asked surprising myself with the calm tone of my voice.

'She ran out. Maurice got straight up pulled some trousers on and chased after her.'

For a moment I was stunned as thoughts slammed into one another. Maurice, Alicia, Tara. Maurice in Tara's bed. Maurice sleeping with Tara. Maurice chasing Alicia. My God! Tara was barely a teenager then. I closed my eyes and tried to concentrate.

Slowly I said, 'But why didn't you say anything. You could have said something.'

Tara shook her head from side to side and said with vigour. 'No I couldn't. I would have got into trouble.'

'You wouldn't have got into trouble; Maurice would have got into trouble.'

'No. It was me.'

'I don't understand.'

'Maurice said they'd send me away. To one of those reform schools for problem children. For promiscuous girls.' The word promiscuous was just a series of hisses and slurs.

'It wasn't your fault.'

'Yes it was. I seduced him. Maurice said I seduced him.'

'No. You were what… fourteen? Maurice was in the wrong.'

Tara continued to shake her head, moving it from side to side in a rhythm with the bottle, moving as if to music. 'It was me. Yes, it was,' she said.

I decided not to continue along the path of 'it wasn't your fault'. Tara was obviously beyond that. 'When did it start?'

Tara looked down and swung one leg off the edge of the step, concentrating on the movement and accompanying it with swinging the wine bottle to and fro. She smiled as if it was a pleasant memory, and we were having a normal conversation about the past.

'The day of the hunt. The day I was marked by the fox.' Again the bottle rang against the railing, making a plaintive ring which echoed around us. 'Do you remember I kissed him?'

The day was familiar, particularly the kiss which had always disturbed me. 'I thought he kissed you?'

'No. I kissed him. That's what he said.' She paused, the bottle made another ringing noise against the stair rail. 'I liked the kiss. I liked it a lot. I told him that. He told me it was alright to like it as long as I didn't say anything or I'd get into trouble.'

Her voice had become childlike, piping up through her woman's form like an echo.

'So you kissed him again?'

'Yes. He let me because I liked it. I didn't tell anybody. It was our special secret.'

'But you were a child.'

Her fingers were fiddling with the edge of her short skirt, the red fingernails vulgar against the black stockings. 'I know it was wrong now,' she replied quickly, 'But I couldn't help it then. I was a promiscuous girl. I wanted to do it. He told me I was the only one to make him feel special. The only one...' Her voice drifted to a sigh. Then silence.

'And when did he rape you?'

'Don't be disgusting,' she said sharply. Briefly she looked at me, and then she focused on the bottle again. 'He never did that. No, he never did that,' she repeated quietly, as if perhaps her whisper was her conscience questioning that long held belief. 'No, I wanted it,' she said more firmly. 'I wanted to sleep with him. He loved me and I loved him.'

She brought the bottle to her lips but didn't drink. 'It started that summer when I moved into the stable room.' She shrugged her shoulder towards the door behind us.

'The first summer you didn't come to camp. The year Alicia went missing.' Tara nodded.

'So Alicia disturbed you and Maurice ran after her. Did he find Alicia?'

'I don't know. But I don't think so. She must have fallen.'

'That's unlikely,' I countered, a hint of sarcasm in my response. 'If that were the case we would have found her or the police dog would have found her in the garden when it was searched.'

The question was did Maurice find her and kill her, and then keep her in the house whilst the police team searched the grounds. A flashback came to me, of Maurice standing at the top of the second flight of stairs in the Manor and saying, 'I've checked in the attic space. She's not there.' Whether it was a true memory, I don't know.

'Do you think he killed her?'

'No, Maurice was gentle, he'd never hurt anyone.'

A sour taste rose in my throat and I thought I would vomit thinking about Maurice maiming Tara's tender flesh.

'You have to go to the police. You have to.'

Suddenly Tara lurched towards me. Clinging onto me like a demented creature. 'Poor Hal,' she cried, 'Always so sad, so lonely.' She hiccoughed letting out a breath laden with the odour of wine. 'Hal, I could make you feel special too,' she whispered, licking my earlobe. It was only then I realised how damaged Tara was. I also became aware of her hand on my crotch. My brain was disgusted, yet my genitals tingled with excitement.

'Stop!' I shouted, pushing Tara forcefully from me. The bottle flew from her hand and clattered down the stairwell, finally smashing at the bottom.

Tara didn't move but remained in a skeletal crouch as I walked away. My uneven footsteps crunched over the broken glass at the base of the stairs. I almost ran up the hill to the Gate House but my right leg was heavy, as if it no longer had the energy to propel me forward. My head was a blur of anger, firstly disgusted with my body's betrayal, and then with Maurice Manning.

My breath came in sobs, I wanted to scream but my lungs were taken up with the effort of breathing. I brushed my eyes with my hand expecting tears but there were none. The grief was deeper within me, unable to be released.

I knew Tara would not go to the police. I could go to the police but what good would that do? Tara would be questioned and gossiped about; Alicia was dead, her bones removed from the Manor grounds and buried in the Manning crypt this morning. Nothing would bring her back. And Charles Maurice Manning was dead and out of the reach of any justice in this world. So only Tara would suffer. As I approached my front door my decision to remain silent was made.

I felt soiled. Tainted by Tara's revelations. I walked into the bathroom and ran a bath.

The water was almost scalding as I lowered myself into it. My skin after days of strip washes was scrubbed so thoroughly I removed several layers of epidermis along with the residual grime. A thick scum floated on the surface like a discarded casing. I put my head right under the water so sound was muted and I was left with the white noise of my thoughts. I remained there as long as I could and then broke the water like an emerging beast.

What Remains 11

Even after my deep clean a sickness remained with me as if something so potent had been planted it could never be erased. I decided alcohol might be the best antidote.

I walked to the pub. Picking up a pebble I threw it at the likeness of Maurice Manning on The Huntsman sign and felt a ridiculous sense of satisfaction as it hit him in the eye. Barklay gave a yap in agreement.

We walked in. There was a reasonable evening crowd in the bar and as the weather was still balmy I could see several groups through the patio doors, in the conservatory and garden.

I headed straight for the bar. Aware I was scratching my hand again I drummed my fingers on the counter impatiently. My need for a drink had become intense. I waited for several minutes whilst Bev chatted on to a couple next to me seeming to take an age pouring wine and pulling a pint. My finger drumming became louder in an attempt to blunt the interval before the anticipated hit of alcohol.

'Pint of Adnam's,' I shouted at Bev.

She appeared not to notice my rudeness. 'Evening. It's Hal, isn't it, Tom's friend?' She smiled taking her time to reach for a glass. 'Adnam's wasn't it?'

'Hurry up,' I wanted to say; 'Can't you see I'm a desperate man?' However, she obviously could not because every action she made was in slow motion.

'I see you've got Barklay accompanying you, but no Tom today?'

'Yes, I've just borrowed him for a while.'

'Well, they say it's a good way of meeting people.'

I didn't tell her in my case it was not working. She stopped pulling the pint and said, 'Anyway, Barklay's always welcome here. He and Tom are regular visitors.'

I was hoping she would stop talking and just pull my pint but she paused again. 'I think sometimes Tom says he's taking him for a long walk and the longest bit is spent here.' She laughed and finally pushed my pint towards me. I did not say 'Thanks' just grabbed the glass. I remained standing and finished half my beer in one long swig.

'You were thirsty,' Bev said.

I slumped onto a bar stool beside me. 'I certainly needed a drink; it's been a long day.'

Bev nodded and then moved to the other end of the bar to serve another customer. When she returned she continued the previous conversation. 'Yes, it was little Alicia's funeral today wasn't it? I went up there. Good to see so many people turn out.'

I couldn't see what was good about it. It made no difference. Alicia was dead.

'To think of her buried under a tree for so many years. It seems right she has finally been placed at rest.'

Light was shining through the final drops of amber liquid as I drained the glass. It made the bar and Bev bulge into a fish eye. Her mouth became a cartoon motif as she continued her mindless gabble. 'At least she's with her family now. She's beside Maurice.'

The mouth moved upwards in a smile which I think Bev thought was angelic but through the refraction of the glass looked more like The Joker.

I nearly vomited into the glass. To think of Alicia lying next to her murderer made me sick. I slammed the glass down with too much force. The sound brought everything into focus. The others at the bar looked round at me. Bev stared.

'Are you alright?' she finally asked.

'Fine, fine. Sorry, sorry.' Gradually the audience turned away. Bev went to serve somebody.

'I can't stay here,' I said out loud but nobody was listening.

I walked out, Barklay at my heels. Once outside again I threw a handful of pebbles at the sign. This time I missed and Maurice's caricature smiled. As I walked down the hill I heard laughing behind me. The kind of laugh given by a man who's got what he wanted.

From the village store I picked up some cheap cans of beer, then replaced them, swapping them for expensive bottles of red wine. Suddenly I didn't care about money. At that moment I decided I would sell the cottage to Grace Elizabeth. I would make her pay over the odds, but then I would be a man of means. I took a detour back to the Gate House so I didn't have to pass The Huntsman again.

I didn't bother to go to bed. I sat in the sitting room drinking from the bottle and watching the change in light through the night and the effect it had on the canopy of trees outside. It was like watching a silent black and white movie. I tried to work out the exact point where night became day but the movement was so subtle it was impossible to mark the exact point of transformation.

As the density of the night made way for dawn I drained the last of my bottles and stretched out along the settee and fell asleep.

Barklay awoke me by barking and I became aware of knocking on the door. I managed to crawl to the door and open it to Gracie.

'Hal, what the hell?' she commented at my appearance. As she walked into the sitting room she repeated the comment. She picked up a bottle from the floor and placed it on the table. 'What happened to you then?'

'I heard some bad news and got drunk. Have you got any aspirin?'

Gracie shook her head. 'What a mess. I presume you looked up the chimney then?' It hadn't appeared so bad yesterday but now through my sore eyes the extent of the mess of soot and grime was apparent. It extended right into the room.

'I'm calling Annie.' She proceeded to phone and then asked, 'And how many bodies did you find?' and laughed.

The sound hurt my head so my answer was aggressive. 'No bodies,' I waited for her to stop laughing and then told her, 'but a diary.' I indicated it on the table.

'Wow,' she picked it up. 'Look Hal, go and get washed and changed, otherwise you'll frighten Annie when she gets here. I'll make some coffee and has Barklay been fed?'

When I returned from washing and changing, Annie was in the room. She was looking at the fireplace, and the soot and dust spreading out from the hearth. Coffee mugs were on the table beside the diary and Barklay had been sent into the garden.

'What an earth have you been up to, making such a mess?'

'Something up the chimney was bothering Barklay,' I told her, 'So I had a look. And I found a diary.'

Gracie handed it to her.

'Well, I never. Whose is it?'

'It's my mother's'

For a moment Annie stood there open mouthed. 'And what does it say?'

'I only read the first page.'

'Do you think we ought to read it?' Gracie asked.

Annie handed the book back to me and I opened the cover looking at the childish scrawl again.

'I think I've got to,' I said. I wasn't certain whether the thudding in my head was simply a hangover or a harbinger. I sensed the diary had been waiting for me.

The start of my New Life. Chantelle Bennett.

As I read them the first page, it felt strange to be voicing Mother's words, because she had never told me about her childhood or how she came to work at Leverbridge Manor. Now it sounded in my aching head like her talking to me from the past.

As I finished the passage Annie said, 'It seems such a long time ago. Why don't I tidy up a bit and you can read it to me.'

Annie got an apron out of her bag and went to the kitchen collecting brushes and cloths from the cupboard and then, as she started to sweep and wipe, I read. Gracie looked on.

April 10th.
I've had such a great day but am SO tired. Can't write much. Georgina was very nice and I think I did o.k. Got to be up at six again.

April 11th.
Working with horses is SO GREAT. They are such beautiful creatures, really gentle and their smell is so warm and soothing. Can't believe I've found this place. There's a word for it I know.

I thought Georgina might be a bit stuck up but she's really great. She's lent me some books about horses so I'm going to read a bit when I've done this. I am going to be the best stable hand EVER.

Serendipity. I remembered. That's the word for it.

April 12th.
Had another fantastic day. I think the horses are already getting used to having me around. 'Another Star' is my favourite, he is a huge hunter which Maurice Manning rides on the hunt. His brother Victor, the 'other Mr. Manning', also keeps a horse there. He popped by and said he was 'very pleased to meet me'. He winked after every sentence. Georgina says he's like that with everybody and 'watch out for your bottom when he's about.' Georgina says I'll be able to go to the next hunt meet, but there's loads of etiquette to learn so I'll need to do loads more reading.

Oh and we had a fantastic lunch today. The housekeeper, Annie, had made us soup as it had been such a cold morning. I have never tasted anything with the power to make me feel warm right from my toes to the top of my head. It was yummy. She laughed when I told her. She is so nice and kind. She caught me off guard though and asked, 'What was really going on?' I said I didn't know what she meant, but she kept on, so eventually I told her about the kid's home and deciding to leave and finding the job here. I pleaded with her not to say anything. I told her I was going to work really, really hard and do everything I was told. 'You realise you don't have to do EVERYTHING they ask,' she said, which I thought a bit strange. She asked me about my age, I didn't see the point in lying to her so I told her I'd be 16 in August. Luckily Georgina was not in the kitchen at the time and Annie has promised not to say anything. I think I can trust her, she seems really kind.

That entry made me pause, and I watched Annie's back as she appeared to be scrubbing with extra force over the already clean hearth. I realised she knew more about Mother's past than I did.

'I'm glad she was nice about you, Annie.'

Annie continued her cleaning and muttered, 'Yes, we became friends.'

'And did she really look older than sixteen?'

Annie paused in her movement but still spoke to the fireplace so the words echoed as they reached my ears. 'Yes, she was mature for her age. You have to realise she'd had a tough time in that children's home. I think she'd learnt to look after herself from an early age.'

I continued to read on.

April 14th.
George came into the kitchen at lunch today. He is the gardener and ever so nice. He made us all laugh at his jokes. I think Annie is a bit sweet on him.'

'Well, Annie?' I laughed.

I imagined I could see a blush edging up her neck below the grey bun.

'Well, George was nice and very good looking. The trouble was when he was younger all the girls in Leverbridge were after him and he was a bit too full of himself for my liking. Mary, his wife, was a friend of mine and I think he treated her badly.'

The diary went on in the same vein for pages and pages. Each daily entry enthused with excitement. Capital letters and exclamation marks abounded.

There were more entries about George and how handsome he was and how he made her laugh. More about Maurice and Victor and how they flirted with her.

I flicked further on to where a photo fell from between the pages. My mother sitting astride a horse. The accompanying text was as follows:

Mr Manning is teaching me to ride. He says I'm a natural. He is really good with the horses. They trust him. You can tell in the way they nuzzle up to him. I said I wished one day I'd be as good around horses as he was. He told me it just took time but I had a natural instinct for it. He said he'd seen it the moment he'd met me, which was kind.

I looked at the photo again. It had a soft focus as if it had been taken on a misty morning in a dewy pasture. I'm pretty sure from the naivety of my mother's diary entries she had no idea of how luminescent she looked in the photograph. Even the riding hat could not quash the golden hair spilling around her shoulders, catching the sunlight and giving a halo effect round her face. Her T-shirt and jodhpurs were tight fitting emphasising her figure; it was provocative enough to be a photo shoot for Play Boy. The thought was such a disturbing one I replaced the photo and closed the book around it with some force.

'What is it, Hal?' Gracie asked.

'They say you shouldn't read other people's diaries, don't they? Well, I know why now. The person writing this diary is a stranger. I can't get my head round it.'

I opened the diary again and passed her the photograph. Gracie said, 'She looks beautiful, doesn't she?'

The photo had drawn Annie's attention and she put her hand out to Gracie for it. She was kneeling in front of the fireplace still, her hair mussed from its bun with the vigour of her cleaning. A grey tendril touched her eyes and I could see moisture in them.

She got up and sat in the armchair, not taking her eyes from the photo.

Further on was a second photo, this one of Mother in a long evening gown. It was taken at the base of a wide flight of stairs; it looked like the entrance hall of Leverbridge Manor. The dress was green, suiting Mother's colouring perfectly. Mother was laughing; I don't recall her ever looking so happy.

I handed the photo to Annie, 'Look at this one, it must be a party.'

Annie whispered her reply as though she was reliving the past and had remained caught up in its memories. 'Yes, that was the hunt ball that year. I think it was her real sixteenth birthday. She was dazzling.' The moisture in her eyes had finally overflowed creating a steady spill of tears down her cheeks. She sniffed.

I didn't know what to say or do. I looked at Gracie wondering if she might intervene with a tissue or a word but she didn't move, so I looked at the entry for Mother's sixteenth birthday and continued to read.

The 12th August.
MY 16th BIRTHDAY. THE HUNT BALL.
IT happened!!! I'M IN LOVE!!!
No time to write more.

13th August.

There was a package outside my door when I got back today. It was wrapped in brown paper and didn't look that exciting but inside was the most beautiful ornament I've ever seen. And it's mine! A bronze statue of a horse. The expression is perfect. It must be worth a fortune. Can't believe I actually own something as beautiful and expensive as this. He must really love me.

14th August.

Had to work again today. But didn't care because I feel so different. Walking on clouds. Nothing else matters except this. I can't wait to see him again. Every moment I'm not with him I ache.

'Doesn't she say who she's in love with?' Gracie asked.

'Not yet,' I told her. I glimpsed ahead. The next couple of weeks' entries continued in the same manner. Short sentences expressing her love but mentioning no name.

Then a word leapt from the page.

SHIT.

I didn't read the next page out.

30th August.
Pregnant. The test was definite. Don't know what to do.

31st August.
Spoke to him. Told him. He says he loves me but can't have a child.

Said he'd pay for an abortion. But I want a child. I want a child to give the love I never had.

1st September.
Decided I want to keep my baby. He was angry. Said I was being selfish.

I told him I'd never tell anybody who was the father, just so long as I could keep it.

He says if I love him I'd get rid of it.
I do love him, but I already love my baby.
What shall I do?
Think I'll talk to Annie.

My expression must have changed because Gracie asked,

'Hal what's the matter. Is something wrong?'

I couldn't read the words, my vision was blurred. August 1979, the baby born the following year must have been me.

My hands started to tremble and I passed the open diary to Gracie.

She took a few moments to read it, and then said, 'So, she must be talking about your father, Hal. He must have been local.'

I couldn't speak; my brain capacity was taken up with filing through males who could have been my father. Top of the list was George Sheldon. That would make Tom my half-brother. Besides being male, I could not think of a single similarity between us.

I looked towards Annie who was still silently looking at the photos in her lap.

'Do you know, Annie?'

For some time she did not move. I thought she might not have heard me. But then she nodded a slow, definite movement. The words which followed were slow and definite too.

'You ought to know, Hal. She should have told you before it was too late'.

What Was Taken 11

'Your mother was a very beautiful young woman, Hal. In the short time she was working here she had many admirers. She ignored them in the main. I guess she had lived with male adoration most of her life. However, I always had the impression she wanted to better herself. She ignored the young lads of her own age; I could tell she was more interested in some of the business men who came up here.' Annie took a deep breath.

'But she had moved to Leverbridge Manor, and there was one man who was more powerful than all the rest. And he enjoyed that position. He liked to think he owned everything, even the people in it.'

She took another deep breath as if having difficulty finding the energy to complete her story.

'Maurice.'

'Maurice Manning?' I asked stupidly, Maurice was quite an unusual name.

'Yes.'

'You're telling me Maurice Manning was my father? I don't believe you.' I was on my feet, stamping my dissent. Pointing my finger at her, I said again, 'I don't believe you!'

Finally Annie looked up from her lap. Her face was calm; the trace of tears now dried remained like the silvery trails of snails. 'It's true Hal, whether you want to believe it or not.'

Gracie finally spoke. 'It can't be true. Hal's right, it can't be true.' She continued to murmur the phrase over and over whilst Annie went on.

'Hal, your mother confided in me. She had no one else. I think I'm the only person who ever knew. But it's true. That's why he left you the Gate House. And the portrait. Have a look at that portrait if you don't believe me.'

I couldn't understand how a portrait could confirm my lineage but I went over to it.

I took hold of the centre and ripped downwards. Mother smiled at me. It calmed me seeing her eyes look at me again, perfectly painted with the exact hue matching the green of the beech leaves outside. Her face was so beautiful it was as if summer had entered the room, I felt warm again. I parted the brown wrapping from her. Her shoulders were bare and I expected to see her clothed in her emerald evening gown. But then I stopped. She was not clothed. She was naked. Her flesh bloomed like the flower of forbidden fruit.

Gracie had got up and was standing behind me. I could sense her revulsion. Hurriedly I re-arranged the brown paper around Mother, as if I was a prudish gentleman.

'Why did Maurice have a nude portrait of my mother?' I demanded of Annie. But she did not need to answer.

'Did you know?' I demanded of Gracie. 'Who knew?' I swung round to look at Annie, 'What about Grace Elizabeth?' I shouted, 'She must have known!'

'I don't think so Hal, at least not for sure. I don't think she knew until the wedding, unless your mother told her before.'

I turned back to face Gracie who had not moved, 'You've not answered me Gracie. Did you know that man was my father?'

Her voice was so quiet in contrast to mine I had to strain to hear her. 'I didn't know Maurice was your father, Hal.'

She started to tremble. Far off I could sense the earth shaking. I wondered if a thunder storm was about to break because there was a roaring in my head.

Gracie started to drop towards the floor. She curled up clutching her arms around her knees as if she wanted to disappear. Then she let out a cry, loud and long, not a scream but a wail. It filled me with horror. Too many thoughts were slamming around my head, the roll of thunder banged on in my brain.

I could not understand Gracie's reaction. Surely I should be the one ranting and raving. This could explain Mother's last letter to me. If he was my father and Lizzie's grandfather that would have made it impossible to marry, wouldn't it? Was I the only one who didn't know?

Gracie was rocking on the floor, moaning as if in physical pain.

'Oh, it's worse, it's worse,' she cried rocking back and forward. She looked so pale she was almost transparent. On her forehead a vein pulsed like a bolt of blue lightening.

'I can't bear it,' she said, and started hitting her forehead on her fists, not gently but hard. The blue veins merged into bruised red purple. I was stuck. The weight of the storm in my head held me.

Thankfully Annie moved forward and bent down to her, holding her fists and cooing, 'No, No, Gracie. There, there.' Her voice came from another time as if Gracie were a child waking from nightmares.

Gracie's eyes looked blindly, the depth of her despair made them black. Tears welled over, her mouth gaped red and salvia dribbled. She looked mad. Still I couldn't move.

My father was Maurice Manning. I contained his DNA. The man capable of murdering Alicia, and abusing Tara, was intrinsically linked with my own body. Twisted into me like barbed wire. I was aware of the world outside. The wind had risen, blowing clouds across the sky, encouraging the trees to rattle above us. The cottage suddenly seemed tiny but at the epicentre; as if we were the cottage in a snow globe and somebody had shaken it vigorously. If I had seen snow falling I would not have been surprised.

With Annie still holding her hands and being unable to hit herself Gracie started wailing again. Annie continued to speak to her softly. Gradually the noise subsided and left Gracie sobbing.

'Hal, get Gracie a glass of water and some tissues.' She said it firmly and I realised she had already repeated it several times.

My legs moved in stilted motion through to the kitchen. I fetched the water and a roll of kitchen paper and took them to Annie. She frowned at the rough paper but began to dab Gracie's face. 'Have a sip of water, there's a good girl,' she continued.

Finally she managed to coax Gracie to sit on the settee. Gracie clutched a damp piece of kitchen paper and rocked slightly on the seat. Every now and again she would gulp and try to speak, 'I can't...' gulp. 'You don't know...' gulp. 'I can't tell...' gulp.

Annie sat beside her, patting her hand. I remained standing. From Gracie's demeanour I realised the storm had not abated. There was more.

I wanted to get it over. Gracie had something else to say. What did she mean by, 'it's worse?'

I had to know. Planting my feet on the floor as firmly as possible I asked, 'What did you mean by 'it's worse', Gracie.'

Annie scowled at me.

Gracie's rocking became more vigorous. Again she had several false starts but then the words came out in a rush, a foul stench from a storm drain released.

'Maurice was my father too.'

I was confused. Gracie was mistaken.

'No, Maurice was your grandfather, otherwise how...?' My question drifted away; the awful truth beginning to seep below my skin as if the barbs of wire were turning. A distant echo was carried on the storm, an echo about a mutant child.

Gracie's voice sounded exhausted as she said, 'Maurice abused my mother. She was pregnant with Lizzie and me before she married.'

How I remained standing I don't know.

'I think he might have started to molest her again. That's when she tried to kill us all.'

Outside I imagined Maurice Manning rising from his grave, monster-like, crouching above the cottage ready to consume us. And me with the same DNA.

Another thought wheedled in. 'And you Gracie, did he abuse you?'

Annie scowled in my direction again. 'I think that's enough, don't you? I think that's quite enough.'

I agreed with Annie. What I'd heard was quite enough but I had to know the full extent of Maurice Manning's depravity. I contained his DNA. 'Gracie?'

The room was quiet as if everything in it was listening, even the portrait of Mother behind her brown paper. The bronze statue on the mantelpiece pricked his ears, and the clock tried to dim its solemn tick... tock.

'Yes.'

The word plummeted into the room. A single hailstone.

We remained silent whilst the earth rotated, moving us through day and night, through seasons and years with no marker to indicate the passage of time.

It was Barklay's scraping at the back door which finally made me move. I let him in, made more coffee and went back to the sitting room. Now the secret had been released I had to know the full story. 'What happened, Gracie?'

I wondered whether she would reply she waited for so long before responding. Barklay appeared to sense her pain and went over and nuzzled her hand. She absently stroked his head and the action seemed to stimulate her speech. She spoke in a low toneless voice.

'Lizzie and me shared a room when we were little. Grandpapa,' she hesitated, choking at the word and changed it, 'Maurice would come and read to us each night. He'd sit in the armchair and tell wonderful stories. He'd base them on fairy tales but embellish them. Both of us loved listening. But when we were nine or ten he stopped, I supposed we weren't kids any more. So when at around fourteen Lizzie and me got our own bedrooms, I was thrilled when Maurice came to read to me again.

'This time he'd lie on my bed with his arm around me. The stories were similar to before and I loved listening to him. He had a deep voice and could do all sorts of accents. Now though, as he told the tales he would stroke me under my night dress. At first I didn't mind, it was soothing and he was gentle but gradually the touching got more and more...' Gracie looked out of the window with the look of an animal, one which was being hunted.

'I told him I didn't like it. He said it was 'just cuddles'. I asked him why he didn't read stories to Lizzie but he said he loved me best and how I reminded him of my mother. And part of me liked that, to be more like Mum and better loved.'

She made a small cry as if a scream was lodged in her throat.

'The cuddles got more intense though.' Gracie was twisting her fingers together and starting to rock again. I thought she was going to start hitting herself but instead she suddenly stood up and then seemed to be unable to move. She continued talking to the chimney breast.

'One night I ran down to Grandmama, my nightdress was torn. I told her what Maurice had been doing. She hardly looked at me, but said, 'I'll have a word with him' as if he were simply leaving the toilet seat up. She did come with me and clean me, found me a fresh night gown and put me back to bed; something she had never done before. She was kind. But later that night I heard raised voices coming from their room and so I crept down and listened.

'It's got to stop, Maurice,' I heard Grandmama say, and then, 'Didn't you learn anything from impregnating your own daughter, driving her to suicide? If you've got to dabble, do it away from the Manor. Use the whore at the Gate House.'

I jolted when I heard Mother being spoken about like that. I remembered Maurice's lascivious features at the cottage door and saying to Mother 'the horse was restless'. Now the inference was so obvious, how could I have been so naïve?

Gracie was continuing her story. 'It took me days to work out what I'd overheard. But then everything clicked, I realised he must be my biological father and the reason why my mother and father had died. That's when I cut my wrists.'

She lifted her hands up so the edge of her sleeve fell back, revealing those white scars on her skin.

I didn't want to believe it. 'But are you sure, Gracie? You were young and upset. Are you sure about what you heard?'

Gracie was still standing, her arms in front of her with her wrists exposed, as if she were holding an empty tray. 'I spent so much time thinking about it, I didn't want to believe it either. But I wasn't mistaken. It's true.'

'And after you cut your wrists, did he stop?'

Gracie sat down again, looking at the scars and rubbing them with her fingers. 'Yes, but I could never relax in that house again. When I came back home the first time he would come to my room to say 'Goodnight' and would ask, 'Did I want a bedtime story?' He tormented me. I couldn't take it anymore, couldn't...couldn't take it anymore.'

She had leant forward resting her face on her knees and her shoulders were trembling, I could hear her crying. I wanted to put my hand out and smooth her quaking back, but could not find the strength to move my arm.

'Did you know Maurice was my father?'

Her reply was muffled but still firm. 'No, no,' she spoke into her knees. 'It never crossed my mind.'

'And Lizzie, how much did she know?'

'I never told her about Maurice being our father. I think she suspected his abuse of me, but I always denied it.'

Gracie lifted her head; her face was an abstract of tears, snot, smudged mascara and smeared lipstick.

I had almost forgotten about Annie. She had been sitting motionless; I doubted she'd taken a breath for some time.

'Annie, did you know about Caro, about Lizzie and Gracie?'

Annie's flesh was the same grey as her hair so she looked as if she were vanishing. Her voice was hardly above a whisper and faded as it reached me. 'I swear, Hal, if I'd known I'd never have let you get so close to Lizzie.'

She was crying but silently. The tears were just another form of greyness, a symptom of her melting away with grief. 'I liked Maurice Manning; I thought he was a decent man. Yes, a womaniser, but just a red-blooded man.'

Poor Annie, I thought. She'd always talked of Maurice with so much admiration and now it had been ripped from her. I thought perhaps she'd once imagined riding off into the sunset with him.

The room became silent again but now heavy with our thoughts. Then Annie hiccoughed, a small sound an insect might make.

'I'm so sorry, Hal. I think I'm to blame. I'm the reason your wedding was ruined. They should have been kinder to you. Not leave you standing at the altar.' She made the insect sound again, a beating of wings against glass. 'I thought your mother would have said something before you and Lizzie got serious. Perhaps she never expected you to become so close. I think had she lived she would have said something, but she never got the chance, did she?' Annie took a deep breath and then continued.

'When I heard you and Lizzie were to be married I knew I had to say something. You seemed to make the decision so quickly. It didn't give us any chance to think things through.'

Briefly she looked up from her lap and shook her head at me, as if I had made things deliberately difficult for her. 'Of course, then I thought Lizzie was Maurice's granddaughter, but I knew even so you were too closely related to marry. I went to Grace Elizabeth.'

Again she paused for breath, as if once more she was building herself up to confront Grace Elizabeth. I had no doubt what a difficult exchange it would have been for her.

'I went to talk to her. Oh, that was a dreadful conversation.' Annie shuddered at the memory. 'All Grace Elizabeth had to say was, 'I don't want people knowing that Ms. Bennett seduced my husband. After all we did for her.' Then she tutted, swore under her breath a bit and called your mother some horrible things, Hal. It was difficult, but there are some things I'm certain of, and this marriage was one thing I knew couldn't happen. So I again found the courage to say I wouldn't let the marriage go ahead and I would tell Lizzie. Grace Elizabeth's mood changed then, she became sweet and told me not to worry, and why didn't I go on a nice holiday somewhere, I deserved a break. She asked me where I would most like to go. But I stayed where I was, 'Mrs Manning,' I said, 'I don't want to cause trouble but I really cannot let this marriage go ahead. If necessary I will stand up in church when they ask for any impediment to the marriage and tell everybody that Lizzie and Hal are related through your husband.' Oh, I thought she was going to hit me.'

She had to pause again and I imagined it was probably the most difficult conversation Annie Taylor had ever had.

'She cursed again, telling me I needed to be careful about what I said and who I threatened. I told her it was not a threat and something I did not want to do, but the marriage did have to be stopped. I think she must have realised I was serious because eventually she said; 'I'll sort it out. I'll talk to Lizzie. I promise. But you must promise me, Annie, that you will not breathe a word to anybody, particularly about Maurice being Henry's father.' I was glad the ordeal was over. I had no doubt Grace Elizabeth would keep her part of the bargain and talk to Lizzie and I had no desire to spread rumours about Maurice, and I said so. So I think we parted with some respect for one another. Poor Grace Elizabeth, I don't think she'd ever seen me so determined. And I did go away for a few days. I didn't think she'd leave you to be jilted at the altar. I'm sorry for that. But there it is, Hal, I guess Grace Elizabeth told Lizzie just before the wedding and Lizzie took off. I'm so sorry, I'm so sorry you weren't told sooner.'

Annie's body remained very still and upright whilst her head moved from side-to-side, trying to negate the memories.

I watched the movement of that grey head, wondering how I could have been left so unaware. Why hadn't Mother told me years ago or Annie or anybody? Was it simply to protect Maurice's good name. But only Mother, Grace Elizabeth, Maurice and Annie knew about my father. Somebody should have told me the truth long ago. One of them should have told me. Maurice was always going to protect his back and Grace Elizabeth would support him whatever he had done. She had tried to remove me from the scene by helping me to get to university. Mother was obviously ready to explain when she sent her last letter to me but didn't live long enough to tell me and then Annie did what she could when she realised Lizzie and I were going to get married. I felt as if I was encircled by them, tossing a ball from hand to hand, and every time I reached out to grab it they would throw it again. I felt impotent, with a storm of hatred building inside me. I had to act and there was only one person left who deserved my anger.

'Grace Elizabeth knew everything, didn't she?' I said.

Gracie and Annie remained silent.

'I'm going to talk to her.' I told them.

I could feel pain. It started from the stump of my leg and burnt its path through my body. A red heat blurring my vision. It raged in me. And then it took over; I was heading to the door before I could stop.

I was outside jogging down the drive. Grace Elizabeth knew everything. She had continually protected her husband. She had let Maurice get away with the abuse and murder of his daughter and granddaughter, and she had not told me Maurice was my father. Perhaps she'd colluded in killing Mother. Or Lizzie. I almost tripped with the weight of the thought. Anyway, Grace Elizabeth would take some of the blame.

As I moved away from the cottage, I heard Gracie shouting, 'Hal, there's something I meant to tell you.'

It was too late now to tell me anything, the damage was done.

I was running now, running to confront the witch of the Manor. Even with only one foot, Gracie's heeled footsteps were no match for mine, but she was still shouting, 'I haven't told you about Lizzie, I haven't told you about Lizzie.' The refrain behind me sounded like 'Lizzie' being shouted over and over. It was more like an incantation than ever.

What Remains 12

I barged in the back door and heard voices in the kitchen. I looked in but it was somebody I didn't know singing to the radio. I didn't disturb them but headed for the back stairs.

When I reached the landing and corridor towards Grace Elizabeth's room I had to slow down. The atmosphere and smell were so different here it was like entering an enchanted world where only soft steps and quiet voices would be tolerated. There was an odour of flowers kept too long in rooms where there was no air flow. It was cloying with the heaviness of dust and secrets. The corridor was unchanged since my visit here with Lizzie so long ago. The walls were painted a deep green making the space dark. The landscapes and portraits of forgotten times tried to envelop the present. One door appeared to be open where the purple and red of the carpet blossomed in a square of diffuse light. I headed towards it, dimly aware of voices carrying from further away.

The door was ajar. At the threshold I paused, aware the room was inhabited. Now my anger had been dampened by the atmosphere, I felt guilty, my natural instincts on trespassing in the Manning's house rose, so I stopped and leaned forward to glimpse the room's interior. From where I stood I could see a large armchair with wingbacks sheltering a small figure. A square of pink fleece, covering Grace Elizabeth's legs, fell to the floor. I could only see a small portion of her face, and noticed the eye in view was closed. In contrast the mouth was wide open, rimmed with cerise lipstick to lips without shape. Her breathing was deep and loud as she exhaled into the high ceilinged space. She was so tiny and fragile it was hard to equate this feeble thing with my knowledge of her treachery. Her skin was the ivory shade of ancient papyrus and equally textured. One hand had dropped to the side of the chair with the limpness of a discarded puppet. Glossy red nail varnish smeared the finger tips in an attempt at youth, but failed with a garish inevitability. The hand was corded with knotted blue veins and punctuated with liverish blemishes.

As the pain in my leg started to rise again I was reminded she was masquerading as a frail old woman. I allowed myself to absorb the pain, digging my fingers into my fist so I wouldn't scream with the intensity of it building up. Enough strength to break the enchantment she had woven around herself.

Finally, I took a step forward and said in a loud voice, 'Don't pretend you're ill or asleep. I need to talk to you.'

Her eyes opened with a flutter and she smiled. 'Why Henry, how nice to see you. Is it pleasant out?' she asked.

I wasn't here to make small talk. 'You have destroyed my life. You and your monster of a husband.'

She continued to smile. 'That's some accusation to greet an old lady from an afternoon nap.'

'You're no sweet old lady, you're a witch. A witch protecting a monster.'

'Henry, give me a moment, I don't know what you're talking about.'

I shouldn't have let her move, I shouldn't have let her get up or tidy herself because suddenly I lost my advantage.

'Have a seat and calm down.' I did as I was told.

She went to her dressing table and brushed her hair; she took off her slippers and replaced them with a pair of heeled court shoes. Returning to the winged armchair she picked up and folded the rug which had been covering her. She had metamorphosed from frail old woman to the formidable matron I had always known. I was on a lower armless chair and it gave the impression that I was attending a queen on her throne.

'Now what is all this about?'

I struggled to keep my voice firm and not fall into supplication at her feet. 'I know everything. I know

Maurice was Lizzie and Gracie's father. I know he was my father too. And you knew all along and protected him.'

She said nothing but held me in a gaze I could not look away from. I wondered whether she would deny my accusations. She did not. Her voice was matter-of-fact.

'I didn't actually know Maurice fathered you. Not until your mother finally and belatedly, told me when you'd gone to university. How could she have been so stupid? If Maurice had told me I would have sorted it. Your mother would have been forced to get rid of you. You would never have existed. That would have solved a lot of problems. I'd still have Lizzie here for one thing.'

The idea of non-existence appeared appealing at that moment. I could see a smudge of the lake through the bay of the window. It hovered like a mirage. If I hadn't been born maybe Alicia wouldn't have gone missing, Lizzie would be alive and Mother would not have committed suicide. Yes, it would have been better if I had never been born. Grace Elizabeth's voice continued to speak at me.

'Do you think I'd want you for a son-in-law? As soon as I found out you were romantically involved I did everything I could to keep you and Lizzie apart. That had nothing to do with who fathered you. Why would I want her hanging around a no-hoper like you?'

My voice sounded weak as I said, 'All you had to do was tell the truth and then I would have stayed away.'

Her voice remained strong and steady. 'As simple as that! For you maybe. But Maurice was a respected man. What would a story like that have done to him, to the whole great Manning family?'

'I don't care. Look what it's done to me, to Lizzie and Gracie, to Tara and Alicia.'

'You're so selfish, Henry Bennett.' She shook her head. 'You're like your mother. Whining and complaining, thinking Maurice owed her something. Oh, she came here to tell me you were Maurice's heir and how much we owed her. Ha! That was a laugh. We owed her nothing. We had given her everything; a home, a job, kindness. As for Maurice leaving the Gate House to you, I've no idea what he was thinking. He did that without my knowledge. But you are right, I should have forbidden you from seeing Lizzie from the beginning, but I was kind. I let you play together, let you into my home. A snivelling bastard!'

She had taken so much breath to exhale the word 'bastard' she was silent for a moment. 'So that offends you does it? Well, how do you think I felt when I walked in one day to find your mother draped naked over my chaise longue, having her portrait painted. She bewitched Maurice, made him simple-minded. I think he had some idea of having her live here as a concubine. That was never going to happen.' She sniffed and straightened her shoulders as if she might be appearing weak. 'And yet Henry Bennett, even though your mother was a harlot, I was good to you. I even helped you get to university; all you had to do was stay there, stay away from Lizzie, away from Leverbridge. But no you had to come back and contaminate us.' She was still shaking her head.

'I came back because my mother died.'

'You came back and stayed. Weak, that's what you were, what you are, Henry Bennett. If only you had stayed away.'

Somehow the air was changing in the room as if a weather front was pushing a fog towards me, covering me with blame I could not disperse.

'And why bring Tara and Alicia into your little heart break?'

I was certain she must know about Maurice's abuse of Tara. 'He abused Tara, since she was a young girl. Like he did Caro and Gracie. He was depraved.'

'How dare you make accusations about my husband? He was twice the man you'll ever be. Yes, he had his weaknesses, but don't we all? You wouldn't say such things if he was alive, but now he's dead you think you can sully his name.'

For a second I wondered if I was wrong; perhaps she didn't know about his abuse of Tara. But catching a glimpse of the steel in her eyes I knew I was not wrong. She would die before admitting Maurice's wrongdoing. She may even have become so blinkered to it she was trying to erase it from her mind. I wondered what she knew about Alicia's death.

'Did you know he killed Alicia? He murdered her.'

I couldn't interpret her expression. Colour was creeping into her cheeks, whether from anger or remorse I couldn't tell. 'Now you're being hysterical, Henry,' she said quite calmly. 'Too highly strung, just like your mother. I wouldn't be surprised if you felt the need to cut your wrists and take the coward's way out. Just like she did.'

The venom of her words struck home. My mind went blank; I could not remember why I was in her room. Then I glimpsed the edge of the lake again, it reminded me of something. It reminded me of the day Alicia had gone missing.

'He murdered Alicia. How can you sit there and not say anything, when you know Maurice was a murderer.'

'We don't know what happened to Alicia.'

My mouth kept talking, making up words and stringing them together. I stood up. 'Yes you do. Maurice would have come to you when he killed her. Maybe it had been accidental but you would have told him exactly how to keep it covered up. I bet you even had George Sheldon dig a nice big hole where she could be buried, deep enough never to be found.'

She stood up then. Even with her shoes on she was a foot shorter than me. But I was intimidated by her, she had a way of holding herself that created those missing inches, and a steel aura which matched any height or weight advantage I had. For once I was glad of my prosthetic foot, it remained solid when the rest of my body was trembling.

'Henry, you're obviously overwrought being back at the cottage. You always did have far too much imagination. Like your mother who lived in some sort of fantasy world where she imagined she was a Princess and was entitled to live at the Manor itself.' She muttered under her breath, 'Silly creature,' and shook her head.

The tactic worked again; it altered my train of thought. 'Don't talk about my mother like that! She was worth twenty of you. A million, a trillion.' Even to my own ears I sounded like a spoilt boy in a playground fight.

Grace Elizabeth's tone remained calm and clear. 'I think you'd better go now or I'll call the police.'

'Good. I'll tell them everything.'

'And who do you think they'll believe?'

She held my arm and rotated me and I was unable to resist the movement. Now I saw my reflection in the dressing table mirror. I looked wild; my black hair was sticking up, my face a shade of blue white which should be reserved for ghouls. To add to the effect my eyes were bloodshot. Beside me she was dainty and dignified.

She spoke at my reflection, 'Perhaps I'll tell them it was you Henry. You made Alicia do some stupid dare. There was an accident. What would you do? You wouldn't tell the others. No, you'd take her to your mother, she'd sort it out. Make the nasty accident go away. Hide the body at the cottage and then ask her good friend George to bury the body later. Is that what happened Henry? It sounds plausible to me.'

Indeed it did. In the mirror her eyes were the colour of coal, the pupils expanding and contracting like a hypnotic charm. I was nodding.

'Your mother couldn't live with the guilt after all; no wonder she eventually took her own life.'

I regarded the tormented man in the mirror. 'Was it suicide?' I posed the question to our reflected doubles.

'What do you think, Henry? Do you think your mother could really keep quiet when I told her you were Lizzie's half-brother? When she finally thought she'd got some sort of leverage. Something to blackmail me with? You're the one who thinks I'm capable of being an accessory to murder. So what do you think, Henry?'

Watching her in the mirror, with a smirk of triumph on her face, I became certain that she had been involved in Mother's death. I would never know the details but, I wanted her to admit it. 'I want to know the truth.'

'No, you don't. Not really, Henry. You're weak and scared. A coward. You couldn't handle the truth if it hit you.'

We glared at each other through the mirror. Then, she smiled. Her hold on my arm though light made me incapable of lifting it and striking her.

'I'm tired now, Henry. I think you'd better go.'

'How can you stand there and let Alicia rest beside Maurice for all eternity?'

She laughed then; the sound circled the room and echoed off the glass of the mirror. I thought it might shatter.

'Come off it, Henry. Neither you nor I believe in eternity. One life time is enough. Now get out!' The words hissed through the air.

I walked out still in a trance, unable to resist her order. Once in the corridor the overpowering stale odour possessed the air. I wondered what sort of flowers she used. It was like being trapped in a musty old book, one bound up with tragic tales and secrets. I was surprised I was actually able to leave and hadn't been placed under a spell to entrap me there for ever.

My steps back to the cottage were slower, my leg continued to throb. Only once did I turn to look back at the house. There was a figure at the window on the stairway above the main entrance. Gracie must have returned to the Manor. The afternoon light was bright causing a sunburst effect on the glass pane and in the refraction her image was split into two as if she were talking to her twin sister. She held her hand up in a wave like gesture. I turned away.

In the circumstances I think I behaved with a surprising calm. Only Barklay was in the cottage when I returned. I went into the bedroom and packed a bag.

Then, calling Barklay, I put him on the lead and climbed into my mini.

As I drove down the familiar street, across the bridge I knew I would not return. I dropped Barklay off. I apologised to Mandy for it being short notice, 'But something important has come up,' I told her. I was pleased Tom wasn't about. If Mandy noticed my ruffled demeanour she didn't say anything. Mandy thanked me for looking after Barklay. I gave him a final pat and told him, 'Sorry.'

Then I was on the road. Putting my foot down, taking the corners much too fast. I wound the windows down so the air rushed in stinging my face and blasted Muse on the player. I left the Leverbridge boundary as if I had reached warp speed and had made my escape from a black hole.

Rain was driving towards me like a hail of grey arrows through the darkening sky. It was difficult to see but still I did not slow down. Occasionally headlights swelled towards me becoming momentarily bright then disappearing. It was other worldly. And I was reminded of the time years ago when I been in a similar state. On that occasion I had been riding a motorbike and had lost my foot. The memory did not make me slow down. I had become reckless with my life. I even felt slightly disappointed when I arrived back in Milton Keynes in one piece.

What Remains 13

My bedsit smelt like an old shoe when I unlocked the door. There was a pile of junk mail on the floor inside. I grabbed it and dumped everything in a bin. The kettle appeared to have developed even more lime scale than when I had left, like an unchecked skin disorder. I rinsed it and made a cup of tea, it tasted tainted.

Ignoring the unfriendly atmosphere I went straight to bed. I did not bother to undress, just kicked off my shoes and prosthesis and then slid under the duvet. It felt damp because it had remained unaired and unwashed. I didn't care. I sipped my tea and then dozed.

I awoke to a loud noise which had shaken the building. A second crack of lightning struck, momentarily illuminating the room and reminding me I was no longer in the Gate House. The furniture looked wrong as if it had been creeping closer as I slept, ready for some dreadful spectre to leap at me. Now the darkness made me blind and I could smell the stagnant atmosphere loading the air with sulphur. I was pleased when the lightning sparked again so I could make out the room about me. After my accident I had occasionally awoken from dreams where I had been constrained in a coffin.

I thought of Maurice lying in his crypt and wondered if the air had a similar taint. Alicia's bones would be confined forever next to his.

I don't know whether I slept again or not, but gradually dawn came. I hadn't closed the curtains and the light intensified, revealing the grime and rubbish I had accumulated over time. There was no sunshine. It was a drab day with a sparse rain falling from a leaden sky. Somehow the thin walls of my flat allowed the weather to permeate the building, so it seemed I was dwelling in fog. I wondered whether Leverbridge actually existed or whether

I had somehow been briefly transported into a parallel world where the heat was unrelenting. Perhaps I was mad and lying in a damp dim room in a mental institution. My existence was a continuation of cold and grey. Happiness was simply an illusion I had created in my diseased brain.

I turned to the digital clock to check the day and time and cling to some semblance of reality. In luminous green figures it told me it was 08.00 am. Below in smaller figures was the date. 03.07.2010. I picked the clock up and threw it against the wall. It made a feeble chirrup as it slid down the wood chip. I turned away. If this was reality I would rather be mad. I scratched my hand wanting to take chunks out of my flesh. Why wouldn't the memory of Lizzie Manning leave me alone? The date was the eleventh anniversary of my non-wedding.

What Was Taken 13

Remembering that day was like walking from a dark room into dazzling sunlight. The sensation was painful as I pictured it through eyes squeezed shut, searching for the shapes of that beautiful day in the glare of light. As the objects became clearer my spirits lifted. I thought my wedding day would be perfect; the culmination of all the difficulties I had gone through to reach a point when I would stand beside Lizzie, vowing to be together forever.

The idea to marry had struck quite suddenly when Lizzie and I had managed to meet one Sunday morning. We were wandering in the gardens behind Tom's bungalow, ambling between rows of poly-tunnels and neat beds of vegetables with shoots visible in the dark earth that I had helped to tend. Bright green fronds in orderly rows growing under a spring sky.

I don't think Lizzie or I had spoken for some time; we were just enjoying being close to one another, holding hands as we meandered the gardens. It must have been the bells from the church sounding which gave me the idea because suddenly I dropped to one knee and asked her, 'Lizzie, will you marry me?' Obviously she was taken aback, because she gave a giddy little laugh as though I had made a joke. I laughed as well; I had surprised myself too. However, the idea took hold and I said,

'I'm serious,' and repeated, 'I'm really serious.' And I held onto her left hand tightly wishing I had a ring to put on it, even a strip of birch bark.

She said nothing. My knee felt cold from pressing into the soil of the path. Still she said nothing. I tried to work out what she was thinking, perhaps she was worried what Maurice and Grace Elizabeth would say. 'We could run away to Gretna Green.'

At that she laughed again and said, 'We shouldn't run away, Hal, but I will marry you.'

I almost fell over with the relief of her words. I pulled her down to me and then hugged and kissed her and we rolled over and over like playing puppies. When we'd come to a stop, I looked up at the cloudless sky, giddy with the sensation of happiness and rolling around. As the sky stopped rotating above me I had an uncomfortable thought.

'Should I ask Maurice's permission to marry you?' I was shaking at the thought as I asked. Lizzie said it wouldn't be a great idea. 'It's best if we just arrange it all, and then tell Grace Elizabeth. They can't stop us then, can they?'

I let Lizzie deal with it all. Lizzie had money of her own and didn't ask me for anything. I think Gracie helped and was sworn to secrecy. I told Tom, and asked him to be Best Man. He was shocked we were getting married but promised to keep it quiet.

There is something joyous about planning things in secret. It added a frisson to the event. I couldn't believe it was really going to happen.

Again I became aware of the benefits to being a Manning in Leverbridge. Lizzie knew the vicar of the church and organised the wedding date and reading of the Banns. At that point we had to let people know.

Lizzie went to Grace Elizabeth. 'She wasn't very happy about it. But I told her everything was arranged, and either we had her blessing or not. Finally she agreed. I think she realised she was not going to talk me round. In fact, she said she'd pay for our honeymoon!'

There would be a small reception at the Manor afterwards and then we'd be on our way to Bali.

So plain sailing then. I'd forgotten to beware of calm water which had in the past just led the way to despair. I thought my luck was changing.

Through the week leading up to the wedding, I floated. I helped in the market garden but hovered above the ground rather than placing my feet on it.

And Saturday dawned. A lovely summer day. Tom's Mum was excited as we got ready in our suits saying how smart we looked, asking Tom again and again if he'd got the rings and his speech. Both she and George said it was as if a son was getting married. I had spent over six months with them and did feel like part of the family.

George drove us all up to the church, Mary still making sure Tom was organised and brushing imagined flecks of dust from the lapel of his suit. She had put together corsages; carnations with a gypsophila spray. Her hands shook as she pinned mine on.

Then we went into the church and waited. Just the four of us at first, sitting on my side of the aisle. I had a few moments to sit and look at the wonderful architecture of the building that had been there for centuries. I looked at the font where Lizzie had been baptised. I saw coloured light spill through the stained glass.

Then the Manning side of the family entered, Lizzie's cousins, even Nigel. None of them spoke to me. Victor came in a few minutes later, a woman hanging on his arm. She was at least ten years younger than Victor and in her high heeled shoes towered over him. They did come to say hello and I stood up to shake Victor's hand. He clasped my shoulders and said in his jovial manner, 'Well done, son, well done. I'm proud of you. Marrying a woman like Lizzie Manning.' He winked several times and continued patting my upper arms until I felt bruised. Finally his consort managed to drag him away and I sat down again.

Eventually Gracie came in with Grace Elizabeth. At least Gracie came over and said I looked very handsome. She tried to hug me and her hair caught in the corsage. It became more tangled, the more desperate we became trying to release it. Finally I took the flower off and left

Gracie to fiddle with it in the pew opposite, next to a silent Grace Elizabeth.

A piece of organ music was played and in the interval afterwards there was a shuffling of feet and some murmuring, and I realised the time for Lizzie to arrive had passed. Tom told me not to worry, 'Brides are always late, it's tradition mate.' I nodded.

Another organ march played and when it finished I was even more aware of the impatient coughing and fidgeting. I looked round me. I nudged Tom and asked him to see if he knew what was happening. He went over to have a word with Gracie.

He returned a moment later shrugging as he sat down. 'Well, Gracie didn't actually see Lizzie this morning...' I could sense my pulse quickening; surely Gracie would have helped Lizzie to get ready? '...Grace Elizabeth said Lizzie had got up early this morning. Lizzie said she'd got something to do before she came to the church. Gracie assumed it was a surprise for you.'

The vicar came down to speak to Grace Elizabeth wondering if there'd been a hold up. I went over to join the conversation. In my new shoes my footsteps tapped over the stone flags, over somebody long dead's grave. Grace Elizabeth was just saying, 'As far as I know there is no problem. I left Lizzie getting dressed, making some final adjustments. Maurice was meant to bring her down. I thought they'd be here by now.'

'What has Maurice said to her?' I wanted to ask, but couldn't get the question out before Gracie said, 'I'll ring the house.' She walked up the aisle, getting her mobile out, I followed her aware of my steps ringing out into the empty space at the back of the church.

The sunshine was warm as we waited for a response. 'Nobody's picked up,' she finally said. 'They're probably on their way.'

'What the hell's happened?' I demanded. 'She wouldn't stand me up like this. Do you think Maurice has said something?' I could sense tears in my eyes.

Gracie hesitated, as if she wasn't certain what to tell me. 'No, no. What could he tell her that would stop her coming? Let's just go back in and wait. They're probably on their way now'.

I shook her hand off me and walked to the church gate. I heard a car and felt relief, but the car carried on. It wasn't her.

Slowly, I made my way back into the church, wondering if this could truly be happening. Lizzie had to come. Organ music was playing and people were talking quite openly now. At the front Grace Elizabeth, the vicar and Gracie were huddled. I couldn't hear what was being said. I sat down next to Tom again.

Mary leaned over and whispered, 'It's alright Hal, there'll be a simple explanation.' But I couldn't think of a single explanation let alone a simple one which would mean Lizzie hadn't turned up for our wedding. All I could think was that for some reason Maurice had forbidden her to leave.

There was a clap of hands; the noise echoed off the struts and arches above us. I looked up to see Grace Elizabeth standing at the front of the church on the knave steps taking the lead. She did not look at me as she said, 'I'm sorry everybody, but we seem to have a problem. There will be no wedding today.' I felt as if I had been hit. I wanted to run at her and say, 'No! You can't just dismiss my wedding day like that.' But when I tried to stand, I couldn't and when I tried to speak my mouth wouldn't open. She walked down the aisle without looking at me. It was only as she passed my pew I noticed her eyes glistening with moisture and wondered whether she was close to tears. Gracie was hurrying after her; she was too caught up with

Grace Elizabeth to stay with me. The rest of the Mannings filed out.

The vicar came over to me and suggested we say a prayer before leaving. I bowed my head and words washed over me.

Over the next week I tried to find out what had happened. Lizzie seemed to have disappeared. Grace Elizabeth and Maurice were never available for me to speak to and Gracie didn't have much to tell me when she spoke to me. She told me Lizzie's disappearance was being investigated and left it at that. Lizzie's recently acquired mobile number didn't work.

After a month when still nothing had been heard I decided to leave.

What Remains 14

I don't know how long I remained cocooned in my bed, occasionally writhing and screaming and kicking out. I hoped a nurse might come and hold me down and tell me I was having a psychotic episode and not to worry, because an injection would take all the pain away and let me sleep. Nobody came. Finally I lay back exhausted. Specks of blood from my torn hands soiled the sheets.

Far away I could hear a bell ringing. It went on and on. Perhaps an ambulance called out on an emergency? When I came round again the bell was sounding once more, it was getting closer. They were coming for me after all. At some point I went to the bathroom to relieve myself. I avoided contact with my reflection; he was unshaven with red rimmed eyes. He was not the sort of person you would want to talk to. He looked like a mad man.

As I hobbled down to the kitchen area the bell rang again. This time I realised it was the telephone. I hesitated before answering. I picked the phone up and held it to my ear. I would wait until the voice spoke and I could decide whether to hang up.

'Hal, Hal, are you there?' Tom's voice paused. 'Is that you, Hal? For fuck's sake say something.'

'Yes, it's me.' I decided not to tell him I felt like an impostor, and very possibly I had been possessed by demons and was not Hal Bennett after all.

'What's going on? Mandy said you suddenly had to leave. Is everything alright?'

'I was wrong. I couldn't cope in the Gate House.'

I looked at the back of my hand, it resembled an abstract tattoo, the scrapes might actually be letters, perhaps an 'L'.

Tom was continuing, his words a blur. I thought he was asking me to come back to Leverbridge. 'You've got to come back, Hal. You need to sort the Gate House out.'

'I can't.' I said.

There was definitely an 'I' and possibly a 'Z' as well. Far from removing Lizzie from me, I had branded her initials onto my skin.

'You don't sound well,' said Tom.

'I'm not.' Then I tried the old excuse. 'I've come down with a cold.'

Tom was being remarkably perceptive this morning. 'I don't believe you, Hal, you never were any good at lying. Did something happen at the cottage?'

I moved to the settee, it was cheap leather and as I sank into it, squeaked as though surprised to be used after my week away.

'Gracie came over. She was worried about you. Has something happened?'

I sighed. How could I tell him what I had found out about Lizzie and me? It might not take many words but in the scheme of things was like an atomic bomb. Once told the mushroom cloud hung over everything.

'Look Tom, I don't think it was a good idea for me to come back to Leverbridge after all. It's only got bad memories for me.'

'So you're telling me you're living a happy existence up there in sunny Milton Keynes? I don't believe you, Hal. I think you need to come and sort things out here. Gracie was pretty insistent she had something important to tell you.'

'Let her call then. Whatever she's got to say she can tell me over the phone.'

'No, she insisted she needed to see you. But she was too upset to make the call. What the hell have you done, Hal?'

'Thanks for your vote of confidence, Tom. Did you consider it might be the Mannings who have done something? I've just been used.'

'Just come back then. Sort things out. You never know, it might make you feel better.'

'Thank you, Dr Sheldon. I'm going to get dressed now.'

As I replaced the hand set I could hear his frantic voice calling, 'Hal, Hal, don't go...'

Through the afternoon the phone rang several times but I ignored it. Nor did I bother to dress. My dressing gown, stained and threadbare with age and neglect was adequate for living a half-life. I lounged on the sofa and drank tea. I had not bought milk, so it was black and bitter. There was half a packet of digestive biscuits which I ate. They were stale. An afternoon quiz show came on and I watched contestants open boxes, whilst the audience screamed. I imagined being on such a show and opening boxes one by one and finding they contained nothing at all, which would make the audience yell at me for losing the contents.

The phone rang again and I picked it up and shouted, 'Leave me alone Tom!'

I should have slammed it straight down again, but waited long enough to hear a quiet female voice echo down the line. 'It's me, Hal. It's Lizzie.'

The audience on the TV screamed louder.

'What?'

'It's Lizzie.'

They were clapping and cheering.

'You're dead,' I told the disembodied voice at the end of the line.

I craved one of the cigarettes I'd given up years ago, just to experience the inhalation and exhalation of smoke, so I could be certain I was breathing.

'No, Hal. I'm alive. I really can't explain everything over the phone. Please will you come back? I want to explain face-to-face.'

I couldn't think straight. I watched my hand replace the phone in its cradle and then turned back to the TV where streamers and confetti were raining down on a contestant's head. She had just won quarter of a million pounds.

The programme was just as much an illusion as Lizzie's voice had been. How could somebody win so much money just by opening boxes? It was not an illusion, it was a conspiracy. Just like the phone call, it was a hoax.

The leather of the chair creaked as I moved, as if to say, 'Leaving so soon?' Because hoax or not, the voice of a Manning had called me and I had to obey.

I travelled back late on the Thursday evening. I was pleased the dark stopped me seeing my surroundings. I felt I was in a tunnel with no alternative, not even a light at its end.

The gates in front of the Gate House were locked and my thoughts were scrambled so I couldn't remember the key code. I parked and walked in the dark through the woods. There were rustling noises as if creatures were running from me and the whisper of the tree canopy, which always made me think of secrets being shared. I had forgotten how well I knew the path, because it wasn't difficult to negotiate my way even in the dark.

I stood in front of the Gate House using the light from my mobile to illuminate the keyhole. I crept into the cottage like a thief. Again it felt as though I had disturbed air that wanted to remain dormant. I wished Barklay was with me. The lamps I switched on created pools of light rather than flooding a whole area, so individual spots on the floor were illuminated; a box here, my mother's last letter on the floor, her diary on the coffee table. In the shadow I sensed her portrait, acknowledging my presence.

I managed to make myself some tea and had a slice of toast even though the bread was edged with mould. I knew I would not be able to sleep, the cottage was too dark and quiet for peaceful rest. Instead I lit a fire and started to burn the contents of the boxes. Newspapers and letters burnt vigorously as though the flames had been starved of food. The yellow and red tongues licked the edges like salivating dogs and then devoured the singed shards.

I heard a noise outside and thought it must be a fox coming to investigate the activity at the house.

At the base of one of the boxes I found the plaque Gracie had removed from the bench years ago. I doubted the fire would manage the metal and so I placed it beside the horse on the mantelpiece. Firelight flickered over the bronze giving the ornament a wide eyed look as though it might rear up at any moment.

By the time dawn came, most of the boxes had been emptied. I refrained from burning Mother's diary or last letter. The portrait had a narrow escape. I had dragged it over to the hearth but then could imagine burning flesh as though it were real. I added its brown wrapping to my furnace and then placed the portrait back in the corner, facing the wall as if in disgrace.

It was only as I made my way to the kitchen I noticed something white on the doormat. It was a letter written on such fine paper it was no more than tissue. It was so delicate in my fingers I wasn't even sure it existed. And that was partly because the writing looked a little like Lizzie's. The message said: *Meet me in the churchyard.*

What Was Taken 14

From a distance the woman laying flowers by the crypt resembled Lizzie. It was certainly a slim, golden haired creature bending over. She looked like an angel. As I walked closer I told myself it couldn't be an angel or Lizzie because the hair wasn't golden enough, even though it glowed in the early morning light. Anyway there were no such things as angels and Lizzie was dead. I continued towards the grave. As my feet approached behind her she turned. It was her. There were fine wrinkles around her eyes and her skin was tanned, but it was definitely Lizzie.

'Lizzie, it is you.'

It was spoken on one exhaled breath so I was without air. The fact she was alive made me light headed. My mouth opened and closed, gulping like a stranded fish.

I wanted to rush to her and embrace her, but she was a body resurrected and I knew I must not. One step I thought, one step and I would be close enough to hug her. I could take one pace on my prosthetic foot, into a space which didn't exist. But now that was forbidden. If we had known we were brother and sister from the beginning we would have been able to hug, but now with all that had passed, I could not touch her.

I wondered if she reflected similar thoughts to me, as she had moved one foot in front of the other as if she were preparing to fling herself into my arms but then remembered the barrier between us.

'Hal.' She smiled. 'I'm so glad to see you.' Her words came from another era when men and women remained apart. When I did not reciprocate her smile she said, 'Oh God, Hal. I'm so sorry, so sorry.' She was shaking her head.

There was no point in apology. I walked past her leaving a wide space between us and looked at the stonework of the grave.

'Why did they bury her with him?' I asked a cherub carved on the side.

Lizzie answered me. 'It's the Manning crypt. Alicia was a Manning after all.'

'But he killed her.'

'Nobody knows what happened.'

'I do.'

I kicked some soil at the edge of the monument and began to scratch my hand. Then I walked away. I was not even out of the churchyard when I heard Lizzie's footsteps running after me.

'Wait, Hal, you have to tell me. Remember, I've been away.'

I let her follow me back to the Gate House. I wondered whether she had been told of my amputation, whether she thought she could detect a limp as I walked.

My steps barely hesitated as we passed the gates with their scrolled letters. I unlocked the cottage and let us in.

'It's amazing to be back here,' she said following me into the cottage. She walked into the sitting room and headed straight for the mantelpiece. She picked up the statue of the horse. 'I'm so glad Maurice left the Gate House to you, it's what you deserve.'

I was numb watching her there, stroking the horse as though she had never been away.

'Are you saying I deserve all this heartbreak?' I shouted. I had never experienced pain like it. All the pain I had experienced from my lost foot was nothing compared to this. It was so intense I wanted to scream, my guts were burning as if being consumed from the inside.

'I hate it here,' I yelled. 'I hate it here without Mother, without you. It just reminds me of everything I have lost.'

I sat down and put my head in my hands and wept.

I could hear her repeating, 'Hal, I'm sorry, I'm so sorry,' over and over but she remained at a distance.

'Why didn't you tell me before? Then I could have gone away and moved on with my life. Instead you ran away. You left me living a lie. You let me go on loving you, missing you for eleven years...and for what? For nothing.'

'I'm sorry. I should have trusted you. I should have told you but I was so confused. I had to come to terms with Maurice being my father. Being your father. Of him abusing my mother; of hurting Gracie. When Grandmama talked to me the night before our wedding it felt as if my whole life was being torn apart. To be honest it was like sleep walking. I got in the taxi Grandmama had called, went to the airport and flew away.'

She put the horse down for a moment and stood twisting her hands together. 'And then suddenly I was living a new life. It was easier to keep going, not look back.'

She picked up the horse again and stroked it gently.

'What happens now?' I asked. 'Are you going away again?'

'I don't think so. I think Gracie needs me, I shouldn't have left her.'

'You shouldn't have left me, either,' I said, but my voice was surprisingly level.

'I had to though, Hal.'

Through the pain in my stomach a small spark of hope flared. 'You and me though, we could be together. Only a few people know we're sister and brother and they're not going to say anything. We don't have to have children. We could live very quietly.'

I watched Lizzie's tanned face blanch. 'Don't ask me to do that, Hal,' she said, making me think she may have considered it herself. 'What about you, will you stay here?' she asked me.

'Is there any point?' I asked the question of myself as well as her. She did not reply. I had no answer either.

For several minutes we remained silent. I could hear her fingers moving over the brass of the ornament again and somewhere in the world outside a horse whinnied a telepathic response.

'There's something else,' she finally said.

I was so numb I could not perceive what else there could be. I did not reply but simply looked at her. This time she returned my gaze and I realised it was the first time we had looked directly at each other. The lovely flecked golden eyes were undimmed.

'Gracie says she killed Maurice.'

'What? That's ridiculous.'

'So you don't think it could be true.'

I was shaking my head, but suddenly realised I could believe it. I stopped my head movement. 'Well, I suppose so. But how? Surely they'd have been suspicious?'

'She says he had been ill for a few days anyway and she injected him with insulin. He fell into a coma and she held a pillow over his face. That was it.' She took a deep breath before asking herself as well as me, 'But they would have asked questions, investigated if she'd done that, wouldn't they? And where would she get insulin from?'

It did sound farfetched. But I thought of Tom's bathroom cabinet with its supply of insulin and needles. About how close Gracie and Tom had become. About the tag on the champagne bottle, '*I did it!*'

It appeared Lizzie knew nothing about Tom's diabetes. With my knowledge, murder was more plausible. 'I think she's bluffing,' I said, looking away from Lizzie's stare. 'Why would she wait until now? She's had good reason to hate him for a long time; she'd have done something before now.'

I took to shaking my head again; it helped to soothe the agitation I felt.

'Apparently she was worried about Eliza; she said something about bedtime stories.'

I had no doubt then that Gracie had helped Maurice on his way to Hell. But I didn't care. Nor did I care exactly how she had carried it out to get away with it. I just wished she'd killed him a long time ago. Long enough so it didn't affect me and Lizzie. It was all too late.

And now Lizzie was making to leave. Putting down the ornament, picking up her bag. I could do nothing. I stared at the horse, willing it to race into action so I could throw myself onto its back like a Wild West hero, swoop up Lizzie and ride away into the sunset together.

I knew my story didn't have a happy ending.

'I'd better go,' she said, 'leave you to decide what you're going to do.' And I realised I was still rooted to the spot.

An Empty Tray

It was only as I heard the door click shut that I moved. I got to the door in time to see her walking towards the Manor. I wanted to shout after her, demand she came back. My mouth didn't obey.

I stood outside and watched her walk away from me. Her swaying figure moved down the drive. She passed the stand of trees into the dip so for a minute I could not see her, then there she was again finally making her way to the front door. She did not look back.